For you de

The ✓H.

Tack Chest

Jeff Hawksworth

http://www.jeffhawksworth.com

The Tack Chest

Paperback Edition First Publishing in Great Britain
in 2014 by aSys Publishing

eBook Edition First Publishing in Great Britain
in 2014 by aSys Publishing

Cover and internal illustrations taken or adapted for this book by
Teresa O'Neill Photography

ISBN: 978-0-9930718-7-4

aSys Publishing
http://www.asys-publishing.co.uk

Contents

Disclaimer .... *iv*

Acknowledgments .... *v*

Prologue *1*

Chapter One *7*

Chapter Two *27*

Chapter Three *60*

Chapter Four *77*

Chapter Five *97*

Chapter Six *127*

Chapter Seven *159*

Chapter Eight *170*

Chapter Nine *206*

Chapter ten *223*

Chapter Eleven *237*

Chapter Twelve *244*

Books by the Same Author *247*

About the Author *254*

Disclaimer

Acknowledgments

I have come to realise that there some things an author needs, in abundance. In fact, they are the very lifeblood of the process.

Approval and encouragement. An author feeds off the support of those around, to an extent that is difficult to measure.

Generosity too. All my books have required research; lots of it and whilst libraries, travel and *Google* play their part, so much is gained from people who are willing to give up time and share their knowledge.

I have been fortunate in all respects.

In this instance I would like to thank Tom Sykes of the *Coleshill Auxiliary Research Team, (CART),* for his wonderfully succinct delivery of a wealth of information about *Churchill's Auxiliaries*. The unit described in this book is fictional but the *Auxiliaries* were very real and I'd like to take this opportunity to salute a little known force of extremely brave men.

My thanks also, to Arthur Battelle who furnished me with all I needed to know about *Fordson Major* tractors and Pete Rix, who worked his magic on a decrepit photograph of 'Dolly Grey'.

Teresa O'Neill exceeded my expectations once again with her photography while Nicola Makin of aSys Publishing managed to turn another manuscript into this book.

Pam, Linda, Sue and Steve, who searched the early proofs for blunders, with continual encouragement and a generous absence of overt criticism.

FINALLY, MY WARMEST THANKS TO YOU,
BECAUSE YOU'RE READING THIS.

Prologue

Serendipity. The dictionary defines it as 'The faculty of making fortunate discoveries by accident'.

I simply think of it as a time when the fates decide to deal you a handful of trumps or four threes, though in my case the former usually arrives when I'm playing poker and the latter during a game of whist.

Not that I'm cynical. It's just that I need to emphasise what a remarkable hand I was dealt the day I met my cousin Audrey for lunch and mentioned the chest.

Grandma had passed away and Audrey was co-executor of the estate with her brother-in-law, who was a legal executive, which made the division of labour a matter of form. He would deal with probate and she would clear the house.

We were talking about family history and how important it was to get old folk talking while they were still with us, something we'd signally failed to do with Grandma, though there were boxes of photographs and postcards in her wardrobe.

Mention of them reminded me of an image that must have had some impact on me since I'd seen it as a child and that *was* a long time ago.

It was of a dappled grey shire horse, groomed magnificently and clearly others had thought so too. She was standing side on to the camera and the man holding her leading rein stood just beyond her head, but a black, wooden chest stood between them with a magnificent silver trophy standing on it.

Audrey thought for a moment before, "I think I remember that picture, do you want me to see if I can find it?"

"Yes please." I said, "Though it would be lovely to find that chest as well, especially if it's still got any of the tack in it."

Two days later she called me, "John, I've found the photograph and there's a note on the back. Her name was *Dolly Grey*."

I was pleasantly surprised, "Well done you. Does it mention what the cup was?"

"Actually, there were two trophies, but no, sorry, that's all that's on it."

It would have been nice to know, but finding the photograph was bonus enough. I asked, "Any chance of borrowing it, I think I'd like to get a copy made."

"Of course, I'll keep it out, but there's something else as well. Grandma had a box at the foot of her bed, which she used as a linen chest. It's a bit tatty; she covered it with a rug, but it looks a bit like the one in the picture. You're welcome to it if you want it; only it had blankets in it, not tack."

I had nothing to lose, "Yes please, if you could hold on to it, I'll pick it up at the weekend."

"Great, I'll put the photo in there too."

* * *

When I called in to collect it, we both compared the chest to the one in the picture. It was a different colour, certainly. The one in front of *Dolly Grey* was beautifully finished in black lacquer, while the one before us had been coated with a dark brown varnish or paint. But it looked right. The size seemed to match and the frame-work around the lid seemed the same. The clinchers for me were the handles on the sides, which looked identical. As Audrey had said, it *was* tatty but I could sort that out and now that I was satisfied with the provenance I knew exactly what I was going to do with it.

Stripped, sanded and varnished, or maybe oiled, I'd decide at the time, it would serve as *our* linen chest and I would hang a framed copy of the photograph on the wall behind it.

Coffee'd out once again, I left Audrey to carry on sorting Grandma's stuff out.

Yet for some reason I didn't get around to doing anything with the chest for nearly a year. I dumped it in the garage when I got home and what with one thing and another, forgot about it.

But it wasn't the only thing just dumped in the garage; lots more went in there too, until the shambles had to be sorted out. Which was how I came across the chest again and decided to do something with it.

That's the way I operate I'm afraid. I do forget about jobs, but once the mental 'go' lever is thrown over, I become fixated. It might be seen as strength or a weakness, my wife Liz has alternating views on the matter.

In any event, I dusted it down and left it in the middle of the hallway; a good place to put something if you want to keep it in mind.

First off, I was going to tackle the awful wallpaper someone had lined the box with. Buckets of hot water and a scraper would soon shift it.

The chest was around three feet wide so reaching the handles was only just possible and then I was forced to sidle out of the front door, to do as I was told and make the mess halfway down our driveway. It was the weight and awkward gait that caused me to trip on the step, resulting in an ungainly exit that became a staggering run as I fought to stay upright. Somehow I managed it, but crashed into the side of Liz's car. I glanced back at the house and was relieved to note that she hadn't seen anything. Her car had so many dents a couple more wouldn't be noticed.

But the impact must have dislodged something, because when I pushed away from the car I heard a distinct 'clonk'. Bugger! I set it down on the floor and inspected it for damage, but found none.

I opened the lid and inspected the interior, but found none.

I picked it up, shook it and it clonked again.

It didn't make sense; the chest was empty and apart from the handles I could find nothing that *could* rattle, or clonk.

The chest was a straightforward structure, with four sides that had been jointed at the corners with dovetails and a simple internal frame, to which the base had been nailed with old square forged nails. That much I'd already discovered, by removing one with a claw hammer.

I shook it again. It clonked again.

I sat back on my haunches and considered the problem, until I was left with a single conclusion. Something was inside there and if I couldn't see anything, it must be hidden.

It seemed such a strange notion that I didn't dwell on it when I wandered back into the garage for a tape measure. But before I measured it, I checked again. The framework was exactly as it should be, with corners jointed perfectly and no evidence of tampering.

The tape told me otherwise. I measured the height of the chest on the outside and then on the inside. There was a cavity there, unless the base boards were two and a half inches thick, which didn't seem likely.

I tried to lift the base carefully, using wood chisels but it had been fitted so well that damage was inevitable. So, I screwed a hook into the wood and heaved upwards, until finally, a board split with a loud crack and I was in.

I couldn't see much through the gap, but the cavity looked to be a little under two inches deep, as expected. I could see papers but nothing else, though even that was exciting and now that one board had surrendered the rest would follow easily. I suddenly realised how close I'd come to hosing the inside down with water and wondered what I might have destroyed.

Ten minutes later, the whole false floor was gone and I gazed at someone's secret hoard with a fascination that was tinged with a sense of trespass.

I called Liz out and this time, with two of us carrying it, the passage through the front door went off without mishap. We took it into the kitchen where I lifted the lid and showed her my find; yet neither of us felt able to touch anything.

Until Liz came up with the necessary answer, "We need to be *very* careful now. You get the camera and I'll get a pen and paper so we've got a record as we go along."

We soon realised that we'd discovered something quite magical and strange; all the more so because my father was no longer with us and the cache was his.

We spread it out on the dining room table as Liz catalogued everything and I took photographs, but the process took literally hours. Each new item called for closer inspection and even then, we didn't understand much of the stuff.

Well, see what you think.

Chapter One

The black and white photograph showed a group of children, perhaps fifty or so, standing in front of a dark-bricked building. Blue bricks I decided, and the building had to be a school; built in the Victorian era.

It was a group of two halves, marking a segregation of boys from girls. All of the boys were in creaseless short trousers and two had jackets; shoes too. The remainder wore home-knitted pullovers and knee-length socks showing various degrees of collapse, into scuffed clumpy-looking boots.

The girls were all wearing pinafore dresses that might have been white once and whilst many had shoes, some, including my aunty Mary, had the same sort of boots as the boys.

A stern-looking man with a walrus moustache sat at the centre of the front row. His rather drab looking suit looked in need of pressing and the stubby collar of his shirt hosted a somewhat clumsily knotted tie which disappeared behind a coarse waistcoat that was lumpy enough to suggest he'd stored some potatoes in there. There were no creases in his trousers, or at least none where they belonged and his boots were dull and scuffed. Not that anyone would have described him thus to his face, I'm certain, not with that expression.

Yet his waistcoat boasted a heavy watch chain that looked as though it might have been gold and quite at odds with the rest of him. I decided he'd inherited it.

He was flanked by two fairly young ladies, both with highly polished and feminine boots, heavy calf-length skirts and blouses with very wide collars that lay limply across their shoulders. One had a thin pinched face but a mass of dark hair that was tied up into a bun and ironically her colleague had a round face but short lank hair with what might have been a small bald patch near the front hairline, partly covered by strategic combing. That might have been ringworm, a little gift brought in by one of the farmer's kids.

Everybody wore a severe expression.

Except one.

I should mention that even as a child, Dad had two very distinctive features; that would remain in place for his whole life.

First, a square slab of a jaw that later on in life would clamp a tobacco pipe into place, just like *Popeye*.

Second, a mop of black curly hair that sprang from his scalp like a tidal wave. The thick mop on top was accentuated in his younger years, by the savage 'pudding basin' haircut that left the sides of his head shorn to stubble.

On this occasion though, there was a third feature that set him apart from his peers.

He was the only one sticking his tongue out at the camera.

The school entrance was in view and to one side, stacked in the corner, was a variety of garden tools. There were spades, forks, hoes, trowels and a few I couldn't recognise.

It was obviously a photograph of the period, when slow shutter speeds required sitters to keep perfectly still and therefore fixed expressions were encouraged. Even so, the headmaster's bleak expression seemed to mirror an innately stern and rigid demeanour. One that looked set to wreak vengeance on Dad, once the finished picture was to hand.

I think that was what prompted me to dig a little, but where to start?

Mancetter Church of England School had been closed down long since and the site now contained a few dozen two or three-bed boxes that had been marketed as luxury homes.

The local council couldn't help, or wouldn't, I'm not sure which, but the lady I spoke to was clearly having a very bad day so I left her to continue battling with the incoming calls, while Liz and I called in to the White Lion for a morning cappuccino, *with* malted biscuit for dunking.

Mancetter and Atherstone *coalesced* years ago into a decent sized town, but it still remains a village in many ways. For example, it's still okay to make eye contact with strangers and if you do, it's likely that one of you will strike up a conversation. The locals are masters at giving you their life story in a few minutes before moving on to spend fifteen minutes discussing the seven six five bus service to Tamworth. It was Tuesday, which is market day and the couple we spoke too were surrounded by shopping bags. We never did learn their names, but when Liz explained our mission they were delighted, for the husband had attended the same school, albeit years after dad's attendance *and* the headmaster's, whose retirement marked the end of his reign of terror and the appointment of a kindly and popular headmistress.

We listened to several anecdotal stories which made me realise how little we knew; about Dad's childhood, or how to find out about it and I said as much.

The lady's eyes widened, "I know who can help, hang on." She dived into her pocket for a mobile telephone and after a brief explanation passed it to me with, "It's Janet, my sister's girl. She'll help you, she's a teacher."

She was too, and she did.

That afternoon, the lady I spoke to in the education department at Warwick County Hall was also most helpful. She directed me to the County Records Office who confirmed that they held the school log book and admissions register. I made a note of the record numbers and drove down to the Records Office with Liz, the following week.

After filling in some forms and depositing our coats and bags in lockers, we were allowed through to the temperature and humidity controlled reading room where another lady had me complete the document request forms. Ten minutes later, the books were set before us on cushion-like bases.

We started with the admissions register, at the page for nineteen twenty, given that Dad had been born in nineteen fifteen and five seemed to be a common starting age. Both facing pages were covered with columns that recorded the child's details; start date, admission number, full names, dates of birth, addresses and the name of parent. The final column recorded the date and reason for leaving.

Most were positive reasons such as, *'transferred to High School'*, 'awarded *grant for Grammar School'* or for many of the girls, *'entered into service'*.

Others chronicled the sadder aspects of that age, such as, 'Died *of scarlet fever'* or, *'Succumbed to Diphtheria.'*

Eventually, we were delighted to find the record of my father's admission, numbered 1045 and dated the fourth of October nineteen twenty two. He must have been a very late starter.

The next entry was for Mary, with the same date of joining, though her date of birth was fifteen months earlier, on the fourteenth of January nineteen fourteen. The year war broke out. From all that I've learned since, hostilities between her and Charlie started a couple of years later and lasted until the late teens.

I was startled to note that he left school on the third of July nineteen twenty five; after just three years, when he would still have only been ten years old. The final column told me the manner of his departure but without any clue as to the why. In fact there were just three words;

'Excluded from school.'

My heart skipped a beat and my first reaction was to seek mitigation in numbers. Perhaps that sort of thing was commonplace in those days. I scanned the pages for eight more years and found none. My father was the only child in over a decade to suffer the ignominy of expulsion.

Suddenly, the atmosphere in the reading room became stifling.

I pushed the cushion away and drew the one bearing the log book before us. There would be mention of it in there, surely.

We quickly scanned the entries for that month and drew a blank, which said the same for our expressions when we looked up at each other. Ever the practical one, Liz said, "Okay, let's do this by numbers. He was only there for three years, so let's start at the beginning."

* * *

The log book cover bore the dates 1919 -1962 so nineteen twenty two was a relatively early entry. Like the admissions register, the handwriting was extremely neat and in ink of course, with nary a blot in sight.

The first entry on the page was dated September the nineteenth 1922. It read;

Visit of Mr Paget to examine the school gardens.

There followed a couple of entries; one concerning a School Manager's meeting and the other a record of sending Mabel Harris home, *'on account of a verminous head.'*

Two weeks later another entry recorded her return to school after being declared free of lice by the local Doctor.

But the garden was mentioned time and time again;

2nd January The manure for the school gardens came this morning. The boys have been carting it across to the plots.

26th January The seed potatoes arrived.

17th February Thursday afternoons. Handwork will be 2.40 – 3.40pm. The girls will then be able to go on alone, while I am with the boys for gardening.

20th February As we missed gardening yesterday, owing to rain, we are having an extra lesson today.

23rd February Mr Paget called to inspect the gardens.

But then disaster struck;

26th February Doctor Baxter, MOH, has closed the school until March 29th on account of Whooping Cough.

Since it was the only entry since December to have referred to anything other than gardening I reckoned it was significant. Not for the kids of course, for the gardens.

That much was evidenced in the next entries;

29th March School re-opened this morning. 30 scholars out of a possible 58 being present. Mr Paget called to inspect the gardens.

6th April With Easter behind us, we must address the demands of Mother Nature and prepare the gardens for sowing and setting. There is much to do.

5th May Mr Nash brought strawberry plants this morning. I left Miss Simpson with the girls to continue with the writing lesson while I took the boys for gardening.

He didn't mention the need to make up for lost time, but the entries were eloquent enough. The three R's, (Reading, 'Riting and 'Rithmatic) were relegated to second place in favour of horticulture and meanwhile Mr Paget continued to be a regular visitor.

In fact, we counted the entries for that school year. There were thirty two that concerned the gardens and only six relating to lesser matters, such as choosing the May Queen and dancing around the maypole on the village green. The Maypole was always sited in front of the old Manor House and the butler would be sent out with a slice of fruit cake and soft drink, balanced on a silver tray, to offer it to the queen. It was done with great solemnity and must have been very affecting for the young girl. This much I have learned from old photographs other members of the family have supplied, though it only merited a six word entry in the log book. One of the photos I recall was of the butler bent at the waist as he offered the refreshments to the May Queen. He looked just like *Lurch* from *The Adams Family.*

Another annual event that featured in the log book was the Harvest Festival in September. The entry noted that each child was required to bring some produce, which was sold after the service. The funds were then earmarked for the school outing in June of the following year.

Predictably, the school outing was mentioned. In nineteen twenty three they went to Wicksteed Park, in Northamptonshire and the headmaster noted that, *'A fine time was had by all'*.

I did notice that there was no mention of produce from the school gardens, at any time, let alone for the Harvest Festival.

We returned to the pages for nineteen twenty six, the year after Dad 'left' school, in case an historical item was recorded, perhaps indirectly referring to the crime, but there was nothing.

Liz noticed that something else was missing. In the nineteen twenty five/twenty six school year there were only five entries that referred to the gardens and three of those referred to inspection visits from Mr Paget.

Liz shook her head, "Who the hell is this Mr Paget?"

I shrugged, "Well we're in the right place to find out. Let's ask to see a census."

I left Liz with the log book and sought help again from the nice lady, who suggested I start with the 1922 census and directed me to a computer terminal which provided a link to an ancestry agency. Preliminary notes on their site advised that it was the first census to record occupation, which was a stroke of luck.

There were only three Pagets in the Atherstone and Mancetter wards. One was a seventy two year old, domiciled on the opposite side of town and another was a woman, married to a Mr Donald Paget and sharing the same accommodation, situate 113 Long Street, Atherstone. They were living over the shop I reckon, for his occupation was listed as *Purveyor of fruit and vegetables*. I hurried over to tell Liz about my discovery, in an excited whisper, surrounded as we were by signs that forbade normal speech, "It was a 'fit up!' The old goat was selling the produce on!"

Liz gave out a "Humph!" followed by, "He was in for some bad news." She nodded back towards the books, "Come and look what I found."

The entry was dated the fifteenth of April, nineteen twenty six, the spring after Dad's unscheduled departure. It was written in another hand and titled;

'*HMI Inspection*'.

Obviously the inspector's own entry, it read;

'The schemes in Nature and in the various branches of Handwork need re-considering. The practical work at present done in the garden is concerned chiefly with the cropping of fruit and vegetables. This is felt to be out of place, particularly in view of the proposed expenditure on new gardening tools.'

Charlie

THE GARDEN TOOLS

Charlie's father, Albert Morcroft, hadn't given schooling much thought and neither had Charlie for that matter. There was always plenty of work to do on the farm and had been since he was old enough to carry a bucket. Whenever the subject was raised by his wife Agnes, Albert argued that Charlie had enough to learn about farming without filling his head with letters and numbers. They could come later, when things were easier.

Any correspondence on the matter had been given short shrift, but when the truancy officer paid a visit and threatened prosecution it was time to pay attention. By that time, they had managed to avoid the distraction and loss of labour for eighteen months.

At seven years of age, Charlie was a thin wiry boy, who thought that nine hour days were the norm and school hours relatively modest, though he had yet to realise how much the freedom of the open fields meant to him.

One thing soon became certain; he was not an academic and hated the discipline in school, which in his case routinely involved the cane. That aversion to discipline would stay with him for most of his life along with a hatred of that headmaster.

The different categories of cane, of graduated weight and thickness, were distinguished by a number, etched into the handle and measured the scale of the crime or the progression of repeat offenders, otherwise referred to as *career* miscreants.

The 'Dap' headed the punishment chain and was only used on rare occasions. It was a size ten sandal whose leather upper had fallen apart, but the sole was in dreadfully good order. The cane they called the 'dudgeon' came a close second.

"Morcroft!" One word, bellowed across the classroom or play-ground, signalled another day of discomfort, for hard wooden benches and bruised backsides were never easy companions.

Three years later, on his way home from school for the last time, Charlie cast back and simply couldn't recall a word of praise or encouragement, which was hardly surprising, in a war of attrition.

One day a boy took a football into school, which the boys were allowed to play with during their break. It was made of thick leather and lethally heavy when wet; so much so that Stanley Broughton's attempt to head the ball left him staggering off the playground in a knock-kneed daze.

The headmaster was on playground duty that day and did some-thing wholly out of character when the football rolled to within attacking distance. The boys had no idea that their leader had been an avid *Wolverhampton Wanderers* fan in his childhood and watching the boys play had reminded him of happier times. Once or twice he had to resist an urge to offer them tips, or even the benefit of being refereed, but when the ball was miss-kicked and shot towards him, he reacted without further thought. They watched in wonder as he leapt forward and lashed out with his right foot. It was an aberrational act, of course, and came as a surprise to all concerned, including the headmaster.

Worse, his boot made a sort of 'popping' sound as the upper detached itself from the sole, revealing a large white toe that marked the sorry state of a sock in need of darning. The boys could barely contain themselves, but waited to see if it was safe to laugh out loud. Seconds passed as the headmaster stared down at the damage, until, finally he looked up, with an expression that quelled any shows of mirth, or at least it would have done if he hadn't attempted to march back into school. As soon as the sole began to flap loudly, the boys lost control and when the headmaster failed to respond they took it as a tacit permission to enjoy the moment. Pandemonium broke out.

In fact, the opposite was true. The man was mortified; his authority had been compromised in a way that had made him a laughing stock, all thanks to an act of foolishness with the football; so hugely out of character.

Minutes later, he rang the school bell and sought to make good the damage he had done, by doing something that was entirely *in* character. He caned every single boy.

Even so Charlie was sufficiently impressed with the game to craft his own football at the farm. Since the only opponent available was Mary, he reasoned that a softer construction was called for and in fact she helped him by stitching the sackcloth into something resembling a globe before he stuffed it with grain.

The result was rather large and lumpy but it served its purpose, until their father came in off the fields. They might have hoped he would join in for a bit of a kick-around but the look on his face when he scooped up the ball said otherwise, "What are you playing at?"

Charlie knew better than to make the obvious reply. He couldn't have anyway, for his father didn't miss a beat, "You haven't got time for that my lad and if you think otherwise I can soon find you more work to do, have no fear." With that he lobbed the ball into the rough grass at the side of the barn, where it wintered without being disturbed. The following spring new shoots of wheat burrowed out through the sacking like a green explosion, until drought and over-crowding finished them off. Like Charlie's football career, they didn't last long.

Farming has never been easy, but a tenanted farm in the nineteen twenties was as tough as it could be, which in part, was why Charlie and the headmaster didn't see eye to eye.

The doctrine of the three 'Rs' wouldn't have found favour anyway, but at Mancetter School there was a significant 'gardening' element to the curriculum; far more than was customary at the time, when other schools made do with small plots in a corner. Charlie's headmaster had a much grander operation, comprising two full-size allotments opposite the school, on the ground that sloped down to the River Anker.

Even at such a young age, Charlie had a keen sense of right and wrong. Whilst some boys regarded the gardening as a welcome escape from the classroom, Charlie was overwhelmed by the injustice of it.

Almost every waking hour out of school was spent working on the land yet this great bully kept marching him across the road to cultivate crops. Something Charlie knew more about than the head; an irony that was even more evident when he witnessed the deference his father exhibited on the few occasions that head and parent met.

The injustice deepened further when the children, every single one of them, were required to take produce in from their own gardens, to make an offering at the Harvest Festival. Not even a lettuce leaf appeared from the school gardens.

Yet only the boys were used for the slave labour, leaving the girls to get on with their Handcraft, with or without supervision, though any attempt to further their education in other ways was discouraged. The arrangement served to ensure that there were no academic differentials between the sexes when the HMI inspections took place.

Out in the gardens, any boy with the temerity to slip a strawberry into his mouth faced retribution. Hand inspections, as they left the gardens, were routine during the fruit season and offenders were hauled out in front of the school at the next assembly, where they would be castigated as a thief, before suffering the ignominy of a public caning.

Charlie's duties on the farm often made him late for school and no matter how discreet his entry, the headmaster's reaction was always the same, except for the cane selection and that was more often than not a reflection of the mood he was in. He would never turn to look at Charlie, since by then the register had been taken and the offender's identity was known. He would merely pause, sometimes mid-sentence and say something like, "*Number four* this morning, I think." Charlie would know where to find *number four*, or whatever the chosen number was and return with it, for the delivery of his punishment.

By the second year of school Charlie had found a friend and willing accomplice in Stanley Broughton. Stan's father worked at *Man Abell Quarries* as their explosives expert and they hatched all manner of loud exits for *Sir*. Though neither boy realised it at the time, their friendship was destined for much greater things and would last for life.

Meanwhile, they embarked on a campaign of mischief that was marked by a robust progression through the cane collection. During one assembly, in which both boys were being punished, the head broke off from his labours to wipe perspiration from the cane handle and addressed the school in an aside as he returned the damp handkerchief to his pocket, "Children, you see here, two perfect candidates for the long drop!"

Charlie and Stan had no idea what he meant, but chose to believe that they were destined to be parachutists. That prompted scores of make-believe adventures and feats of derring-do. The school dust-bins became aircraft, flying at sufficient altitudes to permit parachute launches and sticks became super guns. Boxes became enemy tanks and the rest of the school became the *Boche*. Needless to say, the headmaster became Kaiser Bill.

That December they were banned from the nativity play after just one performance. A misguided younger teacher had assigned them the roles of sheep, though as she pointed out later, they would have corrupted *any* role.

The girls in *Handwork* had smothered two cotton bonnets, *girl's* bonnets, with sheep's wool which Stan and Charlie were required to wear on their heads. The teacher draped white table cloths across their backs and finally, to the hysterical delight of the girls, painted the boys noses with black shoe polish.

Nothing was planned, beyond their usual intent on mischief, but the parents who attended that performance were still talking about it years later.

Stan and Charlie struggled across the area of the hall floor that had been designated as the stage, on all fours, *baaing* loudly. Both could hear the tittering of the grown-ups and shared a great hatred of the teacher responsible for their plight, but there seemed little they could do about it, save sulk and blush.

Stan was following Charlie when he inadvertently trapped the tablecloth under one hand and the tautened material arrested any further attempts to 'step' forward. But inertia carried his weight on beyond the point of balance, causing him to pitch forward and collide with Charlie's backside. The tittering became outright laughter.

It was too much.

By the time the three kings arrived Charlie had a plan. In a voice that might have been heard on the front row, Charlie asked Stan, "Do you know how sheep make lambs."

It wasn't a subject Stan had anticipated and he turned quizzically, "What?"

"Doesn't matter, I'll show you."

As King number three, draped in a dark blue curtain and with a cardboard crown on his head, bent down to present Myrrh to baby Jesus the audience were treated to the spectacle of one sheep attempting to mount another.

Few would forget that year's nativity play, for not only did Charlie provide a hideously accurate enactment of procreation, he accompanied it with a baaing that bordered on the lascivious. It also bordered on the insane, for the headmaster was sitting in the front row, just a few feet away, along with the school managers.

A hush fell on the place as the head leapt up and grabbed both boys by the scruff of their necks. With a discreet twist of the wrist, he ensured that the jumper collars were reduced to a choking grip, until Stan broke the silence with an, "ah, ah, ah," in time with each step, as he was marched on tip toe from the hall. It was thanks to the compression of his windpipe, that his calls sounded entirely in character.

He and Stan were introduced to 'Dudgeon' the next morning at assembly. It was more of a walking stick than a cane, measuring a full three feet in length. Coincidentally, their repeated encounters with it provided the boys with three things; marks for life, an unmitigated hatred of the headmaster and a place in the folklore of Mancetter Church of England School.

It took another eighteen months, filled with minor infractions and punishments, before both boys added another significant chapter to their infamy.

* * *

It was Thursday the 2nd of July, nineteen twenty five. A terribly hot and humid day, but the headmaster's belief in the benefits of hoeing was total. "Never forget boys, a good hoeing is a wonderful thing to do at this time of year, for we cannot allow the weeds to flourish."

Those who weren't hoeing had harvested a few rows of lettuce, spring onions and radishes that morning, which Mr Paget took away in his green van. It was a nineteen fifteen Morris Cowley Bullnose which was afforded more care and attention than any other member of the family, for that was how he thought of it. The gleaming machine was his baby.

That afternoon, the boys who had harvested the salad produce were preparing the emptied beds for a second crop while the remainder continued hoeing. All of them were sweating and their dampened clothes clung to them, so that the combination of dust and coarse material chaffed their skin raw. Charlie was beside himself.

At home they had only just finished haymaking, thanks to a cooler than usual June, which meant that they were working at 'catch up' with everything else. But as hard as Charlie had to work on the farm, he had the comfort of knowing that everyone in the family was working just as hard.

This was not the case at school. The headmaster watched over them from the comfort of a folding chair, placed in the shade of the neighbouring almshouses. He would occasionally look up from the book he was reading and shout at a boy, so as to imply a more diligent observance, but for the most part he ignored them.

Relief arrived in the form of Betty Randle, who skipped down the path, counting as she did, "Two four six eight ten . . . " Until she reached twenty and then she would begin again, just to show that she knew her two times table. She had been sent across with a message from *Miss*. There was a visitor who wished to speak with the headmaster. After satisfying himself that the boys were fully occupied, he cautioned them against slacking and signalled Betty to lead on, back to school.

It was more than Charlie could bear.

As soon as the headmaster was out of sight and earshot, Charlie threw down his garden fork and shouted at it, "Bugger, bugger, bugger!"

The other boys sniggered at the profanities and gathered in a loose group to share each other's gripes.

Charlie summed things up, "This ain't fair!"

There was a general agreement and with the topic established, remedies were called for. Of course, the suggestions became more and more outrageous as time wore on. One boy suggested running home, but another pointed out that there would be hell to pay there and suggested running away instead. Circuses, the Merchant Navy, and the Foreign Legion were amongst the realm of potential adventures discussed, but once they had exhausted that line of thought another boy suggested selling some of the produce to passersby. Another suggested selling the tools as well.

Sniggers became giggles that became outright laughter until the boys were shouting in an attempt at being heard, but the mirth became bladder-threateningly hysterical, when Stan pee'd along a whole row of mature lettuce.

Suddenly someone claimed to have seen movement from the school and panic ensued as they hurried back to their tasks. Even then, they continued to snicker when Thomas Chetwynd couldn't find his trowel and was scrabbling along the bean row in a vain search.

It was a false alarm. There was no sign of the headmaster, but the moment had passed and the boys went back to work, albeit in a desultory fashion.

Charlie was left alone with his thoughts, which fortuitously or not, depending on the perspective, fitted perfectly with the next development.

The headmaster's visitor was in fact the head of Atherstone Grammar school, who had decided to deliver an invitation to their prize-giving ceremony in person. After all, it wasn't simply an invitation to attend; Charlie's headmaster was to be the guest speaker. Flattered, he insisted they discuss arrangements over a cup of tea, *with* scones.

When the school bell was rung for home time he sent one of the older girls across to the gardens with instructions for the boys to pack up and go home.

Destiny called.

As the boys filed past, Charlie called out, "Hold up a minute. I've got an idea."

No-one showed much interest, for it was home time, but they paused to hear what he had to say.

"Someone said that we should try and sell the tools, didn't they." There were mumbles of doubt and one said, "That'd be against the law."

Charlie hurried on, "No wait, I've been thinking. See, if we sold them that would be like *stealing*, but what if we just lost them? What if we just left them here, but so they couldn't be found? That'd just be careless."

The boys began to show interest.

He grinned broadly, "Why don't we bury the tools and nick off home smartly. Old hairy face won't know anything about it 'till we're long gone."

Albert White, easily the most timid boy present, voiced a concern, "But he might say we've stolen them."

"Nah, there'd be nothing to prove it, besides, he'll be in as much trouble as us, 'cos he didn't leave anyone down here to look after us. *And*, he didn't actually tell us to take the tools back to school. He's just said to pack up and go home."

Albert was still worried, "But he won't half be mad."

"Why? All we've done is left the tools over here. If they get lost somehow it's nothing to do with us. We just did what we were told,—and went home."

The boys began to nudge each other and giggle at the thought, which implied that they liked the idea, but uncertainty lingered.

Charlie held on to the initiative by snatching up a trowel, "Look it's easy!" He strode onto the garden and used a fork to dig a shallow hole in the potato furrow. The trowel was dropped in and he smoothed the soil back into place, tamping it down with his foot.

The boys knew that they were now part of the conspiracy and began laughing hilariously. Charlie then ran across and made to snatch a hoe from Stan's grasp.

Stan would have none of it, "Gerroff, It's mine!" With that, he took the fork from Charlie and ran across to the rows of cabbage, to do the job himself.

That started the stampede and within ten minutes every tool had disappeared underground, save for a garden fork; the tool used for last excavation. Someone called out, "What are we going to do with that?"

Charlie already knew and pictured the article he had seen in a newspaper the previous year, which featured the Olympic Games in Paris and included a picture of a *Hammer Throw* contestant.

Grasping the fork handle, Charlie completed two spins before committing it to flight, out over the River Anker, where its trajectory ended in a perfect tine-first landing midstream. Since the river was only eighteen inches deep at that time of year the fork penetrated the muddy bed and remained upright; a monument to their rebellion.

Without another word they fled from the scene, each seeking the temporary sanctuary of their home.

* * *

Ten year old boys rarely consider the long-term implications of their actions, at least in realistic terms, but when the school bell rang the next morning and the boys and girls formed up into their respective lines, the headmaster appeared, holding a cane. The girls were sent in but the boys were told to stay where they are.

Absolute silence reigned, until the girls had disappeared and then the headmaster began to speak. He did so with some difficulty, for he was beside himself with rage.

"You despicable creatures!" He wracked his tortured mind for adequate words, "In all my years as an educationalist, past present and future, you will epitomise all that is bad in boys. You are unworthy of an education. Unworthy! *Do you hear me?*" His last words were a shriek, accompanied by a spray of saliva that prompted a few nods of agreement from the boys near the front of the row. He brandished the cane, "*This* is merely an entrée, six stokes of this, in recognition of the fact that you were all party to this heinous crime. But there will be more, much more. I am prepared to call the Police and have you all placed in a Borstal, where you belong, but there had to be a ringleader and I want his name."

He gestured for the first boy to bend, "First, we'll get you into school."

Six vicious strokes despatched the first boy inside but the next was Albert White, ashen-faced and still upright, with his hand held aloft, "Please sir! They made us do it!"

"Who made you do what?"

"Please sir, Charlie and Stan did sir; they made us bury the tools sir."

"Bend."

Albert was horrified, "But sir, why?"

"For snitching of course, you pathetic creature."

As soon as Albert ran inside, crying bitterly, the headmaster addressed the remaining boys, "Inside, all of you. One hundred lines each, 'Oh Lord, I deserve the ten lashes I am about to receive'. Now inside, all of you; sharply now!" He allowed the boys to begin their rush indoors before adding, "Except for Morcroft and Broughton. Come with me you two. You have an appointment with 'Dudgeon' before you go home."

By dint of the boy's body language and his own conviction, the headmaster determined that Charlie was the prime mover. Both boys suffered as many strokes of the 'Dudgeon' and both were sent home with a letter, but Stan's dismissal was for one week. Charlie's was permanent; thanks to the authority afforded the headmaster at an emergency meeting of the school managers the previous evening.

* * *

Charlie's father took the belt to him but it was little more than a gesture. There had been far severer thrashings, but this time his heart wasn't in it. In truth, he welcomed the return of farm labour though he would never have admitted it to Charlie's mother who had a much higher regard for education.

There was another bonus. The Campbell's up at Hartshill were thinking of retiring and had made it known that their milk round was for sale. Charlie's father wanted it and now had the man, or rather boy, for the job.

The loss of the garden fork Charlie pitched into the river was a given, but they never did find all of the remaining tools. The spade and two hoes in the compost heap weren't discovered until the following spring and were by then, quite useless.

* * *

Somehow, perhaps because the authorities didn't want to see Charlie re-enter the educational system, no-one questioned his absence in the following two years, by which time he reached school-leaving age.

Chapter Two

The letter was one of the most puzzling things I found in the chest, not just because of the content, which prompted more questions than it answered, but I couldn't understand why it should have been important enough for Charlie to stash it in the chest.

I noticed that three halfpenny stamps had been used, all a bright shade of green, with the King's head on. That would be half a penny in today's currency, which I thought seemed a lot for nineteen twenty two, the date of the postmark. The envelope was addressed to Mr A. Morcroft and unlike the stamps, had browned with age. When I lifted the flap, it was clear that it had once been white. The letter inside was dated the nineteenth of August; with a sender's address in Uttoxeter and though the paper was also stained with age, the writing remained fairly clear. It read;

Dear Albert,

I trust you are well. We are too.

I have written to the rest of the family and now write to you, because it is your turn for Uncle Edwin.

He is well for most of the time, but he still has funny spells and they can be very trubblesome after a while. I am sure he will be happy with you on the farm and it need not be forever. Just so we share our duty. I do not think any of us would want to see him put in the assilum.

George will bring him on the train two weeks on Sunday. That is the 3rd. Remember us to your family.

Your sister,

Thelma

Okay, so here's a thing. I didn't even know I had any relatives named Thelma, George or Edwin and what was that about an asylum. Sorry Aunty, if you can see this, but I couldn't bring myself to spell it your way.

Tracking Edwin down was going to be tricky. To begin with, I had no idea where he was from, though I did know two addresses he stayed at, assuming that George *did* deliver him to the farm.

But if he *had* stayed there, with my father, why had I never heard him mentioned?

I didn't have much to go on. In fact, there were only two things; firstly, he was family and second he was mildly nuts. I decided that his condition could be rated as such since he was staying with members of an extended family. Severely nuts would have placed him in care; a bit of a euphemism I'll admit, given what we know of those places in the old days. They were certainly bad enough to keep relatives out of them if possible.

Days went by, without particular focus on the matter, but I did keep returning to niggle at it for clues; a bit like an elusive crossword answer. Until one day, I reconsidered the broader question of Uncle Edwin's care. There may have been a *desire* to look after him, but I knew that we were not a wealthy family and in nineteen twenty two, families in our band struggled to survive. Would they have had the time and resources to look after an insane relative? Remember, we were only tenant farmers and Aunty Thelma's letter suggested she had received a limited education. If I accepted that much; there had to be something special about him to take so much on.

I said as much to my cousin Audrey, when she called in for a coffee. During our chat we talked about the chest and its contents. She knew as little as I did, but she did suggest taking a peek at the photograph album Grandma had left. I arranged to call round a few days later and when I arrived a hefty album lay open on the table.

It was fascinating. The first part contained images of people dressed in their Sunday best, posing in front of painted backdrops and looking very stern. As we moved on though, a growing number of pictures were amateur and far less formal, with smiles and laughter. There were lots of wedding photographs and quite a few taken at christenings, but the most interesting were those taken on the farm. Individuals I recognised, my father amongst them, were featured with horses or machinery, working the land at different times of year. They made our family history so much more real, somehow.

Someone had labelled the pictures and most of the names I knew. There was even one of Thelma, a rather stout, sombre-looking woman, contained in a dark dress that stopped mid-calf and wearing a very large felt hat, with a feather sprouting out of it. But there was no sign of Uncle Edwin.

When we reached the last page we both agreed that it had been fun looking through them anyway and Audrey began to heave the weight over to close the album when she decided to glance inside the back of the cover. There was an envelope there; the sort that contained film negatives and we almost dismissed it, but then if the rest had been such fun, what the heck.

She held the envelope up and emptied its contents onto the table. There were just half a dozen pictures and none were particularly remarkable, until the fourth one. It was a young soldier; from the First World War, by the look of it. He was posing for the camera, yet his floppy peaked cap was set at a rakish angle and the top button of his tunic was undone giving the image a relaxed air. But it was his face that affected me. He must have been around eighteen years old, with an expression that revealed a real sense of fun. He wasn't just smiling. It was a far more eloquent reflection of his nature than that.

I turned it over and there, in the same hand that had written in the album, was, *Edwin 1914.*

And then it dawned on me. I must have looked strange, perhaps gaunt, when I looked at Audrey, because she in turn looked startled, "What's the matter?"

"I know what was wrong." I said, "He wasn't insane, the poor sod was suffering from shell shock."

Charlie
UNCLE EDWIN

It was the stare. They called it the *thousand yard stare*.
His mates in the trench knew it was shell shock but the Colonel
back at the chateau, commandeered for the duration, called it LMF,
which stood for *Lack of moral fibre*. Higher up that obscene chain of
command, someone called Lord Gort, was recorded as saying that
shell shock was a weakness and was not found in 'good' units. By
that he meant units that were well led, which is ironic, since in the
early part of the war more officers suffered from it than soldiers
in the ranks. No doubt his take on 'good' units included weaponry
skills as well, which marked a further irony, since in nineteen hundred and ten he accidentally shot his Indian guide whilst moose
hunting in Canada; no doubt prompting an immediate and discreet
return to England.

Edwin's unpredictable behaviour in the trenches became enough
of a threat to morale for him to be sent back from the front line,
but not for long. It was nineteen sixteen and just after the battle of

31

the Somme, when something like forty per cent of the casualties were shell shocked. Hospitalisation was not something the Generals, nor Chancellor of the Exchequer could countenance.

They had to be treated and returned to the front line as quickly as possible, for there was no question of repatriation. One edict declared, '. . . *that good results will be obtained in the majority of cases by the simplest forms of psycho-therapy*'; *i.e. explanation, persuasion and suggestion, aided by such physical methods as baths, electricity and massage.*'

So they sent Edwin back to one of the new neurological centres that had been set up, where they first tried persuasion.

This began with a medical that was aimed at bolstering feelings of well-being. Even an amputee might have been cheerfully told he was still spritely, for his age. In Edwin's case they ignored his persistent cough and laboured breathing; the legacy of a gas attack at Ypres the previous year and focused on his manly stature.

There followed a series of consultations which included simple orders to test his ability to obey instructions, to drill perhaps, or to slope arms; all in the secure silence of a wooden hut; miles away from the trenches. Naturally, Edwin passed with flying colours and at the end of the programme he stood to attention as ordered. The officer rose from his desk and barked, "There! I knew it! You're still a soldier through and through. I knew you weren't a shirker or coward. Now off with you, there's a good chap, we'll have you back with your platoon before nightfall. It didn't have the desired effect on many and it certainly didn't work for Edwin, who dropped to his knees and cried.

The sessions became progressively less tolerant and much more threatening. On one occasion, they tied him, standing, to a wheel of a field gun as units marched by on their way to the front, so that he might have an opportunity to observe brave men, and they, perhaps, to observe a coward.

The pressure to avoid treating shell shock as an illness meant that it was not an admissible defence in a man's court martial; as Edwin discovered the day they forced him to join an execution squad. They made it clear that if the bullet remained in his gun, it would be used on him immediately afterwards, in his own summary execution. The sergeant did point out that five other bullets would be fired at the prisoner in any event, so the end result was assured.

The prisoner was little more than a youth, and had to be dragged out and tied to the post. They had already stripped him of his uniform so that he slumped against the restraining rope in just his combination underwear. Edwin fired when ordered, but he was shaking so badly he probably missed. The others didn't though and blooms of red appeared on the poor man's torso, followed by the final, shaming indignity of another bloom, when his bowels emptied. If anything, that attempt at persuasion, or intimidation, could only make matters worse.

Finally, they moved on to the use of electricity. Not ECT, or *Electro-Convulsive Therapy*, which wasn't introduced until the late thirties. Many of the doctors had unforgiving views of 'Trench Hysteria' and were happy to inflict pain. A common use of electricity involved applying an electrical current to whatever part of the body that was afflicted. Those who were mute would suffer shocks to the pharynx while those who couldn't walk properly suffered shocks to their spines.

It was electrocution, plain and simple; without anaesthetic. So the poor devils felt everything, which in Edwin's case included biting the tip of his tongue off, because the nurse had been too concerned with tightening the restraining straps to notice that the leather bite guard had fallen from his mouth.

It was simply a question of perspective. At some point, the poor wretch's fear of the shocks outweighed his fear of the trenches.

Inevitably, damaged beyond the point of caring, Edwin succumbed and was returned to the front. A week later; just after he had shaved, the fates were kind.

A German sniper shot him.

He was actually putting his helmet back on when the shot was fired, so that instead of penetrating his skull the bullet removed three fingers from his right hand. A perfect 'Blighty' wound. Finally, now that he couldn't even fire a weapon, they sent him home.

He was sent to one of the tented hospitals at Etaples, on the French coast near Le Touquet where he managed to survive the then prevalent risk of infection. Penicillin wouldn't be discovered until twelve years later.

But Edwin was one of the exceptions, because infection *did* kill enough men to fill the largest war cemetery in France. Most were simple lads, who had never seen the sea before let alone sailed across it and who died, on foreign soil, when they were back within sight and sound of the English Channel.

* * *

George and Edwin caught a *Midland Red* bus from Atherstone, alighting when the driver stopped and told them to, just over the canal bridge. He had promised to tell them where to get off, after George explained that he'd only visited once before, though as it happened, help hadn't been necessary, for the two great oaks at the farm entrance were sufficient reminders.

Mary was the first to see them walking up the long drive. Both wore dark suits, lacking any formal creases; showing only those formed in the previous three hours, on public transport.

One had a starched turnover stud collar with round ends whilst the other's shirt was left wanting, though they both wore, formless waistcoats, flat hats and marginally polished boots. The waistcoats looked 'lumpy' somehow, as though they they'd been stung by a swarm of bees. All this she noticed after calling her mother and waiting by the kitchen gate.

What really set the two men apart was their stature. George walked with his shoulders set back and with long elegant strides, looking better suited to leading a funeral cortege, but from that distance, Edwin's steps had seemed so much shorter that he looked as though he was shuffling. He was also hunched over, though the suitcase he was carrying might have had something to do with that.

It was a very battered case. Thelma had bought it at her church jumble sale for tuppence, only to find, when she got it home, that it was locked with no sign of any keys. George didn't have the patience to try picking the locks and smashed them off with a hammer and screwdriver instead, which would have explained why the wreckage was held shut with a length of rope.

Meg came out of the barn and flew past Mary, barking furiously, until she yelled at her. The dog stopped making so much noise immediately, but ran on to greet the strangers; her tail wind- milling in welcome. When it became clear that neither man would offer her a pat she ran behind them and settled down to what nature intended her to do. Darting from one side to the other, she herded them in.

By the time they reached the house, Albert, Agnes and Mary were waiting but Charlie was still checking the sheaves of wheat they had cut almost three weeks earlier. The old sages reckoned on leaving the cut wheat for three church bells, or three weeks, before thrashing but in that time, some of the seeds could begin to chit, particularly on the north side of the field.

Fortunately, it was a Sunday, or they would have all been in the fields. Tomorrow would be extremely busy though and even the neighbours would join them when the threshing machine arrived.

Now, it was left to Albert to greet them, "George, Edwin, welcome to Purley View." He shook hands with George, but when he held his hand out to Edwin, the man dropped his case and extended his left hand, keeping the other behind his back, out of sight. The handshake that followed became an embarrassing fumble that Albert sought to mask by introducing Agnes and Mary.

They hadn't gone into great detail when explaining the situation to the children, saying only that he was a war hero who was sometimes a little funny in the head. Even at eight years of age, Mary could sense a 'wrongness' in the man's demeanour, but he was still a war hero, from a conflict that was still recent enough to affect every community in the country. Perhaps that was the reason she curtsied. Bobbing back up, she blushed and broke into giggles of embarrassment.

It was an awkward start.

They all stepped into the kitchen, where a table was set with cups, saucers, plates and a huge *Victoria* sponge. Nothing more was expected for they all knew that George would need to leave shortly, if he was going to catch the train home, though Albert promised to give him a lift to the station in the trap.

Everyone was polite and the conversation so stilted, that it continued to be a painful experience; until Charlie came back. Albert allowed him time enough for a cup of tea before ordering him out to harness Nelson up, signalling a welcome end to the visit.

This time though, Edwin formed part of the group that stood at the gate, waving goodbye to George, who was struggling to turn around and keep his balance, as Charlie set off at a trot.

Still they waited and waved, but there was a palpable sense of relief when the trap disappeared from view, though no-one knew why that should be, for visitors called in all the time. Even Edwin spoke a few words when they stepped back inside for another round of tea and cake. Soon after, Agnes picked the suitcase up and suggested showing Edwin his room. Ordinarily, he would have shared a bedroom with the male child, but unusually, for that time, they had a spare bedroom, since relatives from Birmingham would often visit at weekends and stay overnight. Even so, it was sparsely furnished. A small set of drawers and a curtained-off alcove served as storage and a small rug beside the bed offered the only comfort from the wooden floor in winter. The bed was a modest double, with an iron bedstead, but the linen was fresh and the fluffed up feather mattress looked like a soft cloud in waiting.

Agnes set the case down and said, "It isn't very posh I'm afraid, but it's yours for as long as you want it."

She thought it was probably his condition that caused him to appear so moved, but with wet eyes and a smile, he said, "Thank you. This will be fine."

"Well, I'll leave you to settle in. Come down whenever you like. Oh." She waved a hand towards the bed, "There's a pot under there if you should need one in the night," and with that she left him, closing the door gently behind her.

Edwin stood in the centre of the room and looked about him. He sat down on the bed then, and quietly wept.

* * *

He was woken at five the next morning, by Charlie and Mary, who were squabbling again. It was impossible to determine what they were arguing about though he would soon learn that a motive wasn't important. The act was quite sufficient.

He struggled into his clothes and went downstairs to find that everyone had already breakfasted. It was a big day in the farm's calendar and they would all need to be ready for when the threshing machine arrived.

Agnes was making bread and Mary was at the sink, washing up. Charlie and his father were outside, loading tools into the cart that had their shire, *Dolly Grey* between its traces. Nelson would be needed later, for the lighter work, but a couple of neighbours would bring their carts too, so transport would not be an issue.

"Good morning Edwin, I trust you slept well." Agnes had looked up and noticed him. "Mary, get your uncle a cup of tea please." She addressed Edwin again, "And there's bread and jam if you'd care for some. Apart from this," she nodded at the dough she was kneading, "We don't cook much on the first harvest morning."

"That will be very acceptable, thank you."

She noted that he had yet to use her name, "Then sit down over there and Mary will see to you. We shall all be down in the west fields today, so you can come and go as you please. If you want to work we won't stop you, but don't feel obligated. We should be just as happy to see you taking the air."

Mary was startled. She couldn't recall the last time she'd heard her mother say so much at one time, particularly to a relative stranger. Or strange relative, she thought, noting how he managed to conceal his disfigurement by drawing his plate to the edge of the table and holding his slice of bread down with just the thumb and forefinger, so that the rest of his right hand stayed out of sight, while spreading the jam with his left hand. It was well-practiced and done without thinking, though it did imply that he didn't want people to see his disfigurement.

A few minutes later, they heard the whistle.

It seemed to be making a slightly wobbly progress down the drive but there was no denying the spectacle of the thing, from the spinning flywheel to the column of dark smoke that issued from the tall gleaming stack. An odyssey of engineering excellence was clanking down the drive, with the threshing machine in tow. The elevator, an inclined conveyor system was attached behind that, so the manoeuvre through the farm entrance had been a demanding one. A few neighbours, the ones not bringing carts, had turned out and were following it, giving the scene an almost carnival air. The harvest was always a happy time.

As it passed the kitchen gate, Charlie read the polished brass plate on the side of the boiler, '*ALCHIN Built 1910*'. Impressive it might have been, but *Fordson* 'F' tractors had been imported since nineteen seventeen and were proving much more economic to run, though the capital cost was still well outside of Albert's budget.

Even so, the cost to hire a steam engine rig was becoming untenable too, thanks to all the new regulations being imposed, such as speed, smoke and vapour limits. Recently, they had even introduced the 'wetted tax', which varied according to the size of boiler.

Soon, the entourage passed by and Agnes sensed that Edwin wasn't ready to join in yet. She patted his arm, "Come back inside Edwin. Mary must join the others now so you may keep me company while I finish the bread."

It didn't take long to set things up. The contractor unhitched the thresher and turned the engine around to face it, before connecting them with a long flat, leather belt that swayed and bounced as the flywheel set everything into motion.

One group, using two of the carts, gathered sheaves in, to where two men passed them up to the man standing on top of the machine. He pulled the sheaves apart before feeding the wheat into the machine, which shed materials from three exits. Two men removed the chaff from beneath and stacked it alongside while two more stacked the straw as it fell off the elevator. Finally, there was the 'sack man', whose job entailed fixing a burlap sack to the exit point for the wheat kernels.

It was dusty, hot and hard work and it was wonderful.

At twelve o'clock, the contractor let out a blast from the engine's whistle and everyone sought a shady spot to sit and eat their lunches. Most had brought their own food, for the first day, but Agnes and Edwin carried freshly baked bread up from the farm, still warm and fragrant, as well as a small churn of cold well water. The next day would be different, they all knew that.

Edwin would speak only when spoken to, though smiled pleasantly enough as he carried the churn around for folk to help themselves, using the ladle provided. Albert had already explained things, so that the men refrained from the usual banter and jesting, keeping exchanges to a polite minimum; often no more than a word of thanks for the water.

Agnes joined them for the afternoon's work, which was declared to be over by six o'clock, leaving the contractor time to go back to the last farm he'd worked at and collect his living van. A four-wheeled trailer with what looked like a large shed on it; painted dark green, save for the small windows, high up on two sides, which had heavy frames that were painted white. It was his home for the duration.

He'd declined Agnes's invitation to join them for supper, but she plated one up and stepped out to pass it up to him when he returned. A stone jar of ale accompanied it and he doffed his cap as he called out, "Thanks missus, that'll do me very nicely."

* * *

The next day began just as early, but at eleven o 'clock, Albert sent Charlie down to the house with word that they were in good time, which meant that they were certain to finish that day. They had only contracted for two days threshing, so if there had been any doubt, dinner would have been in the field again, but this news meant that it would be down at the house.

Agnes had spent the whole morning in the kitchen, accompanied and assisted by Edwin. Whilst it could never be called chatting, they had spoken of a few things, such as family they both knew and places they had both been to. Those other places, across the channel, were never spoken of. Some of the time Agnes described their life on the farm and at one point, when he asked if she would like a cup of tea, she said gently, "Edwin, you may call me Agnes you know. We both have fine names and should use them."

He looked embarrassed, but her smile reassured him, "Yes, Agnes. Thank you." He returned her smile; a contract had been made.

At noon, everyone adjourned to the house for the feast, in a noisy column of celebration.

A boiled ham, cheese, boiled eggs, salted butter, pickles and freshly baked bread with ale for the men and ginger beer for the children. Agnes made sure that Edwin sat at her side, so that she might shield him from unwelcome conversation, though it proved unnecessary. Any word addressed to him was courteous and harmless.

It was over so quickly, though everyone took time to get back into the swing of things. Hard work and full stomachs were poor partners, but they still made for happy memories.

After that day, life returned to the usual routines of hard work and though Edwin made no attempt to initiate conversation or to join in, beyond the necessary norms, such as 'please' and 'thank you', the rest of the family seemed happy to go about their business and leave their visitor to his own thoughts.

Even so, they encouraged him to join them on outings; not that there were many. Sunday afternoon walks were always popular, particularly if there were visitors. The group would keep in single file on the edge of fields with growing crops in, so that conversations would be limited to a few at a time. In consequence, the group split up and the line became extended, which proved vexing for poor Meg, who ran from one end to the other, trying to round them up.

One experience startled them all, in a most pleasant fashion. It was on the second Sunday after their own harvest, when everyone was required to attend church, for the Harvest Festival. Agnes sought out one of Albert's ties and a collar for Edwin's shirt and encouraged him to polish his boots.

Somehow, they all managed to get on to the trap and set off for Mancetter church in high spirits. Mary had even tied ribbons into Nelson's mane which added to the festive air.

They occupied a whole pew and whilst Edwin seemed oblivious to it, Agnes was aware of the glances and whispering. Word had obviously travelled, but what did they expect to see? A madman in a straight jacket perhaps? She became more and more discomforted by it, until at last; the vicar appeared and distracted the gossips by announcing the first hymn.

The local school were formed up in front of the altar and sang '*All things bright and beautiful*'; well enough to have warranted applause if such a thing had been allowed in those days.

But it was the third hymn everyone would remember; the one that followed the readings and prayers and marked the moment for children to take their gifts of produce up to the altar, where the vicar and his wardens would lay them out in a fragrant and colour-ful display. The one chosen was *Come, Ye Thankful People, Come*, one of the most popular in the hymn book, though it began shakily, for the congregation was more interested in the procession of chil-dren. But then, at the start of the second verse something magical occurred. The church echoed to the finest tenor voice they had ever heard. It was pure and clear, and rose above the congrega-tion as though it had taken flight. This time the stares were open and astonished, though the subject of their interest was still Edwin, whose eyes were cast upward while his heart and mind had taken flight to another place and time, when he was whole.

It was short-lived, for as they reached the next verse he broke off, struggling to pull a handkerchief from his pocket, to deal with a bout of congested coughing. It may have been short but it had been unutterably beautiful and a salutary moment for many as well.

* * *

New influences are soon absorbed into busy households and Edwin was no exception. The family simply accepted his presence, albeit a largely silent one, since he still continued to avoid casual dialogues, speaking only when spoken to, which for the most part was with Agnes who was not much for needless chatter anyway. But she was in the house for most of each day, just like him.

The family's acceptance was in part a statement of relief, for if that was the measure of his illness, they could easily accommodate it, though one night, four weeks after Edwin had arrived, Albert did express concern. He had waited until he was alone with Agnes, in the privacy of their bedroom, "My dear, we have always taught the children that they have duties to perform. That's the way of it on a farm. It might be that seeing Edwin doing nothing each day will begin to affect them." He'd chosen his words carefully instead of saying what he really felt. There was no room for passengers. If that man wanted to eat, he'd need to work, though it was a delicate matter for he knew that Agnes had become very protective towards their visitor, who was, ironically, his kin rather than hers.

Agnes knew all this and had already begun to encourage Edwin to help with the chores, but she had also seen enough to know that his equilibrium was a very fragile affair. He would start at loud noises and sometimes, his limbs would twitch and tremble though he showed no sign of knowing it was happening. She'd discovered that the simpler tasks, such as fruit picking held his attention without any signs of stress and gradually, over the following few weeks she encouraged him to take on simple chores like feeding the poultry and collecting eggs.

Even so, Albert remained uncertain until October, when it was time for potato picking. A ragged line of pickers would creep across the field, some of them on their knees and others simply crouched, gathering the tubers into hand baskets. Once full, the baskets were emptied into one of the many large sacks left at regular intervals along each row, which in turn were loaded onto a cart when full. Fortunately, the soil was quite sandy and fell from the potatoes easily, making lighter work than when they'd been grown on heavy soil, but each day began at dawn, when the autumn mist chilled the bones and dampened clothes. The weak sunshine would eventually dry things off but by then, everyone was warm from their exertions anyway.

This time, to Albert's delight, the gang included Edwin, who seemed to be happily lost in a world of his own yet keeping up with everyone else, in spite of having only a finger and thumb on one hand. By the end of the second day it became clear that they would be finished within the week *without* having to employ any pickers from the village.

Even so, none of them realised how fortuitous the date of Edwin's arrival had been, coming as he did, three weeks after they had finished cutting the wheat with the horse-drawn binder. Any of the neighbours and friends who were going to help with the threshing had been invited to attend the event with their own shotgun and take up position around the field for the annual bag of game, which began to dash into the open as the reaping reduced the square of standing wheat to the point where there was insufficient cover. It was an hour or two of great sport and everyone took something home to hang.

Not another gunshot was heard until teatime on the third day of potato picking and then it was two fields away, on Mount's farm. Whether it was for game or vermin no-one at Purley View would know, but Charlie thought how comical Edwin looked as he set off across the field, with his head high and back arched rearward, covering the furrowed ground like one of the hares they'd seen at the harvest. It was such a funny thing to see, that Charlie, in his ignorance, began to laugh out loud. In truth, it might have looked funny to many, but the impact of a swinging basket on the back of his head wasn't. Agnes rarely showed emotion but there were times when her words could carry weight, "Now you have two baskets to fill Charles and while you're doing that, think about the bread you shall have tonight, for that is all there will be on your plate."

Stunned, Charlie watched as his mother strode after Edwin, until he heard Mary giggling from the next row and then he turned, scowling, "Shut up you!"

The kitchen gate was open but he had shut the porch door, which Agnes did too, once inside, though she stayed at the entrance, listening. There was no sign of him in the kitchen and she didn't think he would have gone upstairs in such dirty boots, though moments later it was one of the hob nails that gave his position away, when his twitching limb caused it to scrape on the stone floor of the larder.

Very gently, she opened the door and peered in, whispering, "Edwin?"

The huddled form in the corner by the stone thrall showed no sign of recognition as she stepped forward and tried to get the measure of things. Both arms were wrapped around his legs, holding his knees below his chin, tightly enough now, to contain the twitching. She noticed a few tremors but it was the stare she would always remember. Stares could reflect, interest, concern, anger and much more, but this one was like nothing she had seen before. It was as though he had left this world for another. All this, Agnes would reflect on later, when she was alone, but in the meantime she had to find a way to help him and that had to begin with comforting of some sort.

Minutes later she placed a knitted blanket around his shoulders, and as soon as the edges were placed against his knuckles he grabbed them and huddled into the comforting enclosure. Agnes then poured a small measure of the medicinal brandy into a glass and held it to his lips. His stare didn't falter and he showed no sign of knowing she was there or any inclination to sip the liquor. There was only one other thing she could think of doing. With a small grunt, Agnes eased herself down and around so that she sat beside him; close enough for him to know she was there and for her to feel his tremors. The charged brandy glass was still in her hand and after regarding it for some minutes, she gave it a home.

They remained in that position for over an hour, by which time the stone floor was causing her agony. The stare was still there, but his breathing had definitely become easier and it was time to begin preparing the evening meal. Normally, the midday meal was their main one but during the potato harvest they stayed in the field during the day and had their hot meal at night. At least there would be someone in the next room if he needed help and as she struggled painfully to her feet, another idea came to mind.

She chose a pipe from the rack; the one Albert would be least likely to miss and filled it with tobacco. In the larder, she lit it and coughed slightly while gently tamping the glowing shreds, as they saw Albert do each evening. This time, when she held it by the stem and placed the end against his lips, the fragrant smoke had the desired effect and a hand, the complete one, came up to grasp the bowl.

It was enough; the worst was over, at least that time.

The worst, perhaps, but his attacks were rarely over so easily. Often, he would suffer some more within hours of the main attack, like mental aftershocks.

That night, his scream penetrated the whole house until it was cut off as suddenly as it had started. Agnes donned her dressing gown and made her way down the landing, holding a candle high in the air. Albert had refused to move but Charlie and Mary were standing at their bedroom doors. "Go back to bed, both of you. There is nothing to concern you out here."

Mary obeyed, but Charlie would have none of it and followed quietly, knowing that his mother wouldn't waste time chasing him back to bed. Agnes stepped into Edwin's room and stopped while she cast light into the corners trying to find him. The bed was empty and the door had been closed, so only one place remained. As she bent down to peer under the bed, she heard him too; panting lightly in a terror she would, or could, never know.

She spoke his name and stroked his arm, but there was no response and for the second time that day, even in the weak candle-light, she saw the *'Thousand Yard Stare'*.

His arms were folded up against his chest, but after sinking down onto the bed, she was just able to get a hold on one of his hands. With that, she closed her eyes and eventually, against all odds, fell asleep.

Charlie went back to his own bed, a wiser and better person. He would never forget that night, or that afternoon, when he'd laughed at a man's terror. He hadn't seen his uncle's face on either occasion, which in a way made the sounds in that bedroom more terrible and then there was the smell of urine.

At five in the morning, Agnes was woken by movement and watched as Edwin worked his way from under the bed, before lighting the candle. He looked gaunt and tired, but the 'stare' had been replaced by a cognitive sadness, "I'm sorry Agnes."

She smiled and nodded slightly as she stepped past him to pull a nightshirt out of a drawer. She placed it gently on the bed and patted his arm, "Don't be, you've got nothing to be sorry for. Now change into that and get some rest. I've kept the bed warm for you." At the door she turned and said quietly, "Good night, God Bless."

No-one knew when the next would be or what would trigger it, but in the meantime autumn gave way to winter, when the ground had to be prepared for the following year and chapped hands harvested the kale and swede crops. No matter how many helpers they had, the workload always stretched beyond them and out of reach.

Edwin began to spend more time out in the fields than in the house, something both Albert and Agnes noted with relief, though for quite different reasons. As far as she was concerned, it showed signs of a recovery whilst Albert's view was much more practical. Neither spoke much, when they were working, but Edwin and Albert had taken to sharing some time each evening, with a bowl of tobacco.

He had also stopped hiding in his room when they had visitors although they in turn had stopped trying to make conversation, in favour of a more comfortable discourse with the rest of the family; an arrangement that suited both sides.

One day, early in December, Albert and Charlie had taken some poultry and cheese into Atherstone, to sell at the market, leaving Edwin; who'd declined an invitation to join them, with some spare time. Naturally, he gravitated to the kitchen as soon as Agnes came back from her own chores, later that morning.

As usual, there was little need for talk. Agnes spoke of the Dunkley family, with their fleas, warts, rickets and rats which Edwin found amusing, until suddenly he became still. Some little time passed in silence until he broke it with, "We had them in the trenches; fleas and rats. Big as dogs some of them. Rats, I mean, not fleas." He smiled slightly at the correction. "There were lice as well. They lived in the seams of our uniforms and itched all the time. They deloused us when we were allowed back behind the lines but most of the time we searched for them ourselves and pinched 'em with our nails. They used to go pop."

It was more than she had ever heard him say and desperately tried to think of a response. Finally, she chose the one that came to mind naturally and which therefore mirrored her innate, forthright way, "It must have been a terrible time for you."

He gave a small grunt in reply and silence returned, leaving her to picture what he had just described.

Suddenly, he said, "They made me live in the shed."

Agnes was still thinking about France and asked, "What for?" His response was startling.

"Because they didn't want me in the house."

This was obviously a different topic and the next question felt more awkward, as realisation set in, "Who didn't?"

"Thelma and George." Moments passed, before he added, almost conversationally, "It was cold in the winter."

They had treated him like a dog, when he so needed kindness. She was lost for words, until she remembered watching their approach, up the drive in September. The imagery should have told them then, that he had been treated badly, but they hadn't thought to ask. Not that he would have said anything then, she was sure.

If she ever had chance to speak with Thelma and George, it would be short and memorable, but in the meantime, no good would come of open argument. Her practical nature prevailed and she patted him on the shoulder, "That was a bad thing to do Edwin, but you're here now, so best not think any more on it."

It was the best possible piece of advice, for the poor man had enough demons already.

* * *

Christmas was a time of celebration for everyone. Whilst the gifts might have seemed modest, their real value lay with being home made. Each one represented thought, care, time and skill.

Charlie had whittled walking staffs from some Hazel he had cut and left to season from the previous year, while Mary had crafted knapsacks out of the fabric from an old sofa, which would be perfect for carrying food and drink in the fields.

Agnes, and therefore, Albert and Agnes, gave everyone new gloves and socks. They were highly prized throughout the family for Agnes's socks were thick and warm, though Edwin's present had called for special consideration and she had crafted a pair of gloves that fitted him exactly, in that the right hand one was fashioned for a single finger and the thumb. It was such a personal gift that might have been received badly, so she was relieved to see his delight as he tried them on.

All of the gifts had been made in the previous months, mostly in the evenings; in full sight of everyone, so there were no surprises as such, though to have discussed them at the time would have been a dreadful indiscretion.

That year though, there *was* a surprise. With Agnes's tutelage and in absolute secrecy, Edwin had made shortbread for everyone, wrapping each portion neatly in waxed paper before tying a label on. He was made to stand and take a bow while they all applauded; marking a moment of kinship he would never forget. He wasn't allowed to either, for when the Birmingham relatives visited on Boxing Day each member of the family surrendered up enough shortbread for a tasting, which prompted further praise.

The Christmas fare *was* extravagant though, at least for nineteen twenty two. In addition to their own produce, the farm provided an ample supply of game, some of which had been traded for special treats, so the dinner table was laden with an astonishing feast, triggering more applause, which embarrassed Agnes, who waved her hands dismissively. Mary, who had helped with the meal was less shy, and gave a deep curtsy, without giggling that time.

Afterwards, Albert pulled out a surprise of his own, an extravagance that bordered on the aberrational. With a dramatic flourish that was equally out of character, he presented a bottle of port to yet another round of delighted applause. Even Charlie and Mary were allowed to have some, though diluted with a large measure of lemonade.

It was a Christmas they would all hold dear.

* * *

It might have been the fog that triggered the next one, perhaps by way of autosuggestion. No-one would ever know, least of all Edwin.

It wasn't unusual to have fogs all winter, fossil fuels made sure of that, but the one in January nineteen twenty three had gone on for a long time, lacing the hedgerows with droplets that soon froze at night.

"GAS! GAS! GAS!" The bellowing woke the whole household immediately, so they all heard his headlong dash down the stairs and out of the back door. Agnes ran to the window just as the kitchen gate was thrown open, with enough force to crash against the wall, but by the time she had opened the curtain he'd disappeared into the gloom. She did catch a glimpse of the white tip of Meg's tail, wagging as ever and heading into the eastern pasture so at least they knew which direction he'd had taken.

It was time for the head of the house to do something, "Albert! Edwin's having another turn. He's headed off across the field, towards the road."

Albert grumbled from beneath the bedclothes, "And what pray do you expect me to do about it? Go out and give him a race?"

"He's in his nightshirt!"

After a minute or two of silence, she began to snatch her clothes up from the foot of the bed, "Then I shall go myself. Lie there and be proud of yourself Albert Morcroft!"

"Yeeaarrrgh, damnation!" He had flung the bedclothes off and sat up, tousling his hair further by scrubbing his head with his hands in frustration. "Go Agnes, get me the *Tilley* lamp and then we shall find out who hasn't taken him in yet, for this cannot continue."

Agnes didn't bother answering him as she left the room to get his coat, boots and the lamp ready.

The fog was laden with hoar frost as Albert stepped out of the house, still angry and half asleep, though the bitter cold soon woke him.

The trail across the frozen grass was as obvious as it could have been and just before he reached the bank that rose up to the road verge, Meg trotted back to meet him and then turned to show him the way. His anger vanished when he saw Edwin, curled into a ball, beneath the hedge. He had torn a sleeve from his nightshirt to fashion a facemask out of it and stared at Albert in horror. His voice was muffled by the cloth, "Get down, and protect yourself with something! It's a gas attack!"

Albert could only guess how cold Edwin truly was and knew he had to act quickly. He tried the only tack he could think of, trying to sound relaxed, even jovial, as he joined Edwin in France, "You bloody chump, didn't you here the 'all clear'? The wind shifted and carried it down the line. Come on now, we'll both be for the high jump if they catch us out here?"

Edwin looked uncertain, so Albert tried further reasoning, "Look, would I be standing here like this if there was gas about?" He reached down and gently took Edwin's elbow, "Come on now, I'm catching my death out here and Agnes has a nice cup of tea waiting for us."

The slip from past to present went unnoticed, but the promise of hot tea and Agnes's kindness did the trick. Five minutes later they were supplied, in full measure, while he sat next to the *Aga* stove, wrapped in a thick blanket.

From then on, the family accepted that the attacks would continue indefinitely, though there would be no more mention of finding him another home. Albert had learned a great deal that night, about both of them and in self-reflection; hadn't liked what he'd seen.

Charlie had also changed, as far as young boys can. But when forced to polish his own boots, he would find Edwin's too. Conversation was difficult, but having to attend school was an unhappy experience shared by both of the children, which merited description over the table in the evenings and sparked a show interest on Edwin's part.

Once, when they were alone, Charlie spoke of the punishments meted out by the head and suddenly, Edwin began chatting about his own school days, which sounded more brutal and austere than Charlie's. Even so, it was common ground and from then on, Charlie made a point of finding time alone with his uncle, though the subject and grievances remained the same. It was an accord that was founded on boyhood adversity.

* * *

In the months that followed, he had a few more attacks, as expected, but the rest of the household grew used to them and treated each as part of the Morcroft family life.

Until the seventeenth of March; when Edwin suffered his worst nightmare.

Like most of the other attacks, no-one knew what triggered it, though he had spent the afternoon picking stones in the field Albert had selected for that year's potatoes. Not on sandy soil this time, it was backbreaking work that lacked the satisfaction of other more productive labour and the ground was still so wet that their boots became heavy with clinging mud. Charlie would always swear that the mud had set Edwin's subconscious off, triggering memories of the trenches.

* * *

It was different this time. He knew that he needed to get away from there, quietly and unobserved. If anyone saw him the game would be up, plain and simple.

Edwin slipped downstairs, gathered his boots up and crept out through the back door, easing it shut before putting them on. He tucked the bottom of his pyjama bottoms in and tied the laces securely, for it wouldn't do to have them trailing, waiting to trip him up.

He opened the kitchen gate and started when something moved out from the corner of the wall. It took a second or two for him to realise that it was Meg, no doubt wondering who might be out and about at that hour. Hissing as loudly as he dared, Edwin ordered, "No, Meg! Get back!"

The dog didn't need telling twice. It was raining, late and of no particular interest. With what might have been a canine shrug, she trotted back to the warmth of her kennel.

Edwin had been unsettled by the experience though and his heart was pounding. Now he'd been seen, already, and he hadn't even got away from them yet.

Using every sense he thought he had, Private Morcroft stealthily crept into the east pasture, hunching low as he made his way down to the canal and along the hedge line. At the end, he dropped to one knee and listened. Nothing moved and all he could hear were the drops of water falling from leaf to leaf in the hawthorn. He was set to move out from the cover but shrank back when he heard a distant sound, like breathing and it was getting closer.

After an unreasonably long time, he realised that it was a train, hauling an impossibly long line of open wagons; the sort they always use for men and ammunition. This one was obviously heading back for fresh supplies and they'd be needed, that much was certain, but meanwhile, any men on it now were heading for Blighty; injured probably. That meant it was heading in the same direction as him and almost as slowly; it seemed. Time dragged, until eventually, the clicking, clanking procession passed by, but the pause had given him time to focus on what needed to be done.

The big push was at dawn; he had to get away. Had to.

Dressed only in his pyjamas and boots, though unaware of the shortfall, Edwin scuttled out from the cover of the hedge in a crab-like fashion until he reached the canal. Without any hesitation, though silently enough to ensure the sentries wouldn't hear him, he slipped into the water and made his way across. On the other side, he crept under the hedge and tried to drain his boots by holding each foot in the air, but they were full of *Coventry Canal* silt, not water.

There was no time to take them off, for dawn was closing faster than he was gaining distance from the front line. He could have gone back up the line, to where the railway embankment closed with the canal, but he couldn't bring himself to turn in that direction.

Just one more field to go and he'd be en route, with the chance of hopping a ride, at least for part of the way. He'd have to be off it before it reached the depot.

Edwin crept along the tow path until he reached the main road and paused to make sure the way was clear before running across to the neighbour's pasture, which ran down to the railway embankment. From then on it was straightforward, though the bank was steep and overgrown with brambles. By the time he reached the top his face and arms were latticed with scratches. It was a minor discomfort though, just like the rain.

He stepped along the track, hoping that he wouldn't have to go far before the next train came through and hoping further that it would be travelling slowly enough to board. He felt sure it would be, for the tracks had undergone so many temporary repairs from the Hun shelling that speeds were limited to little more than a walking pace.

His boots made a dreadful squelching sound but he didn't hear them above the deafening silence around him. The shelling had stopped; the push was at hand.

* * *

Constable Bernard Ellis was a traditional copper who lived on his beat, clipped boy's ears when he caught them scrumping apples and sometimes turned a blind-eye when he judged that Justice should have been blind. He was the village bobby and well-respected.

He was reliably honest too, except for one departure from the rules, though he wasn't alone in thinking that the licensing hours were nonsensical, forcing landlords to stop selling alcohol at nine-thirty at night, just when many men had only just finished work. Now that the Americans abolitionists had come up with a total ban on alcohol there were fears something similar would happen here and that *would* constitute a crisis of conscience for Constable Ellis, for he enjoyed a pint or two most nights, when the observance of the '*no drinking on duty*' rule required him wait until after ten-o-clock; an accommodation afforded to him and a few others, at the *Railway Inn*, on Leathermill Lane. It was well off the beaten track and an easy downhill pedal home. In fact, the hill was steep enough for the railway cutting overlooked by the pub, to become a considerable embankment, overlooking the road, within half a mile.

'After hour' drinking still had unspoken limits though and when it was time, a group of shadows would exit the saloon door moments before it was slammed shut and the light inside extinguished, leaving the companions to grope their way home. Ellis was the only one with transport and stood still while he waited for enough night vision, before trying to find his bicycle. Once he'd done that, the front lamp would provide all the light he would need.

A few minutes passed until the footfalls of the others had gone and he was left standing in an agreeable silence. The rain was light now and his cape more than a match for it.

Something like a very distant thunder reached his ears as he moved towards his bike, and gradually increased until he recognised the sound of the Glasgow sleeper out of London. The majesty of those great express engines amazed him, particularly in the dead of night when the approach would be marked by a trail of sparks and embers from the firebox, followed then by a necklace of lights from the carriages. It was a common enough sight at this time of night, but he never tired of it.

As usual, all of his senses save *touch* were assaulted, though the smell of smoke would take a while to waft over to him. But when half of the train had passed he caught a flicker of movement on the track closest to him. He couldn't be sure what it was, for the strobe-like reflections from the carriageways provided little enough to go by, but something was down there, he was certain.

The spectacle of the express had cost him most of his night vision, but he was close enough to his bicycle to find it by touch and to wrench the lamp free.

Whilst the train had employed most of Ellis's senses, Edwin paid it little heed, for it was heading in the opposite direction, but the light shining down from the bridge gave him a terrible fright.

The lamp was barely bright enough to light Edwin up, so with some cause, Ellis couldn't believe his eyes. It *looked* like someone in sodden night clothes, hunched over and it *sounded* like someone trying to squelch through mud.

"Oi, you there. What do you think you're doing?" He heard a small yelp as the figure picked up speed and disappeared under the bridge, clearly up to no good and intent on escape. Ellis still had a fair turn of speed and ran across the road to see the figure appear from the other side. "Oi! This is the Police! Stand still, this minute!"

The whimpering could be heard clearly now but whoever it was had moved beyond the lamp's range. There was no choice in the matter, but Ellis couldn't help thinking of the pie that waited for him at home as he began to give chase, signalling his intentions in the usual way. With all the air he could spare, he blew his whistle in a long shrill blast.

Edwin began to weep as he spoke to himself, "Oh God no, Please God no, they've started already. The push is on already." He knew there would be more whistles, all the way down the line and his mates were climbing over the parapets through a wall of lead and into a sea of cratered, gangrenous filth. "If they had only waited a short while longer I would have made it, for pity's sake!"

Ellis made hard work of keeping to the sleepers. He couldn't use his lamp to see ahead *and* down, so that he often stumbled on the granite track ballast. The figure had disappeared from sight after a hundred yards or so, prompting him to pause when he reached the spot and listen. Slowly, he advanced, until he heard a noise from a short distance ahead, which grew louder as he drew near. It was a sort of mewling, unlike anything he'd heard before, from man or beast, but he was about to bear witness to great suffering, that much was certain.

The figure was curled up at the base of a signal post with one arm wrapped around a stanchion. It was human, just, but when the beam of light fell on it, the scream was more like that of a rabbit, taken by a fox.

While Ellis tried to make sense of what lay before him Edwin glanced up fearfully and saw the shiny buttons of a uniform, "Please sir, just this once, please, I've done my bit. Please sir, can I go and visit my ma and da? *Please.* I promise I'll come back, only not this time sir, I beg you. The lad's will understand." He shrank back into a ball then, whimpering like an animal caught in a trap.

The poor wretch at his feet was no longer a sensible human, that much was clear, but Ellis had heard enough.

He knelt beside the soldier and placed a hand on his shoulder, "Very well soldier, just this once, you look as though you've earned a break. Come with me, I'll escort you to the docks, there's a ship leaving shortly."

Edwin twisted around and flung himself against his saviour, "Thank you sir and God Bless you. I won't let you down, I'll come back, I promise."

"Well in that case, up on your feet soldier, we have a way to go, spritely mind, if we're going to get there in time."

Moments passed for that to sink in and then Edwin struggled to his feet. Ellis tried to sound slightly military without appearing to be threatening, when he asked, "Fair enough, let's be having your name first."

Edwin was too traumatised to stand to attention, but his reply was militarily correct, at least, "R1408 Morcroft, private, Yorkshire Rifle Regiment, sir."

Ellis put his hand on the man's shoulder once more and spoke gently, "Then let's get you home private Morcroft." He removed his cloak and placed it on Edwin's shoulders, "Here, best put this on. I have to get you there in one piece."

It took half an hour to get back but in that time the rain finally stopped and breaks were appearing in the clouds, allowing enough moonlight through to give the two figures form. Little enough was said, but the constable did glean enough to know that Private Morcroft was related to the Morcrofts at Purley View farm.

They were halfway down the drive, with the farmhouse in full view when Edwin slipped the cloak off and passed it back to Ellis, "Thank you sir, I shall not be needing this now." With that he brought his heels together and saluted.

In spite of the mud and grime, Ellis saw that the salute was made with just a thumb and forefinger. He snapped to attention and returned the salute; holding it until the soldier made an about turn and with a back that was ramrod straight, marched towards Purley View Farm.

An observer might have found the scene comical, after all, the sight of a grown man marching in muddy pyjamas and hobnail boots could hardly be called solemn.

Instead, Ellis's eyes filled. He'd seen his fair share of breakdowns, outright insanity even, but he'd never witnessed anything like this.

He stood in the middle of the drive watching, as the receding figure jerked slightly, and spat something to one side; more phlegm from a pair of tortured lungs. Now the bobby's breathing slowed with a leaden despair as he muttered, "God 'elp you Private Morcroft, and God 'elp us all if we can't look after the likes of you."

* * *

Charlie was sent up to check on his uncle when he failed to appear for breakfast. Normally, he didn't need waking, but that meant he should have been up half an hour since.

A few minutes later, Charlie returned, "He says he's feeling a bit under the weather this morning and will stay in bed for a short while longer."

Agnes assumed he was having another turn, of sorts, and planned to pop up and check on him before leaving the house, but while the rest of the family mentioned it in passing, each one was more concerned with the work he or she had planned for the day, particularly now that the weather had cleared up.

Soon after they had left, she took up cup of tea up and noticed the dank smell as soon as she entered the room. Edwin was curled up in bed, and seemed to be asleep, with only his hair showing beyond the blankets, so she crept around the bed to set his cup down and saw the pile of sodden clothes on the floor. She had to draw the curtains slightly, for the light was too poor to make sense of it, but when the sodden mass could be seen for what it was she whispered, "Oh dear, Edwin. Whatever did you get up to?"

The figure under the bedclothes stirred, so she spoke loudly enough for him to hear, "I've brought you a cup of tea Edwin."

The reply was muffled, "Thank you Agnes. I'm feeling the cold a little this morning so I think I shall stay here for a short while if I may." The tremor in his voice made her look closely enough to see that his whole body was shaking, until a bout of coughing took over and she heard him spit phlegm into the handkerchief he must have had under there. She found another blanket to drape over him and gathered the sodden mess up, "I've left you clean pyjamas on the end of the bed. You stay there until you're properly warm young man. I shall look in when I get back."

A small shaky voice came back, "Thank you Agnes. I shall get up in a few minutes."

He was still in bed at lunchtime; dressed in dry pyjamas and Agnes persuaded him to drink some tea and eat a small sandwich, though his heart wasn't in it. By that evening, he seemed a little brighter. His coughing continued, as usual, so nothing was thought of it, particularly when he managed to eat the bowl of broth Mary took up for him.

It was a brief and treacherous relief though.

Agnes heard his breathing as soon as she stepped out of her bedroom door and hurried into him. The bedclothes were a tumbled, damp mess and the room smelled stale, but his breathing was short and laboured, until the gurgling signalled an approaching need to cough more phlegm into the glutinous mess in his hand that was once a clean handkerchief. Albert helped to change his pyjamas and bedclothes, by which time it was clearly time to fetch the doctor. Edwin kept apologising throughout the process, but they could see he was barely aware.

As usual, Doctor Gregson barged through the back door, giving it a cursory tap as he crossed the threshold, as a token gesture of courtesy. His diagnosis was as quick, though he continued with a full examination to make absolutely sure. Even when the patient was an adult, Gregson would step out of the room, to give his diagnosis to whoever had called him, "I'm sorry Mrs Morcroft, he has *pneumonia*, very badly I'm afraid. It's being exacerbated by the existing lung condition."

Agnes spoke quietly enough to ensure that Edwin couldn't hear, "You mean making it worse?"

"Quite so, we need to get him to hospital where they can make him comfortable."

"But will they make him better?"

Gregson shook his head slightly and whispered, "It would be wrong of me to give you false hopes Mrs Morcroft. Even with specialist care his chances are less than fifty-fifty. His lungs are already so damaged"

Agnes straightened up and when she spoke, it was clear that the news was expected, "Then he shall stay here Doctor, with his family."

Twenty years later he might have argued against that decision, but in nineteen twenty two he knew that Edwin was dying and therefore in the right place. He nodded, "Very well, I shall leave you something to rub on his chest, to ease his breathing but then we can only pray. I'll call in tomorrow, about the same time."

Edwin passed away that night.

* * *

The funeral was a modest affair, attended by the Morcrofts, two couples from Birmingham, Thelma and George.

Two years earlier, Field Marshall Douglas Haig had adopted the poppy as a symbol of recognition and since it was too early for any to be found naturally, Charlie and Mary made their own out of wire and coloured paper. As soon as she saw them, Agnes declared that they would be the only decoration to adorn the coffin.

After the service, they all adjourned to the farm for refreshments, though in the parlour, aired specially for the occasion, rather than the kitchen. Thelma had said little but looked as though she'd swallowed sour milk and the reason soon became clear. Charlie overheard her speaking to the folk from Birmingham and went to find his parents, in the kitchen, "Aunty Thelma says that we didn't take proper care of him."

Albert was astonished and knew that he couldn't allow that lie to fester. He began to make his way to the parlour, but was bowled out of the way before he'd reached the door.

Agnes strode into the centre of the room and gazed around while she composed herself. Everyone fell silent and she began, "I should like everyone to know that Edwin enjoyed his life here. We are saddened that he should die here, but he did so, in his own bed and surrounded by family who loved him."

She turned to face Thelma for the last time in their lives, "I wouldn't have wanted him to die in a garden shed."

Chapter Three

I wasn't surprised to find two photographs of a milk dray in the chest because of course, I knew about the milk round, though I hadn't known the horse's name. It looked to be a chestnut though it was difficult to be sure from the faded black and white image.

A man I still haven't identified was featured in one but I knew who was driving the dray in the other picture—that much was easy; it was my father's sister, Aunty Mary. She was dressed in a white wrap-around overall and looked quite stern, which differed from the person I knew as a child, years later, when she had a home of her own. I remembered her warm welcomes and kindnesses, her wonderful cakes and an infectious chuckle that would have been a giggle in someone thirty years younger.

On the reverse of the picture someone had written, *Mary and Nelson.*

The dray was a high-sided cart that resembled a chariot, laden with two large milk churns at the front and Aunty, of course, standing behind them with the reins in her hands.

My own childhood was filled with a strange form of recognition. Local 'grown-ups' would ask my name and the answer would always trigger the same response, "What, the Mancetter Morcrofts?" My nod of confirmation would be met with something like, "I knew your dad and your aunty! They had the milk round up by us. Well I never. Small world isn't it? How are they both?"

Of course, by then they were both out of farming altogether. Dad was working for Nuneaton Borough Council and Aunty was a housewife and mother; baking wondrous things still and cultivating not just one garden, but two more that belonged to neighbours, who either had no time, or little interest in growing their own vegetables. They certainly had an aptitude for picking them though.

By a strange coincidence, on his return from the army, Mary's husband, Arnold, spent most of his working life driving for a feed merchant, delivering to local farms. He would be the only one of the family to maintain daily links with farming.

As I wrote this, one thing puzzled me about the milk round, or rather the milk. I only remembered Dad and Aunty Mary speak of 'running the milk through the chiller'. There was never any mention of pasteurising it.

A modicum of research soon established that they *didn't* pasteurise the milk, no-one in the UK did at that time. In fact, apart from chilling it, they didn't treat it at all.

It appears that Monsieur Pasteur first tested a heat treatment to kill the pathogens in milk in 1862. Surprise, surprise, the treatment became known as *Pasteurisation*. It might have been worse. He could have been a Mr Barber, or even a Mr Pulver.

In any event, he failed to stir much enthusiasm, since the majority of milk sold in Britain was unpasteurised until the late nineteen thirties.

I also discovered that in England and Wales, between nineteen twelve and nineteen thirty seven, some sixty five thousand people died of tuberculosis contracted from milk.

Nous sommes desolee Monseiur.

Charlie
THE MILK ROUND

Charlie lasted a year on the milk round and hated every minute. He reckoned it was woman's work and said as much, whenever the opportunity arose, but the reality was twofold. He hated dealing with the public and his lack of numeracy made Friday night collections a nightmare.

No-one knew for sure how accurate his collections were, but when Mary took the round on, after spending an extra year at school, takings improved significantly; something she would point out whenever *that* opportunity arose.

Charlie might have drawn everyone's attention to her extra schooling but pride was at stake and in any event he was back in the fields, where he belonged.

Thankfully, for all concerned, Mary loved the milk round. It gave her the same sort of freedom Charlie was enjoying; one that wouldn't have been available to her if she had stayed at home and for that matter wasn't enjoyed by many women in the late nineteen twenties. Women in the workplace were a feature of the Great War, but the nineteen twenty six General Strike was changing all that.

Usually, the round was over by late lunchtime, when she was expected to return home to assume the usual role of a daughter on the farm.

Any leftover milk was put into the butter churn, except in warm weather. Then the milk would have to be stored in the cellar until the cool of the evening, when a belated butter- making could take place. Conversely, in the winter they would put boiling water into the butter churn for half an hour. Her mother, Agnes, would labour the need for temperature control, "Let the cream be at a temperature between fifty five and sixty degrees, in Fahrenheit mind, by the thermometer."

Either way, there would be butter for sale by the next day, either to callers or on the round.

There were also eggs for sale, though not many, thanks to Boadicea the pig, who ate any hen stupid enough to stray within snatching distance.

Each day, Charlie and his father would do the milking before seven. Not an unreasonable hour on bright summer starts, but on bleak wintry mornings they would work in the feeble light given off by a couple of *Tilley* lamps. They rarely spoke to each other on those mornings, for there was little to think of beyond the misery of chapped hands and bones that ached with the cold. Sometimes, they would tie a couple of hessian sacks over their shoulders, but the benefit was more psychological than physical.

As soon as the cattle had been turned out and the milk run through the cooler, they would heave two seventeen gallon churns onto the dray before heading into the warmth of the kitchen, where the women; at twelve years of age and a full-time worker Mary refused to be called a girl; would have stoked the *Aga* with logs. Coal was a luxury they couldn't afford, or at least wouldn't be countenanced by Charlie's father, not when they had their own trees to fell.

A large cast-iron pan lay to hand, ready to fry the slices of fat bacon from the side they had cured and hung from a beam in the pantry. It *was* fat bacon too, with just a sliver of pink flesh running through its centre.

But the large kettle was a permanent feature on top of the stove, set to one side, where it would simmer gently. When tea was called for they would drag it over to the centre where there was enough heat for the water to boil almost immediately. That manoeuvre wasn't just for the benefit of the men either. All visitors would be invited into the kitchen and whichever member of the family was closest to the stove would automatically move the kettle into place, so that the water was boiling before the guests had even sat down.

While the tea was 'mashing' visitors would be treated to the sight or sound of a tin being removed from the corner cupboard. It was simply unthinkable not to have scones or cakes to hand for such occasions.

For the men though, on those achingly cold mornings, the ritual of sitting at the table and nursing a hot mug of tea while waiting for the bacon to cook was a comfort they relished. By then it would be spitting in the pan and filling the room with that unique aroma.

Another difference in fare was the bread; sometimes still warm from the oven. It was nutty, crusty and dense enough to fuel the appetites of men who knew only hard work. Any not used to mop up the bacon fat would be laden with creamy butter, salted to taste and topped off with homemade jam.

As soon as the men's breakfast had been prepared Mary would head out to the stables where Nelson waited to be harnessed.

Her father tried to discourage her, but she named most of the animals after historical notables. Her disdainful cat was called Lizzie, after Queen Elizabeth the first, a favourite cow, Cleopatra and her least favourite cow, the one given to lash out with a back leg whenever the opportunity arose, was named Jezebel. The chickens were the exception, thanks to Boadicea, the pig; the attrition rate was simply too high.

Mary's greeting was always the same, "Morning Horatio and how are you today?" Whenever she was alone with Nelson she preferred to call him by his first name and continued with a gentle chatter while she tacked him up. An observer would think she was actually conversing with the animal and though both were oblivious of the other's thoughts each took comfort from the company. As soon as he had backed into the dray's shafts Mary treated him to a small piece of bread she had smuggled out of the kitchen. The practice had gone on for months though she'd been determined never to ask for any, just as the rest of the family pretended not to notice her take it.

It was her favourite time of day, for it was hers, alone. She knew that the men would have ridiculed her daily chats with Nelson which continued as they made their way up the hill to the first call, in Hartshill.

Some were large houses, almost stately, where she was expected to attend the service door at the rear. At one in particular she was expressly forbidden from making contact with or, unless it was unavoidable, being seen by the owners. If she heard them approach, she was expected to move out of sight and remain there until they had passed by.

At Hartshill House, Major Hilliard's son was up from London on a visit one time and offered her a shilling to venture into the garden with him. Although his father had retired there was a distinctly military air to the place and when she mentioned the offer to her father he was furious, saying that instead of the 'King's shilling' she'd been offered a bastard's shilling. She took it to mean an insult by name only and wouldn't appreciate the hidden meaning for many years.

Most of their customers were poorer though and some were well below the poverty line.

These people lived in terraced houses, for the most part and Mary developed her own method of delivery. She would fill a small churn, that was fitted with a hinged lid and carrying handle, before heading down an entry to the backs of the houses. There were two measuring ladles, one for half a pint; the other for a full one and each customer would stand at their back door with a jug, ready to take a measure of milk which was always just a little more than they asked for.

People were friendly then, and helped each other, as far as they could, but that wasn't the same as charity; an act scorned by all, even the would-be beneficiaries. So there were sometimes things Mary did that called for ingenuity.

The Flemings weren't just dirt poor. Mrs Fleming had three young children, poor health, a little income from taking in washing and a husband, who was last seen walking into Nuneaton, three years earlier. Not surprisingly, she was rarely at the back door, so Mary took to rapping on it and stepping inside two or three times a week. The stench was terrible and the gaunt looks of the kids haunted her, but she never showed a reaction. Instead she would chatter on brightly, though without break so as to deny Mrs Fleming an opportunity to refuse the milk being poured into the jug that sat by the back door. "Good morning children, how are you this morning then? Bet you can't wait 'til you're old enough for school. A spot of reading and 'riting does wonders; promise. An' you're poor old mum'll get a break then." The monologue would continue until she was halfway out of the door and then she would move on to the neighbour who was often already standing at her door. Mary would approach and roll her eyes, "Never has her jug ready, does Mrs Fleming, not like you, Mrs Arnold." The fiction was complete and every member of the cast knew it, but a code of honour had been respected.

Once, Mrs Fleming managed to get a word in, "Please, I know you mean well, but this is charity for I can never pay you."

Mary was ready, "Actually Missus, I'm glad you mentioned it, for I haven't known how to ask, but ma has some curtains she wants me to wash and what with the round and my chores, I haven't got time, so I wondered . . . ?"

The poor woman nodded in relief, "Of course I shall wash them for you, if perhaps you could let me have the soap?"

"Lovely, then as soon as the weather gets a bit better, I'll drop them in." Needless to say the weather never did get warm enough for the curtains to be taken down.

After eight or so houses she would reach another entry and return to the street for more milk. Nelson would have moved on and would always be waiting for her at that next entry.

Well, almost always.

There was the bread incident.

Coleshill Road in Chapel End is a steep incline that is set into the side of a hill. On the right, the houses faced onto the street, but at the rear they were full storey higher, to allow for the ground that fell away.

On the left-hand side, the houses were set some way back from the road and the frontage was a bank of concrete steps that looked a little like the seating of a coliseum.

An elderly lady by the name of Enid lived halfway along that stretch; a distant cousin of the Morcofts, from the Birmingham side of the family. Too distant to warrant visits to the farm in fact, but she took it upon herself to meet Nelson as he waited for Mary at the nearest entry and give him a slice of bread. His second treat of the day. The practice had gone on for months, until the day Enid was laid up in bed with a bout of bronchitis.

Nelson waited patiently, occasionally snorting a call for his mid-morning snack, but there was no sign of Enid. His anxiety peaked when he heard Mary walking back down the entry; it was time to take the initiative.

Mary stepped out into the sunshine, just as Nelson began to climb the stairs towards Enid's front door. The going was difficult since the cart needed to be bounced up over each step, but nothing was going to stop him, not even Mary's yells, which became more urgent as the rocking of the churns increased with every bounce and then the inevitable happened. She was struck dumb then, as the churns fell away from the dray and rolled unevenly down the steps at an angle that caused them to oscillate. The tops had flown off on impact with the ground so the milk was ejected in irregular gouts, as though the churns were throwing up.

Mary was at a complete loss and both she and Nelson, who by then had turned to view the chaos, looked on as the churns reached the road and continued down the hill towards Ansley Common.

Eventually, they made it back to the farm to face the hot water. There were consolations; not least of all that three quarters of the round had been completed by the time of the calamity and since Mary didn't receive any wages, she couldn't be fined. She also took comfort from knowing that whilst Albert Morcroft was a strict parent, he had never laid a hand on his daughter.

There were recriminations, naturally, as a matter of form, but having to creosote the chicken shed was not an unduly harsh punishment, though her father did have one more thing to add, at the dinner table that night, "There's no more bread leaving the breakfast table for that animal, Mary. He's cost me enough today."

Mary made it through that autumn and into the winter without further mishaps and in that time, like most home service providers, she made firm friends with many of her customers. Cups of tea at reasonable intervals were always welcome though time and bladder capacity imposed a limit on how many she could have. By unspoken agreement the same stops became the norm each day. No others offered refreshment.

Except for special occasions and Christmas would be a memorable one.

That December, the temperature had remained below freezing since the sixteenth and Mary had even taken to tying sacks across Nelson's back. Going up the steep hill to Hartshill in the mornings, with a full load always warmed him up. The plumes of condensation appearing from his nostrils spoke of his exertions, but as the load lightened and inclines reversed he became lethargic and at times, wilful. Mary's voice also lacked its usual authority, muffled as it was by a thick scarf.

Once, when they should have continued up the Coleshill Road, he turned left into School Hill and headed home, with an eloquent resolve that said, "Bugger this."

They had covered a hundred yards at a fast trot before Mary was able to turn him into a hedge, where he stood and sulked, while his mistress got off the cart, grabbed his bridle and gave him a talking to. Finally, he allowed her to back him round, but neither trusted the other for the rest of that day.

In truth, she shared his misery. The bitter cold and chapped hands made life a misery during the day, but the warmth of the kitchen at home brought on the terrible itchy heat and soreness of chilblains. They tried all sorts of remedies, including soaking the feet in urine, (hers), warm bread soaked in milk, a raw potato dipped in salt and a home-made ointment of beeswax and olive oil. She became desperate enough to heed the advice of an old farm-hand by standing in Nelson's muck heap and for a while, the stench gave her something else to think about.

Her father had muffled the churns with hay and sacking, but that wasn't enough to stop the milk from freezing towards the end of the round. He stopped using the chiller and that helped but the days dregs would always be frozen when she got home which made cleaning even more of a chore.

But in the afternoon of the twenty third of December, the weather changed.

A blustery north-easterly came out of nowhere and brought snow with it; lots of the stuff. By the evening the wind had risen to gale force and by the following morning, huge drifts blocked many of the roads. Not the one up to Hartshill and Chapel End though.

To make matters worse, because it was Christmas Eve and there would be no delivery the next day, Albert had bought some milk in and a third churn was tied to the back of the dray, forcing Mary to walk beside Nelson, in shared misery. The arrangement was that she would remove the extra churn as soon as it was empty and leave it at a customer's house, for collection later, but in the meantime, with snow still falling, the two companions were a sorry spectacle.

It took twenty minutes for the first act of mercy, in Grange Road.

Mrs Albrighton had seen Mary's approach from the front window and was beside herself, "Mary, my dear, you shouldn't even be out in this, let alone walking. Is there something wrong with Nelson?"

Mary shook her head, enough for the snow that lay on top of it to fall on to her shoulders, "No Mrs Albrighton, I've got an extra lot of milk, seeing how it's Christmas Eve."

"O' course, I should've known that. I'll have an extra pint too, if you please? Mind, one of the men should be out here with you. They should be ashamed of themselves!"

Mary gave a shrug of appreciation and ladled milk into the jug Mrs Albrighton was holding. They wished each other a merry Christmas and parted company, but moments later the door opened and a man's voice called out, "Mary, a moment, please lass."

Mary turned to see Mr Albrighton beckoning. She went back and was ushered inside, "I've got just the thing for yer." He winked, "We give ourselves a treat at Christmas." As he spoke, he poured hot water from the kettle into a glass of brown fluid and passed it to her, "'Ere lass, get this down yer. It'll help, I promise."

She took a sip and grimaced as the rum hit the back of her throat, causing her to choke. It tasted dreadful and she shook her head. He recognised the problem immediately and took the glass from her, "'Old on, let me sort that out for yer." A spoonful of sugar made it much more palatable.

The warmth of the drink and inner glow provided by the alcohol was wonderful and she left the house in much better spirits, (no pun intended).

Fifteen minutes later, Mrs Shepherd, in the terrace that overlooked the castle ruins on Castle Road introduced her to a 'hot toddy', though by then Mary knew what was needed and asked for a spoonful of sugar.

Just a couple of hundred yards on brought her to Mrs Carter's house; the first of her tea stops. But it was Christmas Eve and a glass of home home-made barley wine was called for.

Another hot toddy at the Field's house was accompanied by a mince pie that served to slow the ingestion of the alcohol, but Mary's cheeks had become quite rosy by then and she smiled a lot.

By the time she reached the bottom of School Hill she was in fine form; as warm as toast and willing to give old Mr Farmer a yuletide kiss under the mistletoe in exchange for an extra mince pie. Not for her, but for Nelson. Furthermore, sugar was no longer necessary for the rum or whisky, they tashted jusht fine.

Halfway up Coleshill Road, the infamous bank of steps nearly did for her. With another two hot toddies inside her, she extorted another mince pie for Nelson and when her feet disappeared from beneath her, the bucket and ladle were ejected in favour of the precious pastry, an act which called for both hands, on outstretched arms, as she rolled down the entire row of steps. At the bottom, she raised herself onto her elbows, before struggling to her knees and finally legs. Then she stepped across to Nelson, as though her descent had been normal enough to warrant scant attention.

She tried to engage Nelson in conversation, but he only had eyes for the mince pie. As he munched away she rested her head on his and assured him, "You're my besht friend you know; in the whole wide world." Clearly impressed, he nodded his head, sharply enough to snap her mouth closed, splitting her lower lip and chipping the corner off one of her front teeth.

She didn't notice, though the prospect of her father's wrath did penetrate the drunken haze enough to prompt a search for the bucket and ladle.

Somehow, thanks in large part to the remaining customers tolerance and unwillingness to give her any more alcohol, Mary made it to the end of the round, though Mrs Tenant made her husband turn out, to carry the bucket and measure out the milk for the four remaining calls in that row. But when he offered to accompany her home she became slightly belligerent and set off alone, singing carols to Nelson.

Normally, whenever they reached Hartshill Green, just a quarter of a mile from home, Nelson would pick up his ears and feet, though Mary would normally hold him back from breaking into a trot, but in truth, she wasn't exactly sure *where* they were when he did and sought to regain control by pulling him over, just at the point where Nelson was adjacent to a driveway and the dray, next to a high kerb.

With only a light load, the dray bounced up over the step, launching Mary clean over the side and into a bank of snow. The whole thing was too much for Nelson, who opted for home, in the shortest time possible.

Mary still had the reins in her hands and was dragged along, just beneath the surface of the snowdrift, like a giant frenzied mole until her survival instincts kicked in and she let go, just inches away from being dragged beneath a wheel.

The reins did make contact and jerked Nelson's head around as they were trapped under the wheel, but the inertia was enough to snap the leather, releasing the animal from all restraint, save for a light dray. He made it home in less than five minutes.

It was over an hour before anyone at the farm knew it though. The deep snow had made working out of doors impossible so Charlie and his father were in the workshop, tinkering with the seed drill in preparation for the spring. At around three-thirty Charlie was sent into the house for cups of tea and as he made his way through the deep snow he was relieved to see that that the snowfall had slackened off.

Even so, he noted how quickly the snow had covered the tracks made by Nelson and the dray on their return from the round, by then, marked only by faint indentations. For that matter, he mused, the snow must have deadened the sound of their return as well, for he hadn't heard a thing. It was only a passing interest that caused him to try and trace their passage further until he noticed that they stopped short of the yard. They should have continued around the far side of the house, towards the stables, but instead, a disturbance in the deeper snow to one side of the drive suggested that Mary had taken him into the field, down the side of the barn.

Puzzled, he followed the tracks until the dray came into view. It had a distinctly abandoned look, at least in that there was no sign of Mary, but Nelson was still between the shafts, with his head out of sight, helping himself to the hay stored in the barn.

It looked as though Mary had just dumped the dray there and gone inside. Bad weather or not, such a dereliction of duty called for some words of censure. In fact, a great many he decided, as he hurried to the house.

"You idle little shirker, what d'yer think you're playing at?"

Startled, his mother looked up from kneading dough, "Beg your pardon."

"Mary, she's gone and left the dray in the drive without a by-your-leave and now the horse is helping himself to hay out of the side of the barn. Just dumped it she di . . . what's up?"

His mother elbowed past him, rubbing the flour and bits of dough from her hands and arms with her apron. Charlie finally cottoned on as she threw her coat over her shoulders and ran out of the house. There was no sign of Mary and they hurriedly inspected the dray for signs of damage, finding only the broken reins. Agnes guessed what had happened, "He's bolted. How long's he been here?"

Charlie shrugged, "Dunno, we were only in the shed but we didn't hear anything." He pointed at the drive, "The tracks are well covered though, so it's been a while."

Agnes nodded in agreement and hurried to the workshop where she found her husband still hunched over the seed drill. "Albert, get off that thing, You need to go and find Mary. Looks like Nelson has bolted and he's back here, without her."

Albert looked up, without removing his arms from the machine, "If she's daft enough to let that happen she can make her own way home. It'll be a good lesson in this lot."

"You have to go now Albert, you and Charlie, we reckon the dray's been back here an hour or more." She waited as he continued to work, knowing that he was considering the situation in his own way and eventually he straightened up, wiping grease from his hands with an old cloth. He nodded, "I'll go and get my hat and coat."

Charlie and his father left the farm almost two hours after Mary's ejection from the dray. In the absence of witnesses she had lain in a snow drift for fifteen minutes, watching clouds move around the sky in great circles; enough to make her nauseous. Eventually, she succumbed and threw up spectacularly, into the snow beside her.

That was the movement that caught Thomas Tranter's eye as he made his way home from the *Nag's Head* on Hartshill Green. The pub should have closed at two o-clock but on Christmas Eve, licensing laws were given a wide berth. By the time he reached her,

Mary had dragged snow up over her vomit and was patting it into place with exaggerated care.

As soon as he recognised her he said, "Ay up Mary, where's yer 'oss, an' the milk cart?"

She looked up at him, put a finger against the side of her nose and winked, "It'sh a shecret."

He barely understood what she had said, "Beg pardon lass, what was that."

She waved her hand dismissively, as though the secret could be shared, "'E's gone to the North Pole to help out." She was as tickled by the idea as he was puzzled, but it was clear that she needed help. Somehow, he managed to get her to her feet and across the road to the *Nag's Head*.

The landlord looked up from his paper and tried to recognise the bedraggled figure Thomas was trying to get through the door.

Thomas provided the answer, "It's young Mary Morcroft, I just found her in a snowdrift over the road. No sign of 'er horse and she talked some nonsense about it going to the North Pole. Mind, I reckon she's on the outside of some liquor; she's left 'alf a stomach full in the snow."

The landlord called for his wife and between the three of them, managed to get Mary's wet coat off and sit her by the fire. A blanket was wrapped around her and a bucket was placed within reach, in case her stomach chose to empty the remaining half. Throughout it all Mary thanked them and repeated her 'Merry Christmases' until the warmth carried her off to oblivion.

Thomas and the landlord decided to reward themselves with another half of mild while the other few men in the bar joked at Mary's expense.

Over an hour passed before Charlie and his father inspected the snowdrift; Mary's snowdrift that is. It was the first sign of disturbance they had come across and they followed a relatively new set of tracks over to the *Nag's Head*.

The landlord recognised them immediately and pointed across to the sleeping figure by the fire, before calling out, "She did that all by herself and none of it here. All I've done is sat her by the fire and put that blanket on her."

Albert called out, "Mary?"

The familiar voice brought her to and she grinned stupidly at him, "Hellooo Father. Merry Christmash!"

He and Charlie wrestled her back into the coat and as they made their way to the door she tapped the side of her nose with a fore-finger and gazed up at her father, "I knowww you know. Oh yesh, I knowwww."

He glanced at the landlord whose expression seemed to suggest that he shared Albert's embarrassment and they merely nodded at each other before the drunkard's exit was marked by another clumsy encounter with the doorway.

Nothing was said about it the next morning and Christmas dinner was the feast it always was, but after, before presents were exchanged, all but Mary left the dining room and headed for the parlour.

Her penance was the washing up, and she knew it.

Chapter Four

The photograph was quite small; taken by an amateur with something like a box brownie camera, I guessed. In which case, the photographer was probably my Aunty Mary.

Two trees were the subject matter though only one was in the picture. Even so, it was huge. The past tense was appropriate because it was lying on the ground, having been felled by the two men standing by it. It was also a hot day.

How did I manage that bunch of deductions, you may ask.

For a start, I recognised the two men in the photograph. My Dad and my Uncle Arnie;—Aunty Mary's husband. They looked much younger than I remembered, of course and if pressed, I would guess their ages to be around eighteen. They were also extremely hot, for both were in their shirt sleeves; the cuffs open and hanging limply while the fronts were unbuttoned and opened wide. Their trousers sagged beneath their belts in formless, limp testimonies to their labours, which in turn were evidenced by the huge girth of the tree behind them.

It was obvious that they had felled it, for they were holding a very large two-man logging saw between them and a variety of axes, sledge hammers and wedges lay on the ground.

My last but one deduction was that it had been a success. People don't generally grin at failures and those two wore ear to ear versions.

My final deduction was that there were two trees and one was called Romulus, for someone had written on the back, 'Arnold and Charlie and Remus.'

See, elementary, dear Watson.

Charlie

THE OAKS

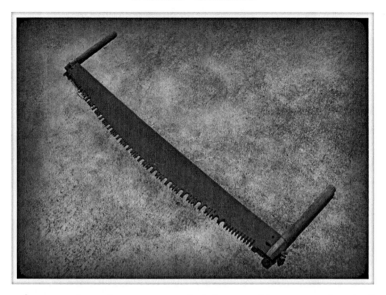

At around ten feet across, at their base and just over a hundred feet high, they were only middle-aged at six hundred or so years old. At least that's what the man from the council said. He also pointed out that they would have been saplings when the *Black Death* swept through the country, which was an appropriate analogy, since he was serving notice on Charlie's father to cut them down within thirty days because they were so badly diseased.

That in its self wouldn't have excited the authority's interest had the trees not been next to a main road, serving as lordly sentinels to the farm entrance. The farmhouse lay several hundred yards away, beyond the pasture that bordered the road so compliance wouldn't entail any risk to property, provided they were dropped into the field.

Since it was May, with the crops set and thriving, but still well shy of harvesting, Charlie's dad had given him leave to tackle the job, rather than call a contractor in; something that would have only been considered as a last resort.

They had been superb specimens and no mistake. So grand they even had names. But they were hollowed by disease now and unlikely to continue bearing their own weight for much longer. When Charlie's father had first taken up the farm tenancy, the landlord had been very specific, "Now, Mr Morcroft, you have two grand oaks at the bottom of your drive, which I am entrusting to your care. I would consider it injurious to me personally if you caused harm to them in any way." He pointed at the trees, "The one on the left is called Romulus and the other, Remus."

Clearly, Mother Nature was releasing Albert Morcroft from his duty of care, but no one was celebrating.

* * *

Charlie had been sitting on the stone wall for half an hour, pondering on the task ahead. Older hands would have found the prospect daunting, but to an eighteen year old it was a grand adventure, though one that would need planning. Tools would need to be selected and sharpened; the cuts planned and what to do with all the brash? Would heaving ropes be enough to influence the fall or would chains be required? He knew that all these preparations would need to be made before his father would spare time to help with the sawing, just as he knew that the job would no longer be his when that happened.

He heard a pair of hob nail boots being stamped on the tarmac road and glanced up to see a young man trying to get mud off his boots. Horse muck as well, Charlie thought, for he had obviously come up from the canal towpath where many barges were still hauled by horses. He turned his attention back to the trees, intending to nod an acknowledgment to the stranger when he passed by, but the clacking steps slowed as they drew near and when Charlie turned the other said, "How do?"

"Not badly, thank you."

The walker seemed keen to make contact and continued, "It's a belter of a day for it."

Charlie frowned slightly, "For what."

The man hadn't expected his attempt at conversation to be answered with a question and in any event, he was not a conversationalist by nature. He *was* extremely lonely though and his spirits were low. In panic, he said the first thing that came into his head, "For looking at trees, I suppose."

An inevitable silence followed, while both of them tried to think of something to say, until eventually, it became too painful and the visitor said, "Well, I'll be seeing thee."

Charlie looked up and gestured towards the trees, "I was just trying to work out how best to cut these two down." After a few more moments he turned to see that the stranger was staring up at the trees also.

Then he spoke, "They don't look too 'ealthy."

Charlie nodded, "No, it's time to get them down I'm afraid. The council have told us we've got to."

The other man looked back at the trees for a few moments before, "There's still some weight there though. 'Appen they'll not be stopped once they start moving."

Charlie had been thinking the same, only moments earlier. "True enough. Mind, that much wood'll see us through a couple of winters."

The other chuckled, "My Da' won't use the stuff. He's a coal man, through and through."

"What a miner?"

"He used to be, when we lived up north. Times have been bad though. It's why we've moved down here so he can get a job in one of your motor car factories. Me too, if I can."

Charlie huffed, "They're not *my* factories. I wouldn't work in one of them; not for all the tea in China."

The other man's tone was neutral and resigned, "We don't have no choice. It's the only work we can get."

This prompted a sympathetic acknowledgement of a clumsy response, "O' course, sorry. Didn't mean to say that."

The other waved a hand in dismissal, "No, 's'alright. Factory's better than down the pit I reckon. I'm still on the waiting list but there's some hope at any rate."

It was nineteen thirty one and hope was still in short supply.

Arnold's father's decision to head South would prove to be a wise one, for the North would remain economically depressed for most of that decade, while the South and Midlands were already showing signs of recovery, thanks to a thriving new motor industry and electrification, which was creating a need for appliances. The South had laid claim to most of the electrical work and the motor industry was centred in the Midlands.

It was time for Charlie to change the subject, "Where are you living now?"

"In Nuneaton. Gadsby Street."

"So what brings you out here?"

"Fresh air I reckon, an' something to do." He was looking up at the trees again, "So how many men will it take to do the job?"

"Oh, just Father and me; when he can spare the time. Mind, he doesn't have much choice about when, we've got less than four weeks to do it."

Arnold sounded almost diffident, "I should be glad to offer a hand if you can use one."

Charlie grimaced, "And you'd be welcome too, in better times, but we can't hire anyone just now."

"No, no, I wasn't expecting payment. I'll do it for nothing."

Charlie was puzzled, "Why would you want to do that?"

Arnold looked embarrassed now, "It'd be good to do some work, any work. For me really, more than for you and I haven't got anything better to do at the moment. Mind, a small bite in the middle of the day would be appreciated."

Charlie was delighted. The prospect of getting on with the job, without his father taking over, was too good to miss, "And you shall! I can promise that much. Would tomorrow be too soon?"

"No, I think that would be wise, while this weather holds fair."

"Then if you could be here for eight, we'll get a head start."

Arnold didn't hesitate, in spite of the four mile walk he'd have to do first, "I'll be here, I promise."

Charlie grinned, "Then let's shake on it. My name is Charlie."

"And mine is Arnold, Arnold Blake."

Neither realised that their handshake did more than close a deal. It would mark the beginning of a lifelong friendship.

That night, over dinner, Charlie announced his plans. Albert had no objection to cheap labour, but he cautioned his son against any temptation to pay more than the agreed reward of food at lunchtime, no matter how well the man worked. He had no way of knowing that, given time, Arnold was going to cost him a great deal more than bread and cheese.

Mary had started her milk round promptly that morning, after cautioning Charlie with, "Don't you dare bring that thing down without me being here. I want to watch and I've got a film in my camera."

Her brother was defiant, "I can't wait around for you. If that thing wants to come down what do you expect me to do about it? Hold it up?"

"It'll only come down if you cut more than you should have."

"I'll cut what I have to. I'm not going to pussyfoot around the job just so you can get back in time."

"You're just being spiteful!"

"And you're wasting time. The sooner you get started the better chance you'll have of getting back here in time."

She had run out of argument and stamped her foot in frustration before running out to the dray; her face flushed in anger.

Agnes was out of sight, in the larder when she spoke, "You two would be better served if you didn't keep arguing."

Charlie was in the porch, putting his boots on and called back over his shoulder, "Don't worry Ma, it keeps her on her toes and anyway, it'll be a lot longer than she thinks before we have one of those down."

It was too.

When Charlie reached the drive entrance, pushing a barrow loaded with tools, Arnold was sitting on the wall waiting and greeted him with, "'Howdo?'"

Neither had arranged how they would meet, though when Arnold failed to appear at the house Charlie hadn't hesitated to heave the heavy barrow down the drive; certain that his helper would be there.

"Good morning Arnold. It's a fine morning for it."

"Aye, as we thought."

Charlie didn't waste any time. He had brought a piece of chalk with him, to show Arnold where the first two cuts would be, so as to leave a wedge-shaped gap facing the intended direction of the drop. He then gestured for Arnold to take one of the saw handles and they began work.

The saw had been well-sharpened and bit into the wood, spraying light grey sawdust out of the cut with each sweep, but Charlie soon noticed an imbalance to their work. It lacked the symmetry of effort called for and he suspected that Arnold was trying too hard.

He was too, for he was desperate to show that he was up to the job.

Charlie called a halt and with the saw left in place, stepped around the tree, "Arnold, if I may be so bold as to make a suggestion and hope not to cause offence?"

Arnold was sweating already, "No, of course not!"

"Well, see, this is a big job and it's going to be a long one, so you will be best served by taking things a little steadier and don't push quite so hard. You'll see, the saw doesn't need it. We have to pace ourselves, so follow me and try and find a rhythm."

It took a little while, but eventually, they managed to find an easier tempo and Charlie heard murmuring from the other side of the tree. He listened carefully and realised that Arnold was singing to himself. It was a slightly slower beat than usual for the song but perfectly in time with the sweeps of the saw. He joined in as soon as he recognised the lyrics and moments later they were both singing aloud, "This . . . old . . . man . . . he . . . played one . . . he . . . played . . . knick knack . . . on . . . my . . . drum . . . "

The sound of a horse covering ground at a fast trot along with the clanking of empty milk churns signalled Mary's return, long before Nelson appeared over the canal bridge with the dray. Both horse and driver were hot and bothered, and Mary's windswept shock of dark hair gave her a slightly wild look. The moment they came into view she yelled, "Stop! Wait for me you little rat!"

She was much earlier than usual and must have finished her round at the run, along with poor old Nelson. They stopped just inside the drive and alongside the tree where she could see that they still had a long way to go. One of the three cuts had been completed and the second was nearly there, which would release a wedge from the trunk. After that, they would need half as much time again to make the single cut from behind and that would be the *coups de grace*.

Charlie turned and looked at the horse, "You shouldn't be pushing Nelson that hard on tarmac roads."

She snapped back, "Mind your own business and I'll mind mine."

Just then, Arnold stepped from the other side of the tree and Charlie flicked a hand in his sister's direction, "This is Mary, pay no heed to her manner."

Arnold showed little sign of hearing what had been said and stepped forward until he could speak softly, "I'm a bit too hot and bothered to shake your hand miss, so if you'd accept that I would have liked to, instead, I'll be grateful."

Mary was flustered. Charlie had only said a local man had offered to help. He didn't say anything about how *polite* he was, or how pleasantly he smiled when he spoke. His hair was dark, like hers, but while her hair fell in great waves, his was straight and neatly trimmed.

She suddenly realised how she must look. Hot, bothered, and windswept. Her hair was a mess. Oh hell, she'd really let herself down by yelling like that. It was all Charlie's fault!

She had to leave, as quickly as possible, "Er, yes certainly. I'll go up to the house and get your lunches." Which she did, at a fast trot, though she didn't return until she'd changed into a clean dress and her Sunday shoes; the ones normally reserved for church. Her hair put up a severe resistance but eventually it was in order too. Then the bread and cheese was transferred from newspaper wrapping to a basket and covered by a clean tea towel. Finally, the water was replaced by milk and she hurried down to the oaks.

The huge trunk seemed to be smiling, now that the second cut had been finished, leaving the wedge they'd removed on the ground in front.

Arnold said as much, when they were sitting on the wall, resting, for Charlie had decided to wait until they had eaten before starting the last cut. They had also exchanged a few words with the people who had started to appear, drawn to the spectacle of such a large tree being felled. When they saw Mary approaching, Charlie realised that they would have an audience for lunch as well, so he pointed out that the fall wouldn't happen for at least an hour and a half. After a quick deliberation, the spectators left a boy at the site with instructions to run up to Hartshill and tell everyone when it was time. With that, the group left for their own midday fare, though some would return sooner, with picnics of their own.

In the meantime, their own lunch was delivered. For once, Charlie refrained from commenting on his sister's appearance, realising that it was for their visitor and any taunting would cause embarrassment to them both

He didn't invite her to join them though.

Arnold did that, "Thank you miss, if you've nothing else pressing, perhaps you would join us."

Mary had a naturally ruddy complexion, from being outdoors for most of her working life, but it failed to conceal her blush as she stammered, "Thank you, but I've left mine up at the house." She flapped an arm in that general direction and made to start back and then stopped, and then started. It was just too painful to watch and Arnold sought to help with, "Then perhaps you could bring yours tomorrow?"

"Er, yes, perhaps I will." She still fidgeted, before seeking the safer ground of addressing her brother, though it was really directed at Arnold, "It's not much, but I hope you enjoy it. I'll come back in while, for the basket."

They had spent most of their lives taunting and teasing each other but Charlie hated to see her struggling so, in front of a stranger and tried to ease things, "Thanks Mary, this'll be fine. Be sure to be back here in half an hour's time though. We'll be starting the last cut then."

She could have hugged him then, but that would have been too much; he was still the rotten little brother who made her life hell.

As soon as they'd finished eating the boy ran up the hill as fast as his legs could manage and in no time a crowd returned. Word had travelled and the numbers had grown from earlier, so that the event took on an almost festive air, not unlike the May Day festivities that had been held on Mancetter Green, a couple a weeks earlier.

Albert decided that it wouldn't have been seemly for him to attend but he and Agnes did go upstairs to watch from the bedroom window.

And so Charlie and Arnold stepped forward to begin final cut, in air of tense expectation. Both men felt it, prompting Charlie to speak quietly to Arnold as they picked the saw up, "Have you ever felled a tree before?"

"No. Have you."

Charlie was too nervous to bluff, "Ye-es, but nothing this big." He paused long enough to clear his thoughts and take a deep breath, "Well I reckon it won't be much different, 'cept for the dent it'll make in the ground. One thing though, you make sure that you've got a clear path away from it 'cos if I shout run, that's what you do. Bugger the saw, or whatever else you've got in your hands. Drop it and run."

Arnold hadn't realised that Charlie was so anxious and now he was too.

It was mirrored in how clumsily they handled the saw. Charlie was about to call a halt when Arnold began to sing once more, "This . . . old . . . man . . . he . . . played   one . . . he . . . played . . . knick knack . . . on . . . my . . . drum . . . " and like the last time, it worked. Except that this time there was an audience; keen to join in.

In no time, the cut was half complete and Charlie called for a halt. By then children were dancing and clapping, while he drove a couple of steel wedges in behind the saw. It was unlikely, but he had to make sure that the monster didn't topple backwards onto the road, or worse, into the crowd. One man called out, "We can huff and we can puff and *blow* the tree down if you like!" The efforts of the crowd to do just that caused great hilarity, until Charlie approached them with his hands held up, for silence. When, eventually, it was quiet enough to be heard Charlie shouted, "Begging your pardon everyone, but we need to listen now, for sounds of it starting to go. If you would be kind enough to listen with us, I should be obliged."

Even the grown-ups hushed their boisterous children as he returned to the saw. With a nod to Arnold, they began the final cut.

It seemed to go on forever, though both men later agreed on the exact moment they thought they sensed movement, yet it was an illusion, perhaps only a shift brought on by the wind, for the sawing continued for much longer. Charlie called for another halt, supposedly to check the wedges and line of cut, but in truth they were exhausted and needed a rest. The damned thing still seemed as steadfast as ever. Finally, they lost patience and threw themselves into their work, in the continuing silence.

The first crack sounded like a gun going off and prompted a host of exclamations from the crowd. Four cuts later and it began to move, like a giant ship moving down a slipway. Charlie shouted, "Back Arnold, out of the way." Both of them ran a few yards and by the time they turned to watch, the great oak was halfway to the ground, exactly where planned. The ground shook when it landed with a huge thump, amidst the crashing of branches and the crowd burst into applause. Charlie was chuckling with relief as he took Arnold by the elbow to turn towards them and together, they bowed. It was a fine moment.

Congratulations were given and hands shaken until finally, they were alone. Mary suddenly called out, "Wait, I've forgotten my camera. Wait here, don't move."

* * *

They brought the other one down the following day, though the crowd was much smaller and Charlie thought, less appreciative. But there were some notable differences.

The most painful ones lay in the palms of Arnold's hands. By lunchtime, the blisters he'd acquired the day before had broken, exposing raw tissue and necessitating the use of cloths wrapped tightly around each hand. But lunch was reward enough, he thought.

In addition to bread and cheese, lunch included slices of bacon with a jar of home-made piccalilli and in place of milk, Mary had provided them with a stone jar of ginger beer. It was a feast and Arnold said as much when they had finished and the basket was being packed. Mary blushed once more and hurried back to the house, promising to return as she had the day before.

When the second tree lay on the ground both men fell silent. The elation they had felt the first time had been a symptom of the relief in completing the job safely, but now their success was blighted by a kind of sadness. Two majestic giants had been slain.

Charlie suddenly realised that in future, he would be reminded of that, every time he passed through their gate. It felt like a family bereavement.

Their spirits were dulled further when Albert finally visited the site. He stepped around the stumps, inspecting the cuts and noting the direction of fall before giving his jaundiced approval, "Well done lad, you've got them down right enough, but why have you left so much in the stumps? They'll have to come out too you know, there's another two hundred square yards of growing land there lad."

Even the mixed praise would have been welcome if it hadn't been tainted with such a monumental task. But something very positive happened that day too.

Arnold fell in love.

He'd had an inkling of course, but when they had finished for the day Charlie asked Arnold to help carry the tools back to the shed and then invited him into the house for a cup of tea, where he could be introduced to Mother. Mary met them at the door and when she saw Arnold's bandaged hands all inhibitions disappeared.

This was familiar territory, for she was often called to deal with injuries and for the first time since they had met, she became confident and business-like, "Let me see those."

Arnold was embarrassed. His injuries were a sign of weakness; of being unused to hard work and he was unwilling to exhibit them in front of strangers, "No, they're fine thank you, just a little sore that's all. They'll be fine by morning."

"Now!"

Her tone startled him into submission, though he couldn't stop himself from wincing when the cloth was peeled away from one of the worst wounds. Mary gasped when he finally offered up his palms for inspection, for both hands were covered in bleeding sores that needed cleaning and dressing. She found it easier then, to continue staring at his hands as she spoke, rather than to his face, "You shouldn't have carried on with your hands in this state. Why didn't you say anything?"

Arnold fidgeted with embarrassment and mumbled, "Because I had a job to do."

It was time for Mary to be shamed, "A job that you weren't even being paid to do!" She gave herself a mental shake; it was time for practicalities. After leading the way into the kitchen she instructed, "Sit there, while I get something to clean them."

Arnold sat at the kitchen table and waited as she filled an enamel bowl from the huge kettle on the *Aga* and set it down on the table beside him, with collection of cloths and a small round tin of *Germolene*. This time, she spoke softly, "This is going to smart I'm afraid. I can't help it, but I'll be as gentle as I can." With that, she took his right hand and held it over the bowl before squeezing warm water over the wounds from a soaked cloth. It was enough to clear the fresh blood and sawdust but gradually, she teased his wounds with the cloth to clean them properly. Once satisfied that it was as clean as they would manage, she placed a dry cloth in her lap and set his hand down on it before wrapping the material over and gently squeezing. Then she placed his hand back on the table and glanced up as she opened the tin, "This is going to drag a bit, but you need to put this on or they could go bad."

He nodded, "That will be fine, thank you."

Mary focused on the job, keenly aware of how much pain it was causing and was relieved to finally tie the bandage off on the second hand.

It should have hurt, but Arnold Blake barely felt a thing; at least not physically. As long as she was looking at his hands he'd been able to look at her and by the time she'd finished he was smitten. There could be no doubt about it; he was sitting next to Mrs Blake.

Fortunately, Agnes hadn't seen the look in his eyes when she came in from collecting the eggs, but she did observe his hands before they had been dressed and gave a nod of acknowledgement, without saying a word.

Charlie joined them for a cup of tea and piece of buttered fruit loaf, though he had a hidden agenda. He and Arnold discussed the adventure, exchanging compliments and laughed at the funnier recollections. Though neither had mentioned it, they were easy in each other's company and worked well together; enough for a friendship to have been established and enough for Charlie to want it to continue.

Charlie urged Arnold to take another slice before voicing his thoughts, "Arnold, thank you for your time and effort these last two days and I want you to know that you'd be most welcome to visit us, at anytime."

It was music to Arnold's ears, for now he had good reason to come and be close to Mary, "Then I shall, Charlie, thank you. I would imagine that you'll need some help to cut those trunks up."

Which was exactly what Charlie wanted to hear.

Mary cut in, "You'll do no such thing!" She nodded at his bandaged hands, "Not until those are better."

Arnold held them up, "They shall be, soon enough, I'm sure."

It was a very satisfactory end to the day and time to leave. As he stood up from the table Agnes walked in, carrying a small sack, "Here, you'd best take this to share with your folks." She passed it to him and made her way to the sink without another word. It was time to get on with their own dinner.

It felt like Christmas in the Blake household, when they emptied the sack onto their own table and unwrapped a piece of home-cured bacon, a loaf, a jar of jam, a spring cabbage, six eggs and some butter.

* * *

It took a week for Arnold's hands to heal; at least, enough for him to get back, though Mary made Charlie promise to exercise restraint and make sure that Arnold wore the gloves they had found for him.

It took a further two weeks to cut the trunks up into sections that were small enough for the horses to drag back to the piece of rough ground behind the barn, where they would stay for two years before being cut up for fuel. They dare not use the new tractor because it had a habit of rearing up and throwing the driver off when such loads were dragged behind and snagged on anything.

The work was interrupted on a couple of occasions, when Charlie was told to go out into the fields, tending crops or livestock, which gave Arnold the opportunity to join in and add further value to his presence, so much so that by the time they had finished the primary job, it was made clear that he could call in anytime; they'd always find something for him to do.

By then he routinely ate with the family and was encouraged to pick a cabbage perhaps, or some strawberries, to take home.

It couldn't last, idylls rarely do, but when word came through that there was a vacancy at the *Alvis* works Arnold had to take it. The only saving grace was that the working week was only five days, unless he wanted overtime, which of course he didn't. The two days he had left each week could still be spent at Purley View farm.

* * *

The woodchips and sawdust soon disappeared beneath fresh grass and weeds, but the two enormous stumps taunted Charlie. A couple of old hands at *The White Horse*, who were not '*Baldheards*', told him what to expect. Most of the roots would be around two feet underground, but there would be plenty of them, covering a lot of ground and then there were the tap roots; plummeting down vertically from the main trunks. He knew he wouldn't have to excavate them, but he'd certainly need to dig his way in and sever them before the stumps could be pulled out. The hour he'd spent pecking at the stony ground had been enough to get a measure of the dreadful task ahead.

One day, Arnold persuaded him to get started and together they exposed a few roots. The soil and stones prohibited the use of saws and axes fared little better, since the 'bounce' of the root limited the tool's effectiveness.

They would have been dispirited had their labours not been interrupted by a visit by Charlie's best friend, Stan. He and Arnold had already been introduced so it was a relaxed affair, finding them seated against the remains of *Romulus*, chewing the cud and sipping Mary's ginger beer.

Naturally, the stumps were the main topic and Stan commiserated as the epic details were imparted. He didn't remind them that they had already told him all of it, for he had an idea and was waiting for the opportunity to share it. Finally, he was able to interrupt, "Why don't you blow them up?"

That was an easy one for Charlie to answer, "I've never used the stuff for that sort of job and wouldn't know how. Besides, it'd cost too much; Father wouldn't hear of it."

"How does five bob's worth of black powder sound?"

"Five shillings? That'd only buy five pounds of the stuff. We'd need more than that I'd reckon, and anyway, how would we set it off?"

Stan grinned, "Leave that to me. Oh, and five pounds *will* be enough, at least for one stump. Then, if it works I'm sure your dad will *stump* up the rest of the money."

"Oh yeah, very funny." It wasn't a joke though. Stan might still be apprenticed to his father, but he still knew more than most about explosives. After all, his father was in charge of them at the *Man Abell* granite quarry, nearby. Besides, Charlie and Arnold were desperate enough to try anything by that time.

The following Saturday was one of those hot, hazy summer days; filled with scents and the gentle murmur of bees or bluebottles.

The heat ensured that it would be early evening before they heard birdsong and in nineteen thirty three there was little traffic on the roads. Periodically, the peace was interrupted by an express train on the *West Coast Mainline* that bordered the northern edge of the farm, but when a breeze carried the smells of smoke and steam over to them it felt more like a caress.

Charlie had purchased five pounds of black powder during the week and added it to the small amount he'd found in the shed. Earlier that week, using a pick and iron rod, he had excavated a reasonable cavity under one of the stumps, per the instructions he'd been given. Stan had also directed them to fill sandbags, but in the absence of any sand they had used earth and wetted it before packing it down.

In the quarry, explosives were strictly controlled and guarded, but they were far less observant when it came to fuse cord, which is why Stan knew they would be able to set the explosion off safely. He arrived mid-morning, with a roll of the stuff around his neck, confident that no-one seeing him pass by would know what it was.

Charlie was impressed, "Well done mate, but will we need that much?"

Stan shook his head dismissively, "Nah, shouldn't think so, but you can keep what's over, I'm sure you'll find a use for it one day."

It was down to business. Charlie and Arnold were happy to leave the explosive element to their expert who placed the powder and cord into position before shuffling out of the hole and directing them to pack the 'sand' bags into position. Meanwhile, he unravelled an appropriate length of cord and waited nervously. He didn't show it of course; after all he was the expert.

Soon, everything was in place and the two labourers were looking to him for further guidance. "Right, Arnold, you go down to the bottom of the road, by the railway bridge and Charlie, go over the canal bridge a wait there. When I blow my whistle, stop anyone from coming any closer. The fuse is set for two minutes, so it won't take long."

Charlie asked, "Where will you be?"

Stan looked startled by the question, "Why, as far away as I can bloody well run of course!" He failed to see why they should find that funny, but both continued to chuckle as they walked to their positions.

As Charlie waited beyond the canal bridge, out of sight, he did wonder whether he should have mentioned this adventure to his father but any qualms were made redundant by the shrieking of a whistle. What would be would be.

At the bottom of the road Arnold had just enough time to step out in front of *Clacketts* coal lorry. Mr Clackett himself was driving and he stuck his head out of the window, "Whassamatter?"

Arnold explained, "We're just about to blow a stump up and I've been told to stop anyone from getting any closer."

Clackett jumped down from the cab and stood with Arnold, as they both looked up the hill in high expectation.

* * *

Major Hilliard, (Ret'd) lived at *Hartshill House*, easily the largest place in the village but modest when compared to Oldbury Hall, a mile away. Even so, he and his wife could barely afford to live where they were. Not that they let it show of course, in fact quite the contrary. Manipulation of credit accounts and a frugal existence in the privacy of their home helped to maintain the myth. Another ploy was that of being seen out on his horse, a grey medium hunter. Someone on horseback still had an air of *presence*, he felt.

He'd chosen that morning to go for a hack, though not much of one, mind. Just far enough to get a breath of fresh air and provide the opportunity to pop into the *Royal Oak*, for a lunchtime snifter.

He'd walked the horse out of the village, along Nuneaton Road and down Mancetter Road until he reached the canal. There he chose to take the canal towpath and save a few hundred yards by cutting the corner. Both horse and rider were dopey with the heat as they climbed up onto Clock Hill, for the last leg. Charlie was on the opposite side of the bridge and had no idea they were there. Arnold saw them, but was far too distant to be heard and Stan was running hell for leather in the opposite direction, across the field.

The terrible *WHUMPHH* startled the horse and rider but it was the shrapnel that set things into calamitous motion. A great cloud of earth grew upwards from the stump, almost as if in slow motion, but the bags of earth contained plenty of stones, that left the scene like buckshot, which then slapped into the poor animal's rump with predictable effect. It reared just once, but that was enough to dispose of its rider, giving it free rein to bolt home, almost trampling Charlie down on the way.

Hilliard landed squarely on his back and lay winded, just as the cloud of earth descended, as though he'd been the chosen target. But whilst he couldn't move he did see a figure appear over the canal bridge and beckoned.

Retribution was called for. In fact, had it not been for Albert's offer of a supply of free milk and vegetables for the foreseeable future, Hilliard would have called the Police. Whilst he saw the latter course of action as justly punitive, it offered little in the way of personal benefit whilst the supply of provisions most certainly would. After extorting an unseemly amount to cover the laundry bill, he demanded to be taken home in the trap; a journey taken in complete silence since Charlie was given the task of driving it.

Arnold had stayed behind to face the music as well, but without need, for no-one laid any blame at his door. Stan, on the other hand, *had* disappeared and was never mentioned.

There was just one other that had been quite forgotten and left unnoticed in the furore. *Romulus* now lay on its side, shattered in defeat.

Joseph Wainwright went home to his small cottage in Hartshill, that night with a tale to tell to his wife. Quite inadvertently, he came up with a delightful alliteration, though he didn't know there *was* such a word. If he had, he would have regarded it posh enough to be pronounced with an 'h', as 'h'alliteration'. Which was ironic, because he rarely used the letter.

He hung his cap on the hook behind the door and turned to his wife, "Saw summat strange today luv."

"Oh?"

"'Illiard's 'orse from 'artshill 'ouse came gallopin' by this morning, wivout 'illiard on it!"

Chapter Five

I expected to find newspaper cuttings in the chest, since most hoards of this sort do, don't they?

But in fact, I found only one, which was front page news for *The Nuneaton Herald*, dated the 24th of November nineteen thirty two. It had obviously been handled well before Dad had stored it, but not just faded or grubby, it was 'blackened' in places, making the print difficult to read. The picture was clear enough though, and featured the remains of a locomotive still upright, though slightly askew. The tender was on its side and appeared to have been dragged further askew by a long line of overturned coal wagons which lay in a sweeping arc, down and along the embankment. The locomotive would have been old at that time, I felt sure. It was fairly short, with three wheels each side and a very tall smoke stack. That, and the smoke box it sat on looked undamaged but the cab at the other end was bent out of shape. In between, the boiler casing had disappeared, leaving an intestinal mess of bent tubes. It had a slightly comical value, though I was relieved to see the headline, which read, 'Driver and Fireman have miraculous escape'. I read on.

The article reported that the boiler explosion occurred just after the coal train had moved off from the signals near Hartshill. The cause was yet to be established, but the driver escaped with a broken leg, cracked ribs and a dislocated shoulder, whilst his fireman suffered concussion, lacerations and non fatal burns.

Not quite what I would call 'a miraculous escape'; more of a painfully traumatic one.

The article reported that fourteen fully loaded wagons had rolled down the embankment, shedding some of the coal they were carrying into the *Coventry Canal* which was causing a temporary hazard to navigation. Every effort was being made to clear the scene and restore movement of both canal and rail traffic.

The reporter had interviewed a number of locals, including one Albert Morcroft, a local farmer whose land lay on the opposite side of the canal. He was quoted as saying, "I am happy that no-one was killed, but it has had no effect on my land so I shall pay little more heed to it."

A full report was offered on page four, which of course, I didn't have. But I *did* have the internet and within minutes I had found the *British Railways Archive*. In no time I had found the accident section which was sub-divided into specific causes, and there it was, under *'Boiler Explosions'; Twenty third of November nineteen thirty two. Two casualties, no fatalities.*

I called up the fifty four page report, which I will not reproduce here, though I did learn a great deal about locomotive maintenance at that time, not least of all, the fact that the boiler in question had been refurbished four times and placed on four different locomotives.

I also learned that normal working pressure was around two hundred pounds per square inch, and that three different drivers had reported much higher pressures, with no sign of the safety valve functioning, by 'blowing off'. One reported a pressure reading of three hundred pounds; the day before the calamity.

In short, very short, it was down to a dodgy safety valve and an extended wait at the signals.

Strangely, I have never heard anyone in the family mention the incident.

Charlie
THE COAL TRAIN

In June, nineteen thirty one, Albert read the newspaper article out aloud to the family. It was a report from the *Meteorological Office* and read;

'*The weather during June has been distinguished by a pronounced excess of precipitation in all districts and by a general deficiency of sunshine. Unsettled dull and wet weather with severe thunderstorms on the 5th, 14th and 19th have prevailed for the first three weeks but it will now be followed by anti-cyclonic conditions and fine weather generally for the last week of this month.*'

It was too. Summer rain was often welcome on the farm, but in moderation. Work still needed to be done and crops harvested, undamaged.

But there were other clouds, that wouldn't go away.

The economic depression, or slump, had halved Britain's world trade and left more than three million out of work. In some areas, mainly the mining and heavy industries in the north, unemployment had been running at seventy per cent where poverty was widespread. There, child malnutrition was evidenced by scurvy, rickets and tuberculosis.

Even the Royal Navy had witnessed a mutiny over pay cuts.

Hartshill and Mancetter were suffering too, for the general strike had been countrywide, and a failure, which resulted in longer working hours for less pay. Yet those miners were the lucky ones. So many men had been laid off permanently.

The Morcrofts did what they could, but the milk still had to be paid for. As a result, the volumes had fallen off and butter production increased, though selling it at the market continued to be challenging.

Spoiled vegetables, damaged swedes or turnips and blighted potatoes had been fed to the pigs but Albert now shared them, by loading whatever he could on the milk dray; for Mary to distribute as she thought fit.

It was all they could do.

Meanwhile, the destitute families continued to scour the slag heaps for scraps of coal that could mean the difference between life and death in winter.

Charlie was harvesting *savoy* cabbages in one of the fields that ran alongside the cut when a barge and butty approached. His father had gone back to do the milking; leaving him to carry on alone for the last hour or so of the day, which was still too hot to wear a shirt. There was always plenty of traffic on the canal, more often than not, carrying coal from the local collieries down to London and he didn't bother to look up. The steady donk, donk, donk of the barge engine passed by and then a female voice called out, "My oh my, with shoulders like that you could be a film star I reckon, or a hero o' some sort."

He looked up and saw a young woman, a little older than him, it seemed, holding the tiller of the butty with practiced ease. The same ease that shone in her smile. She wore a long wrap around skirt and a pale blue blouse that might have seen better days, but still served to enhance the long dark waves of hair that fell onto her shoulders. "Tell you what; you'd be *my* hero if you'd chuck one of them cabbages over for our tea tonight."

She was one of those people who could say almost anything yet not cause offence. It was something Charlie couldn't begin to define, but he didn't hesitate to lob a *savoy* over to her, which she caught easily, before setting it down on the deck. And then she was gone, her boat a slave to the barge in front. He was still staring after her when she glanced back and waved before calling out, "My hero! My Knight!"

It was a refreshing distraction that lifted his spirits, so much so he was still humming a tune as he rounded the corner into the farmyard, two hours later and stopped abruptly when he saw her standing by the wall. Her smile had disappeared in favour of an expression that spoke of anger and embarrassment, "Here, take it back." She thrust the cabbage at him, "I'd've chucked it in the cut but me da' says he's going to come round later and check up." She saw the expression on Charlie's face and hurried on to allay any fears, "He won't, I'm sure, but I ain't going to take the risk neither."

Charlie shook his head, "Why."

She shrugged, "Dad always reckons that you lot ain't got time for us boat people; look down on us like and he won't have charity from the likes of you." She huffed, "He won't take charity from anyone, so don't take it personal."

Charlie was still puzzled, "I don't understand, did you tell him you asked for it?"

"Lord no! If I'd've told him that, he'd've taken the belt to me. Haven't you been listening to what I've been telling you?"

"So how far have you had to walk back?"

"We're moored up at the workshops. They're having to do somethin' with the engine, tomorrow. Soon as that's done we're set for London."

Charlie was still in fine fettle from the earlier experience, and still set on being her hero. With just the germ of an idea and a quarter mile walk to flesh it out, he set off, with the cabbage under his arm, "You come with me. I shall sort the matter out, don't you worry."

"Whatever your game is don't bother. He might not hit you but he ain't goin' to welcome you neither!"

It was Charlie's turn to grin, "Wait and see."

She hurried after him; four paces for every three of his, "Please, nowt any good will come of this."

Charlie was sixteen years old and ready to take on the world, if need be. He had right, a pretty girl and a *savoy* cabbage on his side, "Anyway, what's your name?"

Her sullen reply reflected her anxiety, "Sarah Jane."

"Mine's Charlie, Charlie Morcroft."

* * *

Tommy Finch, formerly known as 'Tommy Longlegs', from the days when the boats had to be 'legged' through tunnels, was taking his ease astride the bow of his barge, with a pipe of tobacco. Moments like this were rare, for the whole ethos of motorised canal freight was to keep moving, until sleep was unavoidable. The workshops had refused his pleas to get on with the job and closed down for the day, forcing him to moor up for the night. The missus was below, cooking, so the approaching footsteps had to be Sarah Jane's. No doubt she was headed for the cabin so he called, "Come down 'ere girl, tell me what he said."

There was an unexpected nervousness in her reply, "Da'ad."

He peered around the tarpaulin cover and was startled to see a youth approaching and carrying what looked like that damned cabbage. He slipped off the boat and stood facing Charlie, noting his daughter's stance and demeanour, just behind, "What can I do for you?"

The tone of his voice indicated what he was prepared to do, if Charlie didn't say the right thing. "Hullo, my name is Charlie Morcroft. We've got the farm back there, the one you passed before getting here."

Tommy just nodded.

Charlie ploughed on though, "It looks like I've caused offence when all I wanted to do is say thank you. Perhaps I should have spoken to you first off, but you'd already gone past me by the time I'd realised that a show of thanks was due."

Tommy was prepared to play along, for the moment, "And why should you want to thank the likes of us?"

"Begging your pardon, but it is usually the likes of you that's washing our banks into the cut but for once there was someone who was travelling at a thoughtful speed. Soon as I realised that, it seemed a natural thing to toss a cabbage over as a thank you. It wasn't an act of charity, I assure you. In fact, I reckon you were doing a charitable thing, not me, and I would be further in your debt if you would accept this please." He held the vegetable out while Tommy held his gaze, but the young whippersnapper had won. It would have been unseemly not to accept. "Then I shall accept it, with thanks, but I cannot undertake to be as kindly to your banks in future."

Charlie smiled, "I understand, but that might mean I wouldn't give you any more cabbages either."

Tommy couldn't help but find favour in this youth. He nodded, "We shall see what the future holds, but in the meantime, you shall have a glass of my wife's barley wine."

Sarah Jane rolled her eyes. She hadn't expected this development and couldn't, therefore, have been expected to warn her young knight about the barley wine.

Tommy banged on the hatch cover and when his wife appeared, made the introductions in a rather oblique fashion, "Elsa, this is Charlie, from the farm over the bridge. Get some o' your barley wine out can you my love."

She had a gentle smile and nodded her acknowledgement of their visitor before disappearing below. Charlie had already seen the likeness between mother and daughter though. Elsa was a striking woman, with a strong head of dark hair still, but her expression and lined features mirrored the harshness of life on the canals, just as Sarah Jane's would, all too soon.

A small ruckus could be heard before three children scrambled up on to the deck to see the stranger. Two more girls and a boy ranging between three and twelve subjected him to open scrutiny before the eldest, a girl, said, "Is you goin' to marry our Sarah then?"

Aghast and fearful of causing offence, Charlie turned to see if an apology was due to Sarah Jane, but instead of indignation he saw a grin that spoke of mischievous amusement. He turned back to the children, "Erm, no, I just called over . . . " He paused, while he wracked his brains for a credible reason that didn't entail mentioning the cabbage again and finally gave up. They would have to settle for 'just called over'.

Elsa appeared, holding four glasses in one hand and a jug of amber liquid in the other. She set them down on the cabin roof and Tommy poured out equal measures before handing them out; the guest first, Elsa, then Sarah Jane and finally, himself. He raised his glass and nodded at the cabbage, "To pleasant surprises."

Charlie took a tentative sip and surprised to discover that he liked it, in fact it was delicious; sweeter than he expected with a malty background. He took a larger swallow and addressed Elsa, "This is very good!"

She held her own glass up and viewed it, "Aye, the recipe's been in the family for I don't know how long."

The twelve year old piped up with a pre-emptive caution, "And it's a secret, an 'all."

Tommy cautioned her, "We'll have a bit less noise from you. Get below now and take those two with you." There was no vocal reaction as they obeyed him, but the sullen expressions were eloquent enough.

Which left the grown-ups to continue with polite, if stilted conversation. The second glass was even nicer than the first and they began to exchange stories from two very different, yet special lifestyles. The two women declined another glass and began to prepare dinner out on the deck, so as not to appear rude, though after one more, Charlie barely knew who was there. He and Tommy were seated on the gang plank by then and had found lots more to talk about.

At one point, after Tommy had spoken of the overheating problem they'd been having, Charlie declared it to be a problem with the pump and offered to set about it there and then. His help was politely declined, as was his offer to help with the vegetables. Eventually though, Tommy stood and indicated that it was time for Charlie to leave by taking the empty glass from him.

Charlie grinned expansively, "Thank you for your hoshpitality," and attempted to stand.

An outsider would not have expected or understood the scale of his collapse, but if pressed, they might have said it looked like a permanent cripple attempting to stand and walk.

Tommy *had* been expecting it and slapped his thigh as he laughed, "There you go Mother. The knees, it goes for the knees, every time!"

Charlie heard him and agreed, though he couldn't understand how his knees could no longer support him.

Sarah Jane moaned, "Da' you shouldn't have let him have that much. 'Twas deliberate and you know it."

Her father didn't attempt to deny it but headed back towards the bows of the boat, intent on finishing his pipe of baccy, "You see 'im over the road and into 'is drive girl, 'e'll find 'is own way 'ome from there."

Somehow, mother and daughter got Charlie to his feet before Sarah Jane slipped under an arm and guided him back to his drive, where she propped him up against a post before saying her farewell, "Oh, my silly, daft knight." With that she kissed him on the cheek and walked away.

Minutes after she had left, he slid gently down to the ground and into a drunken slumber, until the early hours, when the screech of a fox calling to her young startled him into consciousness. Both the stupor and alarm call were timely, for jointly they spared him from familial censure. By the time he reached home everyone had retired to bed.

The following morning, as soon as milking was over, Charlie ran into the barn and gathered half a dozen eggs into a basket; before hurrying down the drive as quickly as he dared, fearing he'd be too late.

The workshops were comparatively small, with a maximum capacity of only six boats afloat and a slipway that could accommodate one more. Another small arm was full of either wrecks or boats in need of much greater repairs, but that morning Tommy's boats were the only ones in the yard and the steady thump of the diesel engine suggested that the work was nearly complete.

Elsa saw him first and stepped off the boat to greet him, "Mornin' Charlie. How are you today?"

The meaning was clear and Charlie was not in denial, "That was a powerful drink Mrs Finch and I had a mite more than I should've."

"Ha! I think you've got my husband to thank for it an' all."

"Well it's your *Barley Wine* I drank so I reckoned it should be you I thank. So I've brought you these." He handed the eggs over and waited for Elsa to return with the basket. She'd disappeared below in some haste, so that Tommy wouldn't see and perhaps refuse to accept them, but Charlie was delighted to see Sarah Jane pop up through the hatch. She grinned, "So, you survived then?"

"I did, thank you." There followed an awkward pause that was broken when the yard foreman stepped out of the engine room and saw him, "What ho, Charlie, I've been hearing about your encounter with Mrs Finch's *Barley* wine. You don't look any the worse for it this morning though." He shared a knowing grin with Tommy who had joined him on deck, but time was pressing.

Tommy shook hands with the foreman and strode back to the stern, "Well you've come just in time to help us shove off. Half a day gone already, when we should be south of Coventry by now." Charlie hurried to untie ropes and throw them onto decks, as the vessels were eased out into the main canal. Just moments later they were underway and Charlie stood and watched them until the first bend. When only half the butty was in sight, she looked back, waved and was gone.

It had been a strange experience, with a certain frisson, yet he did not consider the encounter to be in any way romantic. She was at least nineteen or twenty and therefore a woman, whilst he was still only sixteen. She had teased him and flattered him though, without malice or mischief. It was simply her way and he would have been her knight in a trice.

In the meantime, he still had a field of cabbages to attend to.

* * *

Five weeks later the yard foreman flagged him down as he was leaving the drive, "Ay up Charlie, I've a message for you from one of the Finches."

Charlie was at a loss for a moment, until the messenger added, "Well, perhaps you still don't remember much about that night; you know; the barley wine."

The memory had stayed with him, but not the surname, "Oh I remember it well enough, but I didn't know they'd been back."

"Well no, they haven't yet; they're in Brum dropping a load of steel off before coming up to Baddesley Wharf for another load of coal." He saw the confusion on Charlie's face and explained, "The message was passed on by the Fazzackerlys, who passed by 'ere yesterday on their way up to Stoke. They'd come up the *Grand Union* behind the Finches." He took a breath, as if to indicate that the whole thing was becoming too great a job, "Anyhow, the message was they would like a large fresh lettuce this time, if you please."

"When will they be here?"

"Dunno, they should get to Baddesley sometime tomorrow. Then it'll depend on how long it takes to load 'em. After that they'll be coming through here within a few hours, depending on how long it takes 'em to get through the Atherstone flight."

Charlie knew he meant the eleven locks at Atherstone and how difficult they could be if there was conflicting traffic. The wharf lay halfway through the flight, but it was of no consequence, because he made up his mind to walk along the towpath the next evening and deliver a lettuce personally.

He rarely asked to finish work early, so when he indicated a wish to visit a couple of lads he'd known at school, who lived in Mancetter, Agnes only spoke of a need to wash and change before leaving. His suggestion of taking a lettuce and some tomatoes from the garden seemed reasonable and no more was thought of it, though she noted how spritely his step was as he headed down the drive.

The Baddesley Wharf lay on the south bank of the canal, sandwiched between the Watling Street and the mainline railway; all within a few hundred yards of each other at that point; a testament to the communication pedigree of the *Trent Valley.*

Charlie was several hundred paces short of his destination when the towpath became black and the water in the canal was covered in a black rime. He looked ahead and saw clouds of black dust rise up from where rumbling sounds came from every minute or so and then he turned a bend and saw the Finch's boats, lashed together against the wharf. The vessels seemed to flinch as a steam shovel dumped loads of coal into their holds and the billowing clouds of coal dust made it look as though they had been winded by the impact.

He remained where he was, as figures that looked scarcely human stood by the boats and looked on, until, at a signal from the shovel operator they jumped onto the cargo and set to work with shovels of their own. He could barely see them, but he guessed that they were distributing the load. It seemed like a scene from hell.

He made his way over the Holly Lane Bridge and peered down into the holds where black beetle-like figures strained to move an uneven black mass. Even from his vantage point, up on the bridge, he coughed as the black dust enveloped him.

The 'beetles' made their way out of the hold and signalled for the shovel man to continue, but one of them noticed a silhouette on the bridge and cried out, "Oh bloody hell, you've picked a fine time to call!"

Charlie didn't recognise the figure, but he recognised the voice. Holding the lettuce up, like a trophy, he yelled, "I'm delivering your order."

He waited for a response but saw her say something to the two people beside her and noted how one seemed particularly affected by what she had said. The drama of the scene, the mess, and the unexpected greeting left him feeling unsure whether to go down there or not, so he waited until Sarah Jane shook her head, as if in resignation and signalled for him to join them.

Elsa met him and took delivery of the produce; passing it through the hatch to the youngsters below. Charlie couldn't believe his eyes. The beautifully polished brass and spotless decks had disappeared beneath a thick coating of coal dust. It was as though the stuff had a malignant life of its own.

He turned to be confronted with an image he would carry to his grave. Her features were blackened and streaked with sweat, which was why he realised how beautiful her eyes were. They were the only things that were surviving untouched and shone like dark stars. "What the bloody hell are you doing here?"

"I got your message; about the lettuce."

"So why couldn't you have waited until we came past your place, like you did with the cabbage?"

She sounded annoyed and he became flustered, "I didn't want to miss you." He rolled both hands over, palms upward, "I didn't know what time you come by and couldn't wait by the canal all day. Father would have a fit."

"Well now you've managed to see us at our best, haven't you?"

He still thought her eyes were wonderful dark orbs, shining from the blackened face and then he realised that they held a mix of emotions; of embarrassment as well as anger. There was a change in the background noise and Tommy called out, "Sarah Jane!" They both glanced at the hold as her parents stepped over the gunwale holding their shovels in one hand and pulling cloths up over their noses.

Sarah Jane resigned herself to the situation, with a tired grin, "I could say thank you for the lettuce by giving you a hug, but they look like clean clothes to me. You'd best be off Charlie Morcroft, else you'll get to look like me." She pulled her own facecloth up and turned away without waiting for a reply but Charlie remained where he was, watching as she stepped into the hold.

He was a farmer's son and would never willingly watch others work when he could too, especially when they were women.

The cabin door opened as soon as he tapped it and a young hand took his jacket from him. He then ran across to grab a shovel that had been left against a wall and held it up as an unspoken question. The shovel operator gave him a 'thumbs up' sign and watched the very clean youth set about the business of getting very dirty.

Tommy saw him immediately and dug into a trouser pocket for a neckerchief which he held out; signalling for Charlie to tie it around his face. It looked grubby and when in place, smelled stale, but he knew the work wouldn't have been possible without one. It was incredibly hard work too. The shovels were pointed, which helped, but the uneven lumps often resisted attempts to move them, with wrist-jarring shocks.

Little was said during the breaks. Instead, they watched on in dulled fatigue as the shovel made a mockery of their efforts by shifting hundredweights at a time.

Charlie was fortunate, for the loading was finished within three hours and Elsa left them to sheet up while she heated water. Sarah Jane explained, "We have to sheet up, else too much would 'walk'. Didn't use to be like that but times are bad." Charlie nodded, but he was too tired to make conversation.

Soon, Elsa appeared with a bucket of warm water and bar of soap which she passed to Charlie, "Here lad, go and use the butty cabin and try to clean up as best yer can. There's another bucket in there; use that to get water out of the cut to rinse with but wipe the scum off it first mind. There's nowt I can do about those togs, apart from apologise to your mother if we meet."

Charlie hesitated. The thought of undressing in strange surroundings worried him, until Sarah Jane poked him, "Go on, get on with it, we can't send you home looking like a badger. Me and Da' will mop down while you see to yourself."

It was extremely difficult, in such a confined space, particularly since he tried to avoid splashing water onto the deck but eventually, he stepped out to find Sarah Jane waiting, with her own bucket. She peered closely, "That's not very clean. All you've done is shift it around a bit. If I was yer mother I'd be scrubbing you down now." She waved him to one side, in mock exasperation, "Go on with yer, ma has some food ready."

The light was going, but as Charlie clambered from the butty onto the motor boat, he glimpsed a naked figure on the bow, upending a bucket of water to rinse off. Not a cramped cabin for Tommy Finch.

Elsa had a mug of tea waiting for him and eyed his clothes once more. "I'm not sure what will be done about those."

Charlie shrugged, "They'll be fine. A good soak will do it." She wasn't convinced, but hurried below to fetch another mug of tea when Tommy approached; still wet but decent.

As soon as Sarah Jane appeared Elsa began to serve up dinner. Charlie saw how many mouths there were to feed and tried to decline the unspoken invitation to join them, but Tommy would have none of it, "You shall eat with us Charlie, my lad and welcome."

The stew had obviously been on the stove for most of the day, for the meat was wonderfully tender, with enough gravy to warrant use of the wedge of bread each one was given. As soon as they were all served Elsa picked up her own bucket and headed for the butty. Sarah Jane explained, "She always goes and washes down now. Reckons it's the only time she can have to herself."

They were all too tired to linger and Charlie made his farewells soon after he'd finished eating. He'd covered a couple of hundred yards along the tow path when he heard her call and waited for her to catch up with him, in the hope she might want to accompany him for part of the way. As she drew close, she held up the red neckerchief he'd used, "Here, I've rinsed this out for you. Da' says you should keep it, as a memento."

He took and smiled, "I shall, with thanks and I'll wear it, I promise."

Even in the dark he could see her eyes and then her teeth when she smiled. "Well don't make a habit of this Charlie Morcroft, I can't have you seeing me like that again."

He suddenly felt emboldened enough to suggest the solution he'd already thought of, "Then next time you pass by, could you hop off and come up to the farm. I could always take you in the trap, to meet up with the boats at Nuneaton, afterwards."

She smiled once more, "That's a fine idea. I shall and you can surprise me with a vegetable of your choosing!" They both laughed and she added, "See, I said you were my knight in shining armour." After a moment, "Mind, you're not very shiny at the moment." She rose onto her toes and kissed him on the cheek, "Now off with you. Go and find some more soap."

It was after eleven when Charlie got home and everyone was in bed, so he filled a bucket with water from the kettle on the stove and walked over to the dairy shed, where he stripped off and soaped down properly, before rinsing off with the hose. The clothes were another matter, but his mother already knew of his friendship with a family of boat folk so he would merely explain it away as a chance encounter at the wharf.

* * *

They next came through in the middle of September and Elsa took over the butty tiller so that Sarah Jane could pay her visit. This time her mother insisted that she took some money for the produce, adding that she should buy some eggs as well.

A dull but dry day brightened beyond measure when he saw her ambling up the drive. Her hair was held back by a red ribbon and he thought her complexion was miraculously perfect, knowing that the previous day they would have been loading coal.

She spoke casually, as though they met like this every day, "Well Charlie, what have you got for me today."

He grinned, "Well now you're here in person, you shall come and choose yourself."

It was cabbage, once more, though Sarah Jane picked two of her own. Agnes had instructed him to take her into the house for a cup of tea if she should ever call, which he did. Never one to show her feelings, Agnes *did* demonstrate her approval of the girl's insistence on paying for the dozen eggs, by adding a bag of plums and a jar of gooseberry jam to the basket.

Since the visit hadn't been arranged, the others were out and missed the opportunity to meet Sarah Jane, but Charlie made her promise to call in again. When they left Agnes felt encouraged by the encounter. She knew how insular farming could be and it wouldn't hurt Charlie to meet outsiders. She also knew, that as one of the boat people, the girl would never be allowed to marry 'out-side', so all was in order.

In fact, Charlie was still in awe of Sarah Jane, yet her relaxed attitude had always made conversation easy. She told him about life on the cut and some of the stories that boat people shared, while he spoke of farming and the land so that in no time, the journey was over. As they began the short, steep descent on Tuttle Hill, they saw Tommy waiting on the bridge, arms akimbo and in a stance that spoke volumes. When they drew close he called out, "Come on girl, you were supposed to get some vegetables, not go on holiday! We've been here half an hour since."

Sarah Jane dug Charlie in the ribs and rolled her eyes, "Don't pay any heed." Before stepping away from the trap she looked up and gave Charlie a stomach-churning wink, "See you soon, my knight."

Charlie called after her, "I'll have some 'taters for you then." Almost immediately and for the journey home he chided himself, "What on *earth* made me say that?"

* * *

It was two in the morning when a loud roar began to wake the Morcroft family, but the piece of boiler casing that crashed through the roof completed the job, along with the screeching of tortured metal. They dressed hurriedly and went outside, just as the last of the derailed wagons rolled on to its side and shed twelve tons of coal down the embankment to join the seventy tons already there. The train couldn't have been moving quickly, since quite a number remained on the tracks, their silhouettes only just visible.

There was an area of flickering flames around the locomotive that provided enough light for them to see what had happened. Clearly, help would be needed and Albert began to hurry down the drive, calling for Charlie to join him. They would need to get to the main road and over the canal before they could climb the railway embankment.

Lights had appeared in the windows of the canal yard house, and they had a telephone, so the authorities would soon learn of it, but the Morcrofts were first on the scene, where they came across the guard who had walked up from the rear and was standing beside the locomotive, looking bewildered. The devastation was shocking and one look at the cab convinced Albert that the crew had been killed, but many more would be if they didn't clear the lines. Pieces of steel and pipework were everywhere and many of them were quite capable of derailing a train; one that might be carrying passengers rather than coal. Even at that time of night, the rails glistened like silver ribbons, so any debris that posed a threat could be seen.

They set to work, pulling and heaving metalwork that was still hot, off the rails. Most of the pieces were too heavy to move any further but soon other figures appeared. Both families from the cottages by the iron bridge had the presence of mind to bring *Tilley* lamps which helped enormously, not least of all in locating one of the crew who lay beside the tender and appeared to be regaining consciousness. His face was covered in blood and he'd been burned, they could tell that much from the smell. One man hurried back to his house to get a tarpaulin that would serve as a stretcher while the others continued to clear the tracks. By the time they heard the first Police bells, the permanent way had been made safe, save for the track beneath the wreckage and that would need steam cranes to clear.

They began to search the embankment for the other crew member and soon found him, suspended in a hawthorn bush. He screamed when they tried to lift him out and a closer inspection determined that he had a broken leg. His dislocated shoulder would be discovered later, after many more screams, which finally persuaded the attending doctor to use chloroform on the poor man. By the time he came round, the dislocation had been remedied and he was on the way to hospital.

Also by then, dawn had delivered enough light to reveal the full extent of the calamity. A necklace of coal wagons lay either on their sides or upended, though it looked as though the front ones had remained coupled long enough for the ones behind to overtake them, As a result, the loads had been dumped within a remarkably confined area, leaving a black tide of coal that had rolled down the embankment, across the towpath and into the canal like a lava flow. Even one of the wagons had made it as far as the canal, where it tipped over the edge, leaving the rear end sticking up in the air.

Railwaymen of all grades began to arrive and so did the sightseers. Police kept them off the embankment and there was little enough room on the towpath so most had a limited view from the road, until two or three decided to trespass onto Albert's pastures, from where they would have a wonderful view. He shouted for Charlie to follow him and managed to reach the field entrance in time to stop all but a dozen or so from going on to his land. After a few moments he turned to Charlie, "Stay here and stop any more from going in. I'm off to sort that lot out."

'That lot' showed no sign of moving, even when he explained that they were on private property. Worse, he didn't even know them. They had been on the bus from Tamworth and had alighted for a spot of rubbernecking. Albert wasn't to be ignored, "Fair enough, but I wouldn't stay there much longer, if I were you."

One or two showed interest as he marched up the field and opened a five-barred gate. They heard him call and clap his hands, but turned away when they saw him approaching again. 'Best to ignore' seemed to be the trespasser's policy.

Albert strode past them, on his way back to the road. He pointed back up the field with a thumb and said, "Meet Oscar."

Oscar entered the stage as if on cue. He wasn't much taller than the members of his harem but at over a ton in weight, he was much, much larger. He was also gentle, but that morning he'd been as curious about the goings on as anyone else and broke into a gentle trot, towards the canal, which was nothing compared to the full scale sprint his approach prompted. One man attempted to leap across the small gap, onto the coal and slithered back to waist depth before scrambling out, blackened and embarrassed by the merriment he'd caused in the crowd. He ran up to the nearest policeman and shouted, "Look what that madman has just done. Set a bloody great bull free that nearly killed us, that's what and look at my clothes! We weren't harming anyone officer, now please do something about it."

As luck would have it, he was addressing Constable Bernard Ellis, Hartshill's one-man judicial system and an extremely effective one. He nodded towards the field as he withdrew a pencil and notebook from his pocket, "That's Oscar that is; wouldn't hurt a fly. Now then sir, your name and address please."

The man frowned, "What do you want that for?" He pointed at Albert, "He's the one you should be asking that question. It's his name you should be writing down."

"In good time sir, we shall take the names and addresses of all the witnesses."

"Yes, Yes, I know that, but he's the bloody criminal!"

"Language, if you don't mind sir and if I might correct you on one detail. He is a witness, not a criminal. Now sir, your name, if you please."

A small inflection in the officer's tone made the man nervous, "Are you saying that what he did wasn't wrong?"

"I'm not paid to have an opinion sir, I deal with only the facts; to wit, the bull belongs to that gentleman and so does the field. Whatever he chooses to do with both is perfectly legal. On the other hand, you do *not* own that land or farm it and therefore had no right of way on it. In short, you were trespassing and *that is* against the law. Name and address please sir."

It was a standoff, at least as far as the visitor was concerned, for Ellis looked quite unperturbed. Eventually, discretion overruled valour and the accuser shrank back, as though someone had partially deflated him, "How about we forget all this happened."

"Are you asking me to ignore a crime sir?"

"No, no, of course not, but you have enough on your plate today and who's to say the farmer will want to press charges anyway."

Ellis glanced towards Albert, who was conversing with someone else and unaware of this conversation, "That may well be true sir, in fact I believe it will be the case but then that is an opinion and something I should not have had. In the meantime, your name and address please sir."

Both men knew that the details subsequently provided were fictitious but it was enough that the man should flee to the nearest bus stop and wait anxiously for the next transport away from there.

Albert was speaking to the chap from the *Nuneaton Herald*, who was having a difficult time, for his interviewee clearly had no wish for attention from the press and no intention of attracting any, which was why he'd failed to mention the hole in his roof or the pieces of scrap iron he'd just noticed in the field.

While all this was going on, Charlie continued to guard the entrance and several locals stopped for a chat. Many were mining families, or rather ex-mining families, from the surrounding villages; now well within the poverty band. Their clothes were grey and inadequate, just as he knew their diet would be, too. The Woods, Bedlows, Cartwrights, Wheelers were all good folk who were once proud members of their communities. The Lord who owned that trainload would scarcely feel the loss, but the looks in their eyes when they saw that the huge pile of coal told of a need so primal, it might have represented the difference between life and death. In fact, for some of them, it did.

He wandered down to PC Ellis and exchanged a few pleasantries before asking, "What's going to happen to that lot?"

"Why do you ask, young Morcroft?"

Charlie dropped his voice, "There's plenty around here that need some of that."

The same thoughts had passed through Ellis's mind, but it wasn't to be, "Sorry lad, that lot belongs to Sir Donald and he wants it back. We've been told to guard it, leastwise, during daylight hours. No one's going to try and shift that lot in the dead of night." He caught Charlie's eye, "Are they?"

It was valuable intelligence; that could be relayed to the families. It wouldn't be much, but that night, enough sacks could be brought along the towpath and barrowed up Clock Hill to make a difference.

Meanwhile another incident added to the day's catalogue of events. Barges usually had a draught of three feet and a few had managed to scrape past the hazard, but inevitably, one had a slightly larger load and the bargee knew he would need a decent speed to force his way through. In the event, it proved to be sufficient speed to ensure that his barge was firmly aground. No amount of work, including the use of a couple of horses, would shift it. The only solution would be to bring up an empty barge and transfer enough of the load to float the boat off and that wouldn't happen soon.

It was at times like that when boat people surrendered to the inevitable with an uncharacteristic pragmatism, for there was nothing they *could* do. The nearest company barge was at Coventry so a day would be lost by everyone. By the end of that day there would be thirty pairs of boats moored up in both directions.

Oscar continued to provide a deterrent, but Albert left Charlie in place, just in case. Agnes and Mary had done the morning's milking but there were still jobs to be done, including the evening's milking.

The number of sightseers had fallen and Charlie was becoming bored, when a voice he knew called out, "Where's my vegetables?" She'd clambered over the bank of coal and was marching down the towpath towards him. "Well?"

He thought quickly, "I heard you were coming through so last night I left you a great pile of stuff on the towpath, just there." He pointed at the bank of coal.

She waited until she reached him, "And I'm the queen of Sheba."

"That's true enough and I am your knight."

She thumped him playfully, "So what crusades have you been up to on my behalf?"

"None I'm afraid, though I might be joining in one tonight as it happens."

"Ooh, do tell."

"It's nothing exciting, but it's worthwhile at any rate." He went on to tell her about the mining families who'd been laid off; about the poverty, near starvation, the rickets and disease and then he pointed at the mass of coal, "The man who owns that lot wouldn't even notice it, but he'll do anything to make sure those poor sods don't get it."

She cosied up to him and smiled impishly, "So what's the plan?"

"Some of the folk are coming down tonight and they'll barrow away as much as they can. It won't make much of a dent in that lot, but it'll help them, especially at this time of year."

They stood in silence for a while until she asked, "Why don't they use a barge?"

"Don't be daft, where would they get a barge from and anyhow, in case you hadn't noticed, most of the ones round here are already full of the stuff."

"Exactly! Come with me."

He followed her into the canal yard and strode up to the foreman's house. His pleasure at seeing Sarah Jane was evident when he answered the door, "What a delight to see you and on such an exciting day."

Pleasantries were exchanged and the location of the Finch boats established before she could address the most pressing issue. She pointed at the secondary arm, "Mr Frankland, are any of those boats capable of taking a load?"

"Why would you want to know that?"

They'd known each other for many years, in fact he often reminded her of things she'd gotten up to as a child, much as an uncle might have done and trust was a given, so she told him.

They had no way of knowing and wouldn't, that for years now, he'd been doing as much as he could to support kin who lived in Ansley. Related by marriage, they were one of the unemployed mining families and would have been on the street if it hadn't been for him. Inevitably, he also shared their hatred of the mine owners, or more specifically, Sir Donald.

He cupped his chin with one hand, "Hmm, I'm not sure. Let's go down and take a look."

Minutes later they were looking down at the hulks in the disused arm. They were in varying states of decay but all were full of water and none looked capable of floating let alone carrying a load. Frankland pointed at the two nearest the entrance, "They could carry thirty ton in their day. We could soon get them pumped out but I wouldn't trust them far with that weight on these days."

Charlie asked, "How about six hundred yards? They could moor them up at the next bridge and move the coal up *Apple Pie Lane* over the next few nights."

Frankland shook his head, "Too risky. For one thing, they'd be noticed and for another, they'd sink pretty quickly. *Then*, I'd have to explain how I let them out of this yard and how we were going to get them back." They waited, for he was obviously wrestling with an idea of his own, which surfaced with a slow smile, "How about two hundred yards?"

Sarah Jane asked the question, though she already knew the answer, "Where to?"

"Back here. They can bring them back, we'll cover them with tarpaulins and let them sink back right where they are now. They can shift the stuff over the next few weeks then."

"What about the load?"

He thought for a moment, "If you was to put some boards down in them and was gentle, I reckon they'd still be good for twenty tons a piece. Mind, you'd have to get them back here sharpish, before they sank again."

Charlie began to realise the scale of the proposal and said, "I'd better get word up to the families. They're going to need more pairs of hands, lots more."

Frankland said, "From that, I take it that it's on."

Sarah Jane interrupted, "Yes and I'll be there too."

Charlie hadn't been certain until then, but as her knight he couldn't be found wanting, "And so shall I."

It was Frankland's turn to commit, "Fair enough, I'll get started on pumping them out."

They agreed on an eleven-o-clock start but it was already five-o-clock and Charlie knew that it would take all of the six hours they had to organise things. He left the yard and searched the dwindling crowd but there was no sign of anyone from the families. The nearest lived in one of the cottages on Grange Road, just ten minutes walk away and from there they could start to spread word. After arranging to meet back in the yard at ten thirty, Sarah Jane left for her boat while Charlie set off up the hill and while both were excited, it was only because neither thought of it as theft. If they *had* given any thought to that aspect, they would have probably argued that they were helping with the clearing up.

* * *

That night, an amazing thing happened. Small groups walked quietly down *Clock Hill* and gathered as directed, in Albert's pasture, after being given assurances that the bull had been relocated. By ten to eleven eighteen families had assembled there, though without the children this time. They were expected to pull their weight on the slag heaps during the day but this was different. Working on a shifting pile of coal could be dangerous in the dark and then there was the canal to consider. Few spoke, for unlike Charlie, they knew that night's work for what it was and how a magistrate would regard it, just as they knew that none could afford to forego the chance of getting their hands on so much fuel.

Sarah Jane had yet to turn up so Charlie and Frankland organised two teams of men on ropes; one in the yard and the other on the opposite side of the canal. Then they quietly called out instructions as the first hull was cast off. The men in the yard heaved and seemed to do little more than stretch the ropes, but finally they all sensed movement. It had begun.

The other hull was still being pumped out but Frankland had promised it would be ready in time to take the place of the other.

Once the bows were clear of the arm, the men on the towpath opposite were directed to haul on their ropes and the hull eased out into the canal, gently grazing the corner of the dock on its way past.

But they were miners not boatmen and didn't know how to warp a seventy foot boat along a narrow waterway so progress was difficult. They were forced to stop pulling every few yards, so that they could fend the bows away from the bank, but the loss of momentum cost them time and called for much more effort.

In a heart-stopping moment figures suddenly appeared along the towpath from the opposite direction and without a word, took the ropes from the miners. Within moments it was moving through the water as though it was under power and continued until they heard it run into the pile of coal.

Other figures appeared and helped secure it to the bank while the families who had followed noticed yet more figures, already filling sacks with coal. Only those at the bottom of the pile could be seen, but movement could be heard from above and suddenly two men appeared, carrying sacks and cautiously negotiating their way down the coal. Then, to the surprise and delight of the families, both of them emptied their sacks into the hull.

It was a signal for them all to get started and as the two groups merged on the coal mound, whispered introductions took place. Most worked in pairs, with one holding the sack and the other filling while a small team of men carried the filled sacks down to the boat.

There were forty boat people at work that night, working with over fifty land folk. It was a remarkable thing to see *and* be part of, for it would become part of boating lore, where the deed would remain safe from gossip and informants. The two groups did have one thing in common though and it soon became apparent. They could all handle coal.

* * *

Constable Bernard Ellis stepped out of the Railway Inn, on Leather-mill Lane at a little after eleven-o-clock and considered his options. He could continue down the lane, which became a cart track for a quarter of a mile before it joined the Watling Street. It was a slightly circuitous route which didn't begin with a long downhill stretch the way his usual route home did. But *that* one would entail passing the wreckage of the coal train which, he decided, would be an ill-considered thing to do. With a soft grunt of resignation, he set off down the lane.

* * *

Back at the wreckage a strategy was called for. The towpath was being trampled into a soggy mire and someone pointed out that the authorities would easily see that narrow boats had been used, since the trail didn't extend more than fifty feet. There were more people than the coal pile could accommodate so they had been taking it in turns, which had certainly helped to keep the pace up, but now, thirty or so were employed in beating a trail to the road and back. They also dropped small pieces of coal along the route and within half an hour it seemed certain that the hoard had been removed by road.

Charlie had looked for Sarah Jane but there were too many people and it was too dark, notwithstanding the fact that everyone was soon covered in coal dust and of course, working as quietly as possible. It wouldn't have done to try calling for her.

For their part, the miner's families had never loaded a narrow boat before and were startled by the scale of the task, but eventually the boatmen judged the load to be at the limit Frankland had set and called a halt.

They shoved it off into the middle of the canal and past the empty hull that had already been brought up, so that if any had hoped for a rest they were disappointed. Work began again within five minutes as the loaded hull; now riding much lower in the water, was hauled back to the yard.

Moving the narrow boats was a great deal easier and quicker with the boat men in control, but the whole thing still took almost seven hours. By then though, forty tons of coal had been shifted in two old hulks that would have settled back on the bottom of the arm by mid-morning. Murmurs of thanks and handshakes were exchanged, but they were all too exhausted to linger and besides, they couldn't afford to be seen on the streets. It was important to get indoors before dawn and rid of the incriminating grime.

Charlie was scrubbing down in the dairy shed, as he had the last time he shifted coal, when Albert walked in to start the milking. He stepped past his son without a word, but later that morning when the scale of things became known, something had to be said.

The confrontation occurred in the kitchen, "I did not bring you up to be a thief!"

Charlie tried to make light of it, "I just helped out. The families without work came down and took the stuff. I didn't bring any home."

"Thievery is thievery, whether it's for you or someone else and don't make out that you *just* helped. You spent all damned night out there."

"And I considered it a charitable thing to do!"

"Don't you dare try to justify it! Don't you have the wit to realise that you could go to jail for what you've done."

"I think there would be too many people, good people, there with me, for the authorities to risk that."

"Oh, and who may they be?"

The rapping on the kitchen door continued for a little while, suggesting that there had been an earlier attempt to be heard.

Albert strode to the door with a sense of doom and opened it cautiously, expecting to see a dark blue uniform. Instead a rather handsome young woman with masses of wavy dark hair stood before him. He knew of her, but they had never met before. She smiled, "Hello. Are you Charlie's Dad? My name is Sarah Jane."

He shook the proffered hand and waited in silence, until finally she held up her basket and with a bright smile added, "My Ma' sent me to buy some eggs."

"You'd better come inside."

As they stepped into the kitchen, Sarah Jane smiled at those already there, "Hello Mrs Morcroft; Charlie, how are you today?"

Albert wasn't going to give way to small talk, "So were you involved in last night's affair?"

She nodded and said quietly, "Yes."

In the silence that followed, Albert struggled for the right thing to say. Eventually, he asked, "Does your father know about it?"

"Yes."

"Then it is not for me to reprimand you. That's your father's job. But you may be sure I shall continue to chastise this damned fool!"

"He was there with us, lots of boat folk were."

"Humph!" He stopped short of saying what he thought, which was that such activities were to be expected from water gypsies and finally looked to Charlie, "Just because a lot of people were there doesn't make it less wrong."

"Please Mr Morcroft, I don't want to interfere, but if you please, I'll tell you what my Da' said about it. He knew I was coming here and he wondered if Charlie had asked you, 'cos he should've done," she glanced at Charlie, "By rights, but Da' said, if someone told you that you had to deliver half as much milk again but be paid less than you're getting now, you might think that *that* was a sort of theft. If the milk round was taken off you then, it would be an even bigger theft. Only, Da' reckons that's how them miners must feel, especially when they can't even keep their kids warm and fed."

Just like his son, Albert Morcroft looked into the depths of those dark eyes and fell in.

Not that he could concede in the matter, "Well I've said my piece. You all know what I think and heaven help you Charlie Morcroft, if you try anything like that again."

"Constable Ellis and Mr Frankland."

Albert frowned, "What?"

"They are two folk that we think of as respectable, but they each had a hand in what happened last night, though neither will admit as much, to you or anyone else."

That startled Albert, though he didn't show it. Instead he sought safer ground, "I don't want to discuss the matter any further. I've told you, I have said all I'm going to say, so let that be an end to it."

He hurried outside and set off for the top fields; away from the house and well away from the canal.

Meanwhile, Sir Donald surveyed the scene from the top of the embankment. The chauffeur had stayed with the Rolls Royce, but the rest of the party had accompanied his lordship who turned to the Police Chief, "Near enough half of it has gone. What were your men doing for heaven's sake, helping them load it?"

"No, Sir, we didn't believe that a theft would occur in the dead of night."

"Oh, really? When do thefts normally occur then, might I ask?"

"Quite so Sir Donald, but theft of so many tons of coal, so far away from the road in the pitch dark seemed improbable."

"Well the improbable has become the definite, wouldn't you say?" He looked back at the blackened and flattened grass that served only to measure his loss before stamping his cane on the ground, "This is the work of shirkers. Men who don't know what it is to work for a living. They managed to drop enough where they loaded the vehicles, but too many lorries and vans would have been needed for them to go unnoticed. Someone had to have seen something. Let it be known that I'm offering a reward. Make sure it gets into the papers and so forth. A hundred pounds should do it and then let's get these criminals put away."

"Yes, Sir Donald."

This time the peer turned to face the Police Chief, "Oh, and don't think you've heard the last of this either. Ineptitude on this scale cannot be overlooked."

* * *

Mary inadvertently ensured that the matter was laid to rest when she came home from the milk round, in time to join everyone at the lunchtime table.

As she poured herself a cup of tea, she said, almost conversationally, "The Wheeler's youngest died last night. The Doctor said it was a mixture of bronchitis and malnutrition."

Chapter Six

I've discussed this project with my cousin Audrey on many occasions. After all, it's thanks to her I have the chest and therefore not surprising she should share my interest, but last week she told me a story I had never heard before, which is part of the 'Blake' family lore. Until then, I hadn't realised that there was a connection between two of the articles I had found in the chest. Namely, the photograph and what I call 'the token'.

The token came in two parts, yet was only one. As someone who hates riddles, I shall hasten to explain. It was two wooden chain-like links, fashioned into hearts yet whittled out of a single piece of wood. It obviously meant a great deal to Dad, or he wouldn't have saved it and more significantly, hidden it, in the way he did.

One has the letters 'SJ' carved on it and the other just 'C'. I'm quite happy to assume that the 'C' stands for Charlie and, given the heart shapes, there must have been a romantic connection, which is rather charming, except for one small detail. My mother's name was April.

Sorties around the family failed to shed any light on the matter, but whoever it was, she obviously merited many hours work. The links had been carefully sanded down to a smooth finish and oiled with something.

Liz decided that it was a case of unrequited love, that left dad with his love token, hurt and abandoned, "See," she said, "I feel a *Mills & Boon* moment coming on!"

I scoffed, "My Dad in a bodice-ripper, you must be joking. It'd be for a favourite teacher, more like."

Liz looked startled, "Now it's your turn to be ridiculous. From what we learned he hated the place and everyone in it."

"Well we'll probably never know, because I'm not prepared to start any guessing games, not with this one."

Liz was about to force my hand though, "Well *I'm* prepared to take a few guesses and if I repeat them often enough they'll soon become 'fact'." She made signs of inverted commas with her fingers as she said 'fact' and added "Just like the newspapers do."

I cautioned her, "Don't dick around with my family history."

She ignored me and continued with her train of thought, "Love; that's what I take 'hearts' to represent. Sooooo, if we accept that much, it's fair to assume that 'SJ' was the subject of his affection."

I grumbled, "Yeah, yeah, I think we've established that."

"In that case, who was it? A Susie Julie perhaps, or Stephen John?"

I was becoming a tad irritated by now, "Be real Liz, with a family as big as ours I think his sexual preference was a given and anyway, the alternative was illegal then, so he'd hardly carve something like that for posterity *and* the local constabulary."

She was being mischievous now, "In that case, are there any little Morcrofts running around, we haven't heard of yet?"

"Oh that's great. Next you'll have him down as the local *Don Juan*!"

She chuckled, "Well, I can think of worst things to be. Mind, we send too many Christmas cards out already, I don't want to add to the list." She thought for a moment, before adding, "And just think what that would do to your inheritance."

"I didn't get anything! Well, apart from a mallet and a smoothing plane."

It was going nowhere, at least anywhere sensible so I wandered off to water the tomato plants.

It wasn't going to be that easy to dismiss though. I hate loose ends. It's like forgetting where you put something; at least it is for me. I have to keep searching for it whether I need the damned thing or not. Deep down, I knew that this was one of those loose ends.

As I watched the water pool around the base of the plants my mind wandered back to what we actually *did* know, or thought we did.

Dad could whittle. We all knew that from stuff we'd seen around the house and he was heterosexual, at least enough to father us lot. Then came the difficult bit, but undeniable, he'd made a love token for someone with the initials 'SJ' and therefore not my mother. Yet somehow, I couldn't see him as a sexual predator. I know, that's a bit extreme, but it was my father, after all.

Then something else came to mind; a distant memory, but in the context of fresh intelligence, it became a bit of an epiphany. I remembered mum saying that on their wedding night she burst out laughing when she saw his skinny legs. 'Cockerel's legs' she called them. I hadn't given it another thought, but now I had a fresh perspective.

Wedding nights were very different then, or most of them were, if stories from that time are to be believed. It was a time of discovery and surrender; more often than not, with virgins on both sides of the bed. Nightclothes would have been donned in private and any exploration carried out in the dark. At least that's how *I* thought it usually happened.

Until now, I'd never realised how strange it should be that they'd been ogling each other at that moment. Moreover, mum's pre-occupation with dad's legs implied that she had already become acquainted with other, more fundamental parts of his anatomy and knew what to expect. In short, the wedding night was the first time she'd seen him with his trousers off completely.

Once sex before marriage with mum became a probability, I had to consider everything else in context.

If he was still here, I would have asked him and I think he would have told me too.

Which brings me back to my chat with Audrey and the *second* article.

We were studying the photographs from the chest when she came across one of a charabanc, loaded with people sitting three abreast, beneath a variety of hats and flat caps. The driver was standing on the road, beside his door, wearing a peaked cap and calf length white coat, looking very stern. In fact, no-one looked as though they were enjoying themselves. It was a black and white photograph, obviously, but the coachwork looked dull and might have been a dark brown. A large hand was painted on the driver's door in what might have been red or blue and must have been significant, for the driver had obviously positioned himself strategically, to ensure it featured in the picture.

I found a magnifying glass for Audrey to look more closely at the faces while I looked up 'charabanc' and discovered that the word came from a French phrase meaning 'carriage with benches', which was very apt. This one was a long, open-topped, vehicle that looked a bit like a stretch mail coach and the 'toast rack' seating was so high off the ground there were two running boards that acted as steps.

We were able to identify Agnes, Charlie, Mary and Arnold but found no sign of Albert

Audrey explained, "Grandad hardly ever left the farm, even for day trips, but I think that might have been the trip mum and dad always joked about. They always said that she had only hit him twice and the first was on a charabanc trip to Derbyshire."

I was startled, "You're joking. Uncle Arnold and Aunty Mary *fighting?*"

Audrey chuckled, "Oh no, it wasn't a fight, I think she just thumped him."

"Why?"

"Well she reckoned it was about courting, or the lack of it. She said she had to prise him away from your dad."

"Yeah, they were good friends."

Audrey continued, "Dad always reckoned that he knew mum was the one for him, the first time he saw her. He always said how lucky he was, not just in finding her but not having to take lots of girls out *hoping* to find the right one. He said your dad wasn't nearly so lucky."

I was in a position to differ, "Well I think he struck a chord with someone." I showed her the heart-shaped links, hoping she could shed some light on the initials.

She admired the handiwork, but shook her head, "Sorry, I've never heard anything about these and the initials don't mean anything, though once, mum did mention an encounter he had with a canal girl, but she couldn't, or wouldn't elaborate. She said something about memory blanking out unhappy times, so perhaps that was someone he fancied from afar and made these for."

"Unrequited love you mean?"

Audrey shrugged, why not, "Most young men seem to suffer from it. My dad had it easy and he knew it. His wife was served up on a plate, so to speak."

It was a possibility, but somehow it didn't ring true.

Charlie

OF LOVE AND STUFF

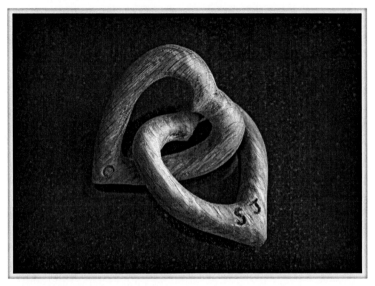

Arnold continued to work on the farm every weekend, though on Sundays he would arrive at eleven in the morning, when the family returned from church. They had invited him to join them but he'd declined, saying that he had chores to do at home on those mornings, which was partly true, but he'd seen them in their Sunday best and didn't want them to know that he didn't have a suit. He was saving hard though and would soon be able to join them.

In the meantime, he still lived for Sundays, when Albert would observe the 'day of rest' by limiting work to light tasks or those that needed attending to every day, such as feeding the livestock and the milking.

By then, Arnold was expected to join them for Sunday lunch as well, though he continued to be on his best behaviour when seated at the table. Any banter with Charlie had to wait until afterwards, when they were outside.

The work continued to be unpaid, save for the food Agnes packed for him each week, but the continued contact with Mary

133

was more than enough reward. That winter, chaps and nips of frostbite were rewarded with concern and treatment and on one occasion, when the return of circulation was particularly painful, she clasped his hand in hers until it eased. They conversed quite freely by then, yet it was still only polite and friendly, when all he wanted to do was embrace her. Sometimes, he would shout at himself on the way home, angered by his own reticence, but one day it would happen, he knew.

Often, after a day's labours Charlie would clap his new pal on the shoulder, "Thanks, Arnie, I couldn't have managed that on my own." It was true too and those were the times he would go home in high spirits, imagining the day he became a permanent part of their family.

Somewhat foolishly, Arnold would use Charlie's tormenting of Mary as a conduit for contact and in so doing, appeared to be taking his side against her, when all he wanted to do was look at her openly.

Mary had caught him gazing at her several times when they were alone, though whenever their eyes met he would quickly look away, embarrassed. She'd seen enough though, and waited. And waited.

At some level, Charlie knew what was afoot, but even at nineteen years of age, he knew little about the subtleties of such campaigns, yet ironically, he knew more than most about the dynamics of a relationship, or more specifically, about procreation. Farming provided ample examples of that, on a scale that would shock most folk, for there was little subtlety in watching one's father provide manual guidance to a bull as it tried to serve a heifer.

But girls were another matter entirely. He knew how to torment them, well one, in particular, but otherwise his attempts to impress girls had fallen short of inept. He continued to see Sarah Jane when the boats passed by, but she was still much older than he was and still given to teasing him.

* * *

Albert chose which church the family attended and thanks to a great variety of reasons, he kept changing allegiances. It might have been a change of vicar; a perceived slight; discomfiture with another member of the congregation or even a sermon he considered to be inappropriate. On balance though, he preferred the Methodist chapel, which Charlie and Mary thought was fortuitous, since that lot organised a charabanc outing twice a year.

The first one that year was set for the Sunday after Easter and bound for Dovedale.

Travel of any sort was exciting, for all ages, but travelling as a group gave it an even greater sense of occasion, with sing songs and shared humour. Shared adversity too, when the transport; provided by Monty Hands, broke down or suffered a puncture.

This was to be a trip of two halves and everyone was dressed in their Sunday best, including Arnold, who had by then, purchased his first suit. Which meant that they were inappropriately dressed for the first activity, involving a walk along the *Dove* valley, or for the more adventurous, a climb to the top of *Thorpe Cloud*; both muddy and sweaty affairs, particularly at the *Stepping Stones* where some children would topple over into the River *Dove*. It was shallow enough at that point to be harmless, but deep enough for hilarity.

After that, they were booked into a tearoom in Ashbourne, where each table would be furnished with pots of tea and a multi-tiered stand, laden with fancy cakes.

It was going to be a defining experience for both Charlie and Arnold.

* * *

Charlie had known Harriet West for over ten years, because her family used to live in Mancetter, before moving to Hartshill, which in turn meant that she had gone to the same school and now attended the same chapel he did.

This also meant that she would have been aware of the thrashing that preceded his expulsion from that school, though she had the good manners not to mention it. Charlie would have been indifferent but Agnes would have been embarrassed by the topic, even after so many years.

Harriet was a chatty sort and since she occupied the seat in front of Charlie and his family, she sought to make conversation on the outbound journey. Her parents hurried off when they reached *Dovedale* but they found themselves seated next to each other in the tearoom. Charlie was flattered by the attention, though he hadn't any idea of how things should progress. In an act of breathtaking irony, Arnold later explained to Mary, "He knew the 'what' but not the 'how'."

Charlie also failed to know a predatory female when he met one.

Her parents were still in the queue for the toilets when she called to Charlie from behind the charabanc. Since it has been reversed into the parking area, no-one could see them, save for Arnold who had accompanied Charlie. She was holding a necklace up for Charlie to take, "This thing has fallen off again. Would you be a love and put it back on for me please Charlie?"

"Of course, give it here." She handed it to him and held her hair to one side as she turned and presented her neck to him with a seemingly fawn-like innocence.

She had a nice smell, he noticed and fine downy hair on the back of her neck, which was a creamy sort of colour. When the clasp was in place she turned back to face him, though only inches away and gave a little curtsey, "Thank you kind sir."

Charlie acted without thought or hesitation. He snatched a kiss and then stepped back uncertainly, expecting to either hear her scream or feel the back of her hand. Instead, she ran forward and flung her arms around him, pressing her lips firmly against his. Neither opened their eyes or mouths, for both were novices at this sort of thing.

Just like Arnold, who stepped smartly around the corner of the vehicle, out of sight, desperately embarrassed and uncertain what to do. Should he leave them to it and find somewhere else to go or should he stay nearby, as moral support.

Just then, Mary and Agnes stepped around the opposite end of the vehicle. His distress was evident though the cause was still out of sight.

"Hello Arnold, anything wrong? Where's Charlie?" Mary had walked down to him and caught his guilty glance. She stepped around him and when she saw what her little brother was up to, it was simply too much.

She turned back towards Arnold and lunged at him with both arms outstretched, striking him with enough force to throw him off his feet and land squarely on his bottom, "Even my stupid brother has more gumption than you Arnold Blake!" With that, she strode back onto the charabanc and refused to speak to him for the rest of the day.

Arnold had a quiet journey home and week to think about it.

Charlie on the other hand, was in high spirits. He and Harriet spent most of the journey talking, though the noise of the vehicle and airstream required them to hold their heads close together, which suited them perfectly. As they turned off the Watling Street Charlie suggested meeting outside the *Picturedome* in Atherstone, the following Friday and received a discreet squeeze of the hand in reply.

What a day!

Harriet's parents didn't agree. In fact, Mr West took pains to explain why, "That's the Morcroft boy, the one that stole all those garden tools and was sent home from school, permanently!"

Harriet tried to defend her new beau, "He didn't steal them daddy, he only buried them, so they could still be found afterwards."

"They never found some of them and that's as good as stealing in my book. I will not have my daughter consorting with a criminal and that's an end to it!"

It was too. On the following Friday evening, Charlie waited for an hour before coming to the same conclusion.

The following day, Arnold felt inordinately scruffy for the task in hand, but the reason he'd attended the farm for so many months was to work and it would have seemed inappropriate to dress up.

The peony plant he carried was almost large enough to hide his torso though, with buds that were just beginning to open into scarlet blooms, just like Arnold's cheeks, when Mary answered the door. "I thought you might like this Mary."

She glanced over her shoulder and closed the door quickly before replying, "Is this a special occasion then. It's not my birthday you know!"

He stammered, "I, I know that, I just wanted to buy you something."

She stood her ground; this was to be a rite of passage, "Why?"

They stared at each other in the manner of a challenge that finally made him throw caution to the wind, "Mary, would you care to step out with me please."

Mary walked past him and said, "Follow me, I'll show you where I should like it planted."

Her tone held no threat, so he followed, happy that she had at least accepted his gift. As soon as they turned the corner of the barn and out of sight from the house, she took the plant from him to set it down on the ground before standing before him with an impish grin, "I should like you to plant it," she placed her forefinger on her lips, "Here, if you would, please."

Understandably, he hesitated as he tried to catch up with things, so she stepped forward and sealed their relationship herself.

Some little time later and empowered by his new status, Arnold asked, "Would you like to go to the *Picturedome* next week?"

Mary smiled, "Yes! I should like that."

"And should we ask Charlie do you think?"

The smile slipped away, "No, I should *not* like that." Clearly, she still had her hands full.

Two weeks later, their relationship had become common knowledge, though the only Morcroft who was happy with the budding romance was Mary.

Albert, if truth be told, was ambivalent about it, since he wanted nothing to do with that sort of thing, but Agnes was alarmed. She also blamed herself for not recognising the signs; ones that in retrospect, were as plain as day, but he had always been Charlie's companion and a great help on the farm.

Her family were farmers, just as Albert's were and that would always be the way of things, which therefore required both Charlie and Mary to marry into farming families, preferably ones that owned their own land.

Now, her only daughter was stepping out with a miner's son from the North.

Albert had tried to allay her fears, "They are both young and from such different backgrounds that the differences will tell soon enough, have no fear."

She did fear the worst though and her dealings with Arnold became, at best, coolly civil.

As did his friendship with Charlie, who, as things progressed, saw their romance as salt on the recent wounds inflicted by Harriet West. He'd tried to make contact with her at the last two chapel services but her parents ensured that they were seated on either side of their daughter *and* on the opposite side of the chapel. At the last meeting, her mother noticed him staring at them, hoping for eye contact with Harriet and the malevolence of the stare he received in return, settled the matter.

He was nineteen years old and had only been kissed with enthusiasm once in his life. The injustice of it affected him badly, since his regular masturbatory adventures seemed so natural and wonderful. The connection with females was obvious and equally natural, so why should it be so difficult?

And now this; his friend had decided that Mary, his own big sister, made for better company. Well, so be it. He could work alone in future, just as he used to.

Of course, circumstances dictated otherwise, because the farming calendar was littered with tasks that needed many hands. Just five weeks later haymaking overrode all other issues, particularly that year, for they had enjoyed a long hot spell that was forecasted to end a few days later. Winter feed was vital to a dairy farm and dampened hay could be ruined by fungus or worse, have sufficient heat build up within the stack for it to set alight by spontaneous combustion, which would take the barn with it as well.

Like many things, a single harvest could mean the difference between survival and bankruptcy in those days, so their differences were set aside in the face of the greater need. The last day was a Monday, and had been cloudy, as if to hurry them on, but the rain held off and by late evening, the barn was full of sweet smelling hay. Agnes had prepared an equally fragrant pot roast that was served with a good deal less frost than of late, since Arnold had hurried straight over from work to provide a timely impetus to the last few hours.

Mary said nothing, but she noted the change and decided that an accord was possible, after all. As for Charlie, well he just needed another two oak trees to fell, or better still, a girlfriend of his own.

* * *

Sarah Jane had called in whenever they passed and always rejoined the boats at Nuneaton, with more produce than she'd paid for. After the coal incident Charlie had been made much more welcome, to the extent that by the time they reached the bridge at Tuttle Hill, the Finches would have moored up and put the kettle on to share a cup of tea. Casual stops like that were unheard of amongst boat folk and a measure of the regard Tommy had for him.

Each visit would close in a similar vein, with Sarah Jane giving him a peck on the cheek and seeing him off with such things as, "Get off with you my knight and get growing some more things for me."

In July though, she strode up their drive in high spirits, similar to those Jack the collie was demonstrating as he danced around her, pleading for a fuss with sharp yelps. In the yard, she met Charlie with, "Where are you taking me tonight then."

He shrugged, "Back to Nuneaton, as usual, I should think."

"That's not good enough. Not this time. You're my knight. It's time you took me somewhere nicer than that."

"Well of course, just give me a minute and I'll check on when the next steamship leaves for Hong Kong."

"Now you're being silly, you haven't even asked if I get seasick."

"Well, you started it."

"But I wasn't joking, about taking me somewhere nice."

His heart skipped a beat, "Do you have anything in mind?"

"Yep, do you have a picture house near here?"

"Yes, in Atherstone."

"Lovely, then I accept your invitation. The boat's in the repair yard. It's coming out of the water later to have the hull re-blacked so we'll be here for two days."

"But why?" He shook his head, as if to clear his thoughts, "With me I mean?"

She stepped up to him and spoke with a softer voice than she'd ever used before, "Because you're my knight and always will be." The kiss on his cheek lingered longer than usual too, but then she turned and walked away, calling over her shoulder, "Come for me when you're ready."

She was so much older than he was; four or five years at least and surely spoken for, though neither of them had talked about such things. He knew that boat people arranged things like that amongst themselves, just as he knew that relationships outside of their community were virtually forbidden.

He was imagining things, he realised. It was simply an unusual twist on their usual banter, brought about by unusual circumstances but in any event, they would both enjoy the pictures.

They did too. The film was a *George Formby* comedy called '*Boots, Boots*' which filled the cinema with laughter. The singer-come comedian stuck to a well tried formula, in which he played a lovable but gauche character, who, against all odds, wins the heart of the most beautiful woman in the film.

Afterwards, as they walked along South Street to buy a cornet of chips each Charlie thought of his disastrous attempt to woo Harriet West and said, "I feel as daft as he was sometimes."

Sarah Jane put her arm through his and chuckled, "You are."

They walked home, all the way from Atherstone, so that it was dark by the time he escorted her into the repair yard. There were no lights in evidence so she whispered, "I'll say goodnight here, save waking any of that lot up."

Charlie agreed, "Fair enough, but pop across to the farm tomorrow, won't you?"

"Course I will, and here's something to go home with." She stood up on tiptoe and gave him a kiss he would never forget. Her full, soft lips parted and met his like a caress. His senses bloomed in shock but he quickly tried to meet the sensory overload by parting his own lips. He was stunned by the sensuality of the kiss, which lingered, yet was over in a trice. Then those wonderful eyes held his as she whispered, "Night, night, my Knight."

She appeared in the farmyard at lunchtime and called his name. He had stayed around the farmyard all morning, waiting and fretting; barely believing what had happened the previous night and fearing the worst. That she might have realised her error and decided to stay away.

"I began to wonder whether you were coming."

She smiled, "I had chores to do and I thought if I timed it right you might want to share your lunch with me."

His relief was clear, "Yes, yes of course you can." It was dull but dry and quite warm. He gave a wave that encompassed everything, "Indoors or do you want a picnic."

"A picnic sounds wonderful!"

"Fair enough, come and say hello to Mother and I'll wrap something up. Once near the kettle, they had a cup of tea with Agnes while Charlie threw some bread, cheese, pickle and ginger beer into a basket. Agnes cautioned, "Don't go taking the last of Mary's beer or you won't hear the last of it."

"I haven't, there's still half a jar in there." He nodded towards the larder, "And besides, we can blame it on Arnold."

It was a cheap shot that might have found some support from Agnes of late, but shortly afterwards she watched them walk through the yard and turn down towards the canal. The body signals were as clear as the look she saw on that girl's face. It was not to be! *Couldn't* be!

It was the finest picnic of his life, and a curious sequel to the previous evening. They didn't mention the parting or what it might have meant, which for most couples would have been a natural thing to do. Instead, there seemed to be an unspoken acknowledgement of a long-overdue ripening, of a relationship founded on years of banter and familiarity, rather than the more conventional form of courtship. Even so, Charlie was still startled by the new horizon and his heart now skipped a beat whenever he looked at her.

But Sarah Jane had known it as something more, long before then.

The field they were sitting in was pasture now, alongside the canal, but he'd chosen it deliberately, for three years earlier it had contained a crop of *savoy* cabbages. The memories they spoke of made him realise how much they had shared and he said as much.

Sarah Jane shrugged, "Yeah, well, I'm pretty difficult to shake off you know." She stood then and dusted herself down, as though she wanted to avoid further discussion, "Come on, you've never shown me round your place."

He stood and dropped the basket onto the arm furthest away from her, in case she chose to link arms again but it was soon clear that she preferred to wander; eager to see things he pointed out. Three fields on they came across Albert, hoeing some rows of parsnips. He walked over to them with a smile for their visitor and gestured over his shoulder with his thumb, "A good hoeing is as good as a watering at this time of year."

Sarah Jane smiled with her mouth *and* eyes, as always, "Then I probably owe you an apology Mr Morcroft 'cos I suspect that Charlie should be out here with you."

Albert smiled and nodded, "He was set on making you welcome and that's fine with me." He added, as an afterthought, "For one day."

She smothered a laugh and said, "Then I shan't be found wanting. Charlie's just showing me round, but as soon as we're done *I* shall come out here and help you, with or without Charlie."

Albert looked on, impressed, "Fair enough!" With a broadening grin he made to start back, "Well in that case, I'll not hold you up."

As they walked on Charlie spoke, "There's no need you know."

She nudged against him, "I shall enjoy it, but we have lots to see first."

It took almost an hour to get back to the yard and as they approached the hay barn Sarah Jane ran to the edge and took a deep breath, "Mmm, I love the smell of hay." Charlie followed her inside and watch her gaze up at the tiered bales, "There's so much of it! Do your animals eat it all?"

"Pretty well, sometimes we sell a bit, if there's enough. It all depends on what sort of winter we have."

She pointed at the top, where there was a six foot gap between the hay and the roof. "Did you ever play up there as a child?

"No, Father wouldn't let us do that."

"That's a deprived childhood, that is. So you wouldn't *dare* go up there as a grown up neither."

"Don't you dare me Sarah Jane Finch!"

She giggled then and suddenly began to climb the stepped bales, calling down when she was ten feet from the ground, "Double dare!"

They were just able to stand at the top, where she'd been waiting for him and this time, when they kissed, his lips opened to meet hers. It was gentle and loving but soon she moved her head to whisper in his ear, "So, if you didn't play up here as a child, let's play up here as grown-ups."

From that moment on he slipped into a dream-like state, gazing in shock as she lay down and held her arms out to him. He dropped down on to his knees and leaned forward to kiss her.

Her arms left him and moved down to struggle briefly with something at their waists before she wriggled slowly and was done. He turned and looked down to see that her skirt was open, exposing her dimpled knees and the whiteness of thighs that were joined by a shock of dark curls. Each image seared through his dream-like consciousness like a strobe. She pulled him over into the opening vee of her legs and fumbled with his belt until he used one hand to help, and then he looked at her beautiful face as she pushed his trousers down and released his erection into the gentle exploration of her hand. Her eyes never left his, as though she didn't want to miss anything his features might reveal and then her arms were around him; moving up his back and drawing him into her.

The shock of her moist softness enveloped him completely. His mind reeled with a sensory explosion he could never have dreamt of as her hips rose slightly in encouragement. He opened his eyes and saw that hers were closed now, but her beautiful lips parted slightly as she reached up with one arm and drew his head down to hers. They kissed briefly, then she eased his head onto the top of her shoulder and placed her other hand on the base of his spine, gently urging him on, until all too soon, his own urgency began to take dominance. His pace and force grew until at last, his orgasm swept through him with a force that was transcendental.

In the calm that followed, he felt as though he'd been in a wonderful dream and then realised that Sarah Jane still lay beneath him, being squashed probably. He made to move but she held him tightly and said, quite firmly, "Stay."

Minutes passed while he rested his head beside hers and closed his eyes, until he felt himself sliding from her. He raised his head to look at her and she gazed back, expressionlessly. After a short while he cocked his head to one side and smiled slightly.

"Kiss me, Charlie Morcroft."

He gasped with relief, and sank on to her lips. When he rose for air she smiled, with her mouth, eyes and hand as she reached up and ruffled his hair, "I heard an Aunty talking to my ma' about it once. She said that if a fella still wanted to kiss you afterwards it was alright but more often than not they were out of the door like a shot."

Charlie couldn't believe it, "Then do you love me Sarah Jane?"

"Bloody 'ell Charlie, what's a girl got to do to make you realise that?"

They both laughed and cuddled and kissed and realised that they had been missing for too long. She pushed him off and said, "Come on, your father will be down here looking for us. You go an' get the hoes while I just attend to a couple things up here and I'll meet you out the back." She met his questioning gaze with, "*Lady* things. Now leave me alone for a minute."

That evening, they were both tired and disinclined to go into town again, so after eating with the Finch's on board the boat, they planned to walk along to the *White Horse* at Mancetter. The boat was still out of the water and it felt strange having to climb a ladder to step aboard, where the smell of paint tainted everything; until a glass of barley wine dulled the senses sufficiently for it not to matter.

It had been a patching job mostly, in the interests of economy, so the boat would be launched in the morning as soon as the yard men turned up. Tommy and Elsa made their farewells soon after the meal, explaining that they would be making an early night of it.

At Purley View Farm, things were far less orderly. Albert couldn't remember the last time he and Agnes had words, but they seemed to be making up for it this time.

He'd spent the evening trying to placate her and counselling for patience, for just like Mary's dalliance with Arnold, he guessed it would be a temporary encounter. Besides, Sarah Jane was one of the boat people and they *never* married outside of their ilk; in fact hardly outside of the family he'd been told.

Agnes would have none of it. It was time for a confrontation; with all four miscreants *and* the other parents. She had agreed to wait and see with Mary, against her better judgement and now, it seemed that lack of influence had enabled Charlie to go off the rails as well. It was also time to put some backbone into her husband, "I will not give these unions my blessing Albert and I *must* have your support. You have been tardy in this affair and now you must stand with me."

He shrugged but said nothing.

"Albert! Do I have your support in this or are you prepared to see this farm and the family's heritage, go?"

He sighed, "Yes Agnes, you have my support."

She watched him sit by the stove, with his back to her and knew he'd have no more to say, but enough had been achieved for one night, "Very well, I shall go to bed. We shall attend to things tomorrow."

Albert stayed silent and when he heard her climb the stairs, opened the stove door and gazed at the dancing flames. The warmth washed over him when he leaned forward and rested his arms on his knees; the silence broken only by the slow ticking of the clock and the snickering of burning wood. Things were so much easier when they were children but now they were adults so many other things needed weighing up.

And what *of* the farm and its future? They were still only tenant farmers, after so many years and there was no likelihood of a purchase, not as things stood. They could barely manage to keep up with the advances in machinery and they always lived on the edge of ruin it seemed, waiting for the natural disaster or disease that would put them on the street.

Mary and Arnold would manage, he felt certain, whatever they chose to do, but what about Charlie. He was faced with a choice of two lives if he wed that Sarah Jane, though that was a long way from certain and just as likely to be a passing fancy. But if they were to wed, he would be forced to choose between farming and the canals, both hard lives.

One thing was for certain; tomorrow would be a difficult day.

It was a warm, moonlit night and rather than climb the haystack Charlie spread a single layers of bales across the floor and lay a clean horse blanket over them. This time she allowed him to explore her in his own way while she pursued her own trail of discovery but soon a mutual urgency called for their union.

Afterwards, they held each other until Charlie whispered, "I have a gift for you; it'll be ready for next time."

She grinned mischievously, "How do you know there will be a next time?"

Charlie was horrified, "what do you mean?"

She giggled, "You are very gullible Charlie Morcroft. I think I shall start to call you 'ashpit' for you'll take anything in."

"That's not fair; you just like playing games with me."

She put her hand to her mouth to try and smother her giggles at that one, until at last, he realised what he'd said and shared the humour. After a while he returned to his earlier concern, "But tell me, will you be back soon?"

"Depends, what the gift is."

"Then you'll have to come back to find out."

"Tell me now. What is it?"

"You'll have to wait and see, or it won't be a surprise, will it?"

"Then it looks as though I shall have to, I suppose."

"How will I know you will?" It was a needless thing to say, but suddenly he realised he had something too precious to lose.

She leaned forward and kissed him, before falling back on her knees and reaching up around her neck to remove a silver locket and chain. She pointed out the initials, 'SJ'; just discernible in the weak light and explained, "It was my grandma's, before she gave it to me and one of the men in the workshops put them initials on for me. Mind, there's nothing inside. I haven't got a picture to put in there yet. Still," she handed it to him, "You can hold on to it for the time being; that'll make sure I come back."

He took it and then an idea struck him He picked up a scrap of wood and opened his clasp knife, "Here." She realised what he wanted to do and leaned forward so that he could take a lock of her hair. When it was done he carefully opened the locket and curled the hair inside until it would close. She saw his grin as he spoke, "Now, I shall guard it with my life."

"Hah, you better 'ad, 'cos your life won't be worth living if you lose it."

* * *

As soon as they finished the milking and loaded the dray, Albert and Charlie went in for breakfast to find Mary and Agnes sitting at the table. The thunderous look on Mary's face was enough for Charlie to ask, "What's the matter with you Mary? Don't go near the milk with that face on."

She sneered, "You'd better listen to what's been said before you get high and mighty."

He frowned and looked at his mother who said, "Wash your hands and sit down Charlie, your father and I have to speak with you."

Charlie was intrigued rather than concerned and did as he was told, pouring himself a cup of tea before he sat and reached for a plate.

Albert was at the sink washing his hands when Agnes began, "Your father and I are very concerned by the people you have both chosen to step out with. Neither of them are suitable choices for the long term." She couldn't bring herself to say either their names or the word 'marriage', "We *both* feel that it would be best if you stopped seeing them and proper too. No good can come of these affairs and you would both be wrong to give them unreasonable expectations."

Albert was still at the sink so Charlie confined his comment to Agnes, "What about *our* expectations Mother?"

"Why, in time, we trust that you will find yourselves wedded to the right sort of folk and hopefully, farmers."

"What if we've already chosen?"

Mary huffed, "I've already said that."

Agnes ignored her, "That is why we've chosen to speak to you this morning. Youth and inexperience make for poor choices, which is why the law in this country says that you must have parental consent to marry at your ages. You must trust us in this. Time and a little more experience will show you how close you came to making terrible decisions, ones that you would have regretted for the rest of your lives."

Charlie could feel his bile rising, "Father, are you of this opinion too?"

Albert looked tired as he turned and dried his hands, but when he sat at the table, Agnes poured his tea, leaving him free to speak, "I support your mother Charlie, which is how it should be."

Charlie *did* have the wisdom to realise that this had been planned and that his mother had never been given to changing her mind in important matters. But her power to affect their choices was limited, "Mary becomes of *full age* next January, so she has only to wait a few months and me only sixteen months more."

"We are worried for Mary, it's true and I pray that she will see sense in that time, but I know that there is enough time for you to come around to the right choice. There are plenty of fish in the sea."

"And in the canal Mother. Perhaps I should go and live there."

Agnes snapped at him, "Grow up boy! You're a farmer, not a boatman and they will say as much. Do you honestly think we can stand by and see you make such a fool of yourself?"

Charlie had heard enough, and stood to go, "You must do as you wish Mother, just as I will."

Mary followed him out and Agnes waited until the porch door had closed before asking Albert, "What do you think?"

He would never fail his wife, they both knew that, but he was too vexed to stomach breakfast. He stood to go and spoke with some sadness, "I think we might be losing our son Agnes; that is what I think."

* * *

Charlie knew to within a few days when the Finches would be coming through and made sure that he could keep an eye out for her. Even so, she almost made it to the house before he intercepted her and headed around the barn. As soon as they were out of sight he gathered her up and hugged her.

She seemed delighted and with eyes shining, said "Now that's what I call a welcome!"

His smile was tinged with something else as he said, "Come on, we need to go for a walk. There are things I need to say."

He took her hand and led her up the hill, towards a track that would lead them to Hartshill, in one direction or to the *Outwoods* at Atherstone in the other. Just yards into the walk he started. After five weeks he'd had time enough to rehearse, "Sarah Jane, my father and mother do not approve of our courtship and I am only nineteen, but I love you and I want to marry you."

She looked ahead as she spoke, "You sure it ain't just young love, or because of what happened between us."

He glanced at her and saw her expression. "Do you think that?"

"I'm just asking, that's all."

He turned her to face him and shook his head, "No, I mean yes. What we did was the most beautiful thing that's ever happened to me, but that was only part of what has happened between us. I've done nothing but think about this over the last five weeks and I realised that we've been courting for three years now, since I chucked that cabbage to you. We just didn't realise it."

She remained solemn, "You didn't."

He let that one sink in before shrugging, "Well I certainly know now. I love you Sarah Jane, please trust me in this."

She sat down on the grass and pulled him down beside her, "Charlie, Charlie, Charlie, I've got some news that might change your mind." She paused for effect, "I'm expecting a baby."

His jaw dropped along with his heart before he whispered, "Who is the father."

She stared at him as though he'd said something very stupid.

He stammered, "I'm sorry, I didn't mean to . . . well." He seemed to wilt as he whispered, "You were my first."

"I've got news for you Mr Charlie, you were my first too. Should've known; a farmer would have scored first time."

This time he took her by the shoulders, "You mean it's our baby?"

He hugged her tightly enough to hurt, but she held on to him, for long enough to blink away the tears that threatened to fall.

They parted and Charlie explained, "This last five weeks I've thought it all out. You may not think so, but Mother is a strong person and will not back down. That is why I'd already decided to leave Purley View, if you'd said yes."

"Whoa, Charlie, you can't just walk away from the farm like that."

"It isn't our farm and never will be. Your life is a hard one, but so is farming. I'll not miss it."

"Well what about my father?"

"I should like to ask his permission to marry you, even if we have to wait for twenty months."

She knew that marriage certificates weren't as coveted on the cut but would it matter in the place they chose to live? She was also Tommy Finch's daughter and a lad off the land had put her in the family way. "You'd better let me break the news to him. I reckon my ma has an inkling already but if you're there when we tell him, he's likely to take a knife and cut your bits off."

They spoke some more, but the copse was nearby and both wanted to make love again. It was a hurried, passionate coupling and the post-coital hug was interrupted by a couple of belligerent wood ants, but it didn't seem to matter. They parted after agreeing that he should turn up the next morning.

Charlie didn't mention it to his parents and had no intention of doing so. He was going to leave on his terms and would not have it said that the woman he loved had entrapped him, but the next morning he walked down to the canal with his heart in his mouth. He knew that he had to go through with it and dare not back down, not when Sarah Jane was at stake.

Tommy and Elsa must have sensed something was up the previous day, since they had moored by the yard instead of going on to Nuneaton as usual and waited for their daughter to return on foot. When she told them her news they remained there for the night, ready to receive 'Charlie bleedin' Morcroft' the following morning.

Tommy was waiting for him, "Charlie, I think it's time I beat the shit out of you."

"I'd rather you didn't Tommy."

"Well, there's a surprise. And why do you suppose I should pay any heed to the man what has sullied my daughter?"

Charlie struggled on, "Because, when I marry her, we shall be family and while I know that you might do as you say and beat me terribly, I shall know where to find you when you grow older and less fearsome. That will be the day I shall repay you in kind."

"My God, you want my blessing for this marriage yet you threaten to harm me when I am old and unable to defend myself!"

"I concede that much, Tommy, for I would be unable to best you before then."

Tommy suddenly seemed resigned to the inevitable, "So you would be taking my daughter onto the bank?"

Charlie thought about his parent's reaction and his hitherto acceptance by the Finch family, "Do you think there would be a place for me on the cut."

Tommy's reaction was instant, "I do! And by God, I would be happy to see as much too! No-one would try and best my family on the cut. You'll be taken care of I promise you." He thumped the hatch, "Elsa, get up here, and bring some *barley wine!*"

Mother and daughter were crying when they fell out of the cabin and Sarah Jane ran over and hugged Charlie, "My knight. I'll make you happy I promise."

Elsa huffed, "Not too often mind, look what's happened already."

Tommy was shocked by his wife's comment, "Ma!"

She stood her ground, "Don't you go ma'ing me Tommy Finch, yer randy old goat!"

Modest volumes of *Barley wine* were called for, in the interests of sound planning. A little patience was called for too, so that Tommy could speak to the company and see if a boat was available for them, but if not, they agreed that somehow or other they would manage on the two to hand.

One thing was certain though; Charlie would be leaving home in five weeks time.

In the meantime, there was a load of coal to be delivered to London, which would be followed by a visit to the Regent's Canal Dock, where the company offices were sited. Tommy was well thought of there and he felt confident that they'd be looked after, which could mean that Charlie and Sarah Jane would have their own boat before Christmas. Heaven help them if it turned out to be a bad winter!

* * *

The two boats were lashed together so that Tommy could steer them through the Braunstone Locks while the women managed the paddles. Often, they would take turns but on this occasion Elsa and Sarah Jane elected to stay ashore and have a natter. It was two days since they had left Charlie, waving madly from the bridge at Hartshill and there was a lot to talk about. Tommy was content to leave them to it, because it would be woman's talk, he was certain.

The weather had been dreadful, with rain and northerly gales bringing an icy chill to October, but a depression had moved in, bringing a spell of mild dull weather.

They completed the flight of six locks in good time and with the top lock virtually flooded, both women had thrown their weight against the lock gates, when Tommy saw his daughter twist around and drop to her hands and knees. He shouted for Elsa who had seen it too and was clambering across the boats rather than waste time closing the gates.

She stooped down and put her hand on Sarah Jane's shoulder, "What's up love?"

"Oh Ma, it hurts and I think I'm showing."

Elsa gained enough purchase to get Sarah Jane to her feet and told Tommy to go and open the butty cabin. By the time they reached the stern, he'd drawn back the bed covers and was waiting to help them aboard.

By then, another pair of boats was waiting to come into the lock but it only took moments for them to be told what had happened. They hurried forward to help separate the Finch boats and moor them against the towpath. Once satisfied that there was nothing else they could do to help, the other family moved on, and Tommy sat on the stern of his boat, alone and anxious.

In the cabin, Elsa made her daughter as comfortable as possible and stayed with her for a time, but they had to keep moving and what was happening was a sad, but natural thing. She stroked her daughter's brow and said softly, "I've left you a bucket, . . . in case you should need one, but call me if you need me." They both knew what she meant.

Up top, she closed the hatch and waited for Tommy to trot down to her. Before he could ask, she shook her head, "She's losing it." Tommy dropped his head and stared at the ground. Elsa went on, "Don't worry Tommy, it happens to lots of women, 'specially their first one. There'll be others, have no fear."

Tommy looked up as a thought struck him, "What about Charlie."

She smiled gently, "Ay with him an 'all, have no fear. Charlie won't let her down, I'm certain of that."

There was nothing else to say, apart from the obvious, "We'd best get on."

Elsa nodded, "Ay, better that we do."

Four and a half hours later, when they were just clear of the Buckby flight of locks, Sarah Jane called out, "Ma! Ma!"

Elsa gave the thirteen year old girl the tiller before stepping down into the cabin and then she saw the blood. Sarah Jane had tried to use the bucket but it was everywhere. Now she was curled up into a foetal position and whimpering with the pain. Elsa gagged slightly at the horror of it, but snatched a pillow and forced it between Sarah Jane's thighs, "Please love, I want you to hold that there, as tightly as you can, I'll be back in just a minute."

She fled from the cabin and ran along the gunwale to the bows, where she could make herself heard. Tommy's head snapped round and as soon as he saw Elsa's frantic waving, he pointed at the tow rope. As soon as he was satisfied that she knew what to do, he put his engine into reverse. Had she not been gathering the tow rope in, it would have wrapped itself around the prop and if something bad was happening that was the last thing they would need.

As soon as they were within earshot she called out, "She needs a doctor Tommy, go and find one. Me and the kid's will moor up."

He shook his head, "No, we've got to keep moving, the Watling Street bridge is down here a ways, you can moor up then."

She trusted his judgement enough not to argue, and soon realised what he meant. They were travelling as fast as they could; around five or six knots. He might have made better time on foot, but the same distance would then need to be covered back to the boats by the doctor.

Thirty minutes later he signalled to her and let the speed bleed off as he gathered the tow rope in, but as soon as his boat nudged itself to a standstill against the bank he leapt off and ran for the bridge ahead, leaving the others to moor up.

He could hear traffic and scrambled up the bank onto the main road. There was no sign of a building but a car approached as he stepped into the road, waving his arms.

The driver stopped and leaned out of his window, "Anything wrong?"

Tommy explained and the driver signalled with a nod, "Hop in, you can make the call from the *New Inn*, just down the road."

It took almost an hour for the doctor to collect him from the pub and be shown to the boats, but it took less than four minutes for him to leap off and run for his car. Things became a blur for Tommy after that. He stood at the roadside, as directed, waiting to show the ambulance where to stop and saw it approaching, a long way off, on the straight Roman road.

They asked few questions, but hurried to get Sarah Jane onto the stretcher and to hospital. Tommy returned to the boats, to look after the children so it was Elsa who held her daughter's hand when she passed away, minutes before they reached the hospital.

The doctor had feared the worst and called at the hospital shortly after. He sought out a member of staff and was told the diagnosis before he went to find Elsa. She was in the waiting room, slumped against the wall; weeping and when he crouched down to take her hand she sobbed, "Why?"

"I'm very sorry, Mrs Finch, it was an ectopic pregnancy, which caused a haemorrhage. You couldn't have known that and everything you did was the most you *could* have done, in the circumstances." He wrapped an arm around her shoulders, "Come on, I'll take you back to your husband."

He offered to accompany her down to the boats but she shook her head, "No thank you Doctor, I'd rather be on my own."

Tommy had stayed up on deck, rather than go to bed, so he saw the figure approach in the dark and jumped off to meet her. As they drew close his heart knew the answer, even as his head dictated the question, "What's the news love?"

He rushed forward as she emptied her lungs in a series of exhalations. By the time he reached her the wracking sobs took hold and his began too. They remained like that; on a muddy towpath, in the middle of nowhere, for a very long time.

* * *

Two days later, at breakfast time, Mr Frankland knocked on the kitchen door and Albert answered it.

"Morning Albert, I'm sorry to be bothering you at this time of day, but is Charlie in please?"

Albert noted the man's expression and said, "Of course, please come in."

"Er no, thank you. Begging your pardon Albert, but I've had strict instructions that I must speak to Charlie alone."

"Very well, I'll get him." He went inside and moments later Charlie stepped out, "Hello Mr Frankland, what can I do for you?"

"Charlie, lad, could we have a word, in private like?" He indicated with a wave that they should move into the yard, away from the house, so Charlie slipped his boots on and followed.

Agnes stood away from the window, so that she couldn't be seen from outside and watched as Frankland relayed whatever he'd come to tell. It seemed to be a long message and eventually Frankland grasped one of Charlie's arms.

He shook it off and walked away and didn't return for two days.

No one would ever know that he had lain on the bales in the top of the barn for some of the time and one night, he'd slept at the side of the towpath, beside the bridge near Baddesley Wharf, wrapped in the horse blanket.

Meanwhile, the family discovered what had happened. Mary was distraught and privately, Albert thought of those wonderful eyes and that natural charm, yet he was wise enough to stay silent when Agnes said, "Well, perhaps a greater will than ours saw the folly of that match." Albert didn't respond but he *did* grieve for his son's loss.

When Charlie returned nothing was said, save for the single occasion, when Mary followed him into the workshop and hugged him. "Little brother, you stood up for us. I am so sorry for you, but I tell you this, I *shall* marry Arnold and I should like you to give me away."

* * *

The funeral was at the church they were to be married in. A small, grey, stone affair, on the outskirts of Dudley. It was full of Boat people, except for one, who sheltered at the back, by the vestry door.

The coffin was covered in flowers; a testament to the beauty within and the family followed, still looking stunned in disbelief.

Only Tommy had seen the outsider and just moments after they had moved into the front pew, he stepped back out into the aisle, signalling to the minister to pause. There were gentle murmurs of care and concern as he walked back down the aisle to the very back, where he found Charlie, who saw his approach and collapsed back against the wall, sobbing quietly.

Tommy's eyes were moist when he stepped up and placed a hand on Charlie's shoulder, "Come with me lad. I want you with us today."

Charlie shook his head and tried to speak through the sobs, "I can't, not like this. I'll stay here."

Tommy leaned in and whispered fiercely, "You were going to be family and you *shall* be today." He wrapped an arm into one of Charlie's, "Come on, she'd have wanted it, remember that."

The two men walked up the aisle, crushed by grief. As they passed one row, the man on the end leaned in to his neighbour and whispered, "Who's that?"

As luck would have it, his neighbour had been one of the 'forty', "He was Sarah Jane's betrothed. It was 'im and Sarah Jane wot organised the coal train do on the *Coventry*."

"Wot, up near Atherstone?"

"Yeah."

"Aaahh."

Yet still, neither of his parents said a word or indicated any sympathy until a week after the funeral, when he had to go into the house for a pair of scissors and found his mother alone in the kitchen. She waited until he was on his way out before speaking, "I was sorry to learn of . . . "

He turned on her with a savagery that stunned her, "NEVER! NEVER, utter her name in my presence!"

He made for the door and stopped, it was time she knew, "I tell you this Mother, when it is time for Father to finish you will have to sell, for that will be the day I leave farming forever."

* * *

In spite of Tommy's reference to family, they never saw or spoke to each other again. The link between their two worlds had been broken.

Chapter Seven

It was an impossibly small photograph, though that at least saved it from being folded, as I know it would have been otherwise, since the dog eared edges indicated that it had been kept in either a pocket or wallet for some time and referred to frequently.

There were six men seated on a bench outside a pub; that much I knew, since they all had tankards in their hands. Yet there were no smiles. It was as though they were gathered to consider an agenda of some gravitas.

Someone had written on the reverse in ink that by now had faded to pale sepia and was barely readable.

'THE BALDHEARDS 1938'.

I'm reasonably literate but that word was a new one and reference to the dictionary confirmed it. Further exploration of our language via the internet and our library also failed to identify it. I even wrote the word in large letters on a piece of paper and put it on our kitchen table while I sat to consider my options. Was it ancient British? After all it did have an Anglo Saxon ring to it.

Further searches included an exchange of emails with the English department of Birmingham University and all failed to solve the puzzle. But each failure seemed to elevate the importance of the word. It had to mean something, yet there were no clues in the picture or other papers.

The note remained on the kitchen table while all that was going on, perhaps in the hope that having it to hand would trigger a new line of thought, until one morning, as I cradled a mug of coffee and stared at the thing my wife mumbled through a mouthful of toast, "Balderdash."

I looked up, my brow creased in mild irritation, "What?"

She nodded at the sheet of paper, "Balderdash, you can spell balderdash with those letters, you know, like an anagram."

Charlie
THE BALDHEARDS

Charlie eased his way into the bar of the White Horse with caution, so as to avoid any contact with his left arm, which was cradled in a sling. Protruding from it was a white globe of bandaging that would have made his hand look like a boxing glove had it not been for the two fingers protruding from the front; the fore and little fingers to be exact. Between them lay a space marked by bloody spotting that spoke of terrible injuries.

By the time he reached the bar, Thomas Wandrill, the landlord, had already pulled a pint of best bitter and set it down on the pocked mahogany, nodding a greeting and murmuring, "That looks right bad there Charlie."

Charlie dropped a shilling into the man's hand and grasped his tankard, "Aye, it's not been pleasant I can tell you."

He didn't elaborate, for he was late and the group were already seated at their table.

Wandrill felt more was called for though. He was a large man, with a mop of reddish brown hair that extended south into two large 'lamb chop' sideburns. Affable for the most part, but he could also be a stern host when house rules were broken. "Hang on lad." He grabbed a shot glass and turned to the optics behind the bar for a tot of rum. "There you go, on me, I reckon you could do with a stiffener tonight."

Charlie looked up in surprise, "Why thank you Tom, that's a very Christian thing to do. I shall remember that." Wandrill nodded and turned to serve another.

Saturday was the single night of the week that was his alone, to do as he pleased and not as the farm demanded. Not that Albert demanded such a commitment, which if true, would have implied that life on the farm had become harder since the loss of Sarah Jane. In fact, the opposite was true and to say otherwise would have been unfair to Albert, for he had privately shared his son's loss and would have gladly allowed him more free time if it had been requested.

But Charlie had sought and gained comfort from hard work; though conversely, his Saturday evenings assumed an almost religious importance, even though he'd done the same thing each week, every week for the last four years.

Every Saturday night, as soon as the milking was done, he would rush indoors, wash, change and leap on to his bike for a ten minute dash to the *White Horse* at Mancetter. He would always forego dinner, knowing that a hunk of bread and ripe cheese would be available at the pub; along with a dip into the landlady's jar of pickle. You may make of that what you will, but Charlie would and could only think of the savoury relish that was meant to accompany cheese.

On this occasion he couldn't cycle to the pub, on account of his disability, at least not safely, notwithstanding the fact that the journey home was often a hazardous affair anyway, thanks to the *Bass* brewery.

"I'm sorry I'm late lads." He placed his tankard amongst the others on the table before returning for his glass of rum and as he sat down he raised his injured arm slightly by way of an explanation.

At 43 years of age Abe Thomson was the most senior of the five men already present and by unspoken agreement was the spokesman, "That looks a bit of a bad do Charlie." Murmurs around the table leant support to this view.

Charlie attempted to grin but winced as he did so, before adjusting the sling slightly, "It most certainly is."

He couldn't help but notice that their eyes were drawn to the seepage of blood evidenced on his dressing where the two middle fingers should have been and looked down at it himself as if mourning the loss of digits.

Abe continued, "We're pleased to see you could make it mind." Further nods and murmurs followed and most saluted with their tankards as they supped a little more ale. All were keen to know what had happened but none would ask, it simply wasn't done, though an explanation was expected and Charlie knew it.

He took a swig of ale and set his tankard back down amongst the variety of vessels on the table. Some were pewter, some pot but they were all different.

One commemorated the coronation of Edward the Eighth, just two years earlier in 1936. When he abdicated in December of the same year, so he could be the third husband of Mrs Wallis Simpson, the *Baldheards* tried to persuade the tankard's owner to destroy it. But tankards were expensive and this one held a smidgeon more than a pint; not much more, but the owner reasoned that over a year he would have supped one more pint than the rest and for not a penny farthing more. He therefore compromised by applying a splash of black paint to the embossed image, which then seemed to commemorate an act of regicide.

Their tankards were not labelled and didn't need to be for the landlord knew and cared for them as though they were his own. At the end of each Saturday he would clean them and set each on the shelf that ran above the bar. Allowing someone other than its owner to sup from a tankard was an unthinkable crime.

Charlie was hungry and glanced at the plates two of the lads had before them; each laden with a chunk torn from a cottage loaf and a generous piece of ripe cheese. Its age was evidenced by the white mould on the rind and the traces of moisture on the inside surfaces marked the demise of a couple of maggots. The surviving halves were still inside and would be relished along with the home-made pickle.

There were always two cheeses on the counter. The one crusted with age, with a population of cheese maggots was there to meet local demand. Another, under a glass dome, was for the 'tourists'. Creamily fresh, with a light rind and void of visible life, or flavour, the locals would argue.

But Charlie decided to postpone the cheese until after he'd told his story.

"S'all thanks to my sister's pig." The atmosphere changed as all those present paid heed, along with any others who were within earshot.

"It was my sister Mary's pig. Like her, bloody stubborn an' well, *belligerent*. I wanted to call it Mary, for obvious reasons but my sister always gets 'er way and it got called Boadicea, in fact all our pigs have been given that name, over the years." He shook his head in exasperation, "I have nothing but trouble with her animals. I reckon they end up taking after her.

Once, she, that's the pig, decided to go and visit the neighbours. You know, the Watsons, over at Hill Farm.

Mary hadn't fixed the sty gate properly because she had a bucket of mash in her hands and that's usually enough to keep the animal inside the pen and halfway in the trough. Only this time it was like the pig had planned her move, like an ambush I suppose. Mary had half-emptied the swill when she heard Boadicea give a bloody great squeal, like a battle cry and she was off! Out of the yard and down the lane, with Mary chasing after her and yelling her head off.

Well Boadicea put on a hell of a pace and Mary was left stand-ing. I heard the din and come out of the shed to see what was going on. I'm still not sure who was the loudest,—the pig or my sister, but one thing was for sure, one of them was having fun and the other wasn't.

Bye, that pig could run!

I joined in the chase and we followed her back up off the lane onto the track to Watson's place. We'd lost sight of her by that time but there'd been so much rain the ground was soft enough for her tracks to show up."

He paused to take some more ale, before continuing, "Anyhow, we finally got to the Watson's place and there she was, stood at their back door. I still reckon she'd knocked on it 'cos a moment later Billy Watson came to the door in his stocking feet. By the time we got close up he was grinning and scratching his head.

Soon as he saw us he laughed out loud and pointed at Boadicea"

"Looks like this old girl 'as 'ad enough of your company young Charlie. I reckon she's picked me now."

"Meanwhile, Boadicea was shaking her head, so that her ears were flapping up and down, like she was demanding to be let in, or fed at the very least.

He was going to have a bit of sport with me, I could tell, and I was having none of it.

I said, well now, Mr Watson, we were a bit short of peelings tonight and she looked over this way as if there'd be a morsel or two included in a visit to a neighbour. I said to 'er, now don't go thinking you'll get any more up there. Their 'taters are so small they can't afford to peel them. I could see that she didn't believe me though and before I could stop her she was over the wall and heading this way.

Billy pursed his lips and looked thoughtful for a bit."

"Well, I can see how she might have made a mistake, as you say, 'cept you're forgetting that I keep all the smaller 'taters to one side so my pigs get the whole thing, not just the peelings. Bit of a treat like."

"He reached down and scratched her behind an ear. You could tell she was loving the attention and he looked me straight in the eye."

"Only, I don't have a pig this far forward so I reckon this one realises she can have as much as she likes. Makes me think she's as bright as she looks. In fact I reckon she's adopted me. I'll be sure to look after her and I'll tell you what, I'll send some black pudding down when the time comes. As a token, like."

Charlie looked around the group, "I knew I had to keep my wits about me, for Billy is as sharp as they come.

That's very generous of you Billy, I said, and next spring, when your heifers come through into our north pasture, as they have done for the last four years, I'll be sure to send some stewing steak up.

Billy's grin came back and he said, "Now I couldn't ask for anything fairer. What's her name then?"

Our Mary barked at him, "Boadicea!"

"Whatta?"

"Boadicea!"

"Weren't she that mad woman warrior?"

Our Mary was getting fired up by now and shouted back at him, "She was a hero."

Billy gave a grunt, "She was a woman first an' foremost an' from what I heard she didn't do much cooking an' cleaning." He held his hand up then, to stop Mary from yelling back at him, "I'm very sorry deary, but that sounds like a free-thinking woman to me. A suffragette pig you might say an' I've got my principles. She can't stay here I'm afraid."

He spoke to me then, "Go to the barn Charlie, you'll find some twine behind the door" He chuckled at us, "I'll wait while she tows you two 'ome."

"I can hear him laughing at us now"

Charlie took another swig and eased his arm into another position. "You know, she had a special look about her did that pig. I've never seen the like before and it was more noticeable when she was planning on some more mischief. Talk about bold. She could look you in the eye and never back down. Believe me, I tried. I think it would be fair to say that she hated me and the feeling was mutual.

'Course, since then she'd been to see most of the neighbours. She was so bloomin' quick. I've lost count of the number of chickens she had; the ones stupid enough to get up on the sty wall. In fact she never missed one and by the time I'd got there, no matter how quick I was, there'd be just a few feathers left."

Dan Pickering, one of the younger members of the group, interrupted, though he spoke for everyone, "Charlie, can we ask to hold up for a moment, while we get another drink?"

Charlie jerked up and winced with the pain sudden movement triggered, "Blimey, no of course not, you should have said." He grabbed his tankard and emptied it, "I'll get myself a refill too, while you're at it."

The rum remained untouched; he realised earlier on that it had a strategic value.

Once they were all seated Abe signalled that Charlie should continue. By now, the folk sitting around them had given up any pretence of not hearing and had turned their stools around to listen.

"Aye well, this is the difficult bit and strange too, for she had once last trick to play on me.

Tuesday morning I was all set to have the last laugh. I went to peer over her wall first thing, just to see if all was well, but I couldn't help but point out that her travelling days were over.

Mary would have nothing to do with it so Mother had to stoke up the boiler and old Joey Feltham came down to help with the butchering. Him and dad went in to get her, all set for trouble. Dad told me to stand to one side and come up from behind if a shove was needed.

Well, they got a rope on her and were ready for anything, or so they thought, yet she came trotting out of the sty like a lamb, even though the slaughter bench was there to see.

We should have known better.

They started to relax and commented on how placid she was, when all of a sudden she flicked the rope out of Dad's hands. I don't know how she managed it, I didn't see, but one thing I did notice was how she was heading at me!

Dad and Joey were quick off the mark, trying to stamp on the end of her rope and I tried to make a run for it, but the next thing I know, she's taken a lump out of my arse! Bloody hell it hurt. I'd show you the bandages but Tom'd soon have me out of here if I dropped my trousers."

The group grinned and nodded in agreement.

"I don't know what else she'd have had if they hadn't got hold of her then an' of course she switched into full panic after that. It took all of us, Mother as well, to pull and push her into place.

Joey finally despatched her and after we'd hung and bled her, mostly at any rate, Dad told me to take the head off and take it into the house, ready for Mother to do the brawn.

Now all through this, I'm certain, that pig's eyes never left me, even after we'd got her hung. It's uncanny, but not only could I have sworn she was looking at me, but the eyes were still glinting, with malice. That's the only way I can think of it.

Anyway, I got the knife and saw ready and Dad stepped to one side to let me get at the carcase. The first thing I did was untie the noose so the rope was out of the way."

Charlie looked down at what was left of his hand, "An' that's when she got me. I didn't get chance to react. In a flash, she took two fingers off.

Pfff, you should have seen the blood. Dad fainted, clean away. Sat right down and rolled over. Joey and Mother wrapped my hand up and then Joey hopped on his bike to go down to the telephone box and call for an ambulance.

They couldn't do anything mind, just cauterised the stumps, wrapped them up and sent me home, this morning in fact."

This was the moment he had reserved the rum for. It was time for a little theatre. He grasped the glass and threw back the rum, choking as the alcohol scorched his throat.

He set the glass back down and shook his head in wonder, "You know, Joey *and* Dad said they'd never seen or heard the like of it before. The kicking just after slaughter is to be expected but to see a nervous reaction like that, so long after, was something else.

I've got my own thoughts on the matter though. Like I said, I could swear her eyes never left me and somehow, don't ask me to explain, but somehow, she kept something back, some mean spark, even after death, knowing she'd get one last crack at me."

In the silence that followed Abe pulled his pipe and tobacco pouch from his pocket and seemed to be lost in thought as he kneaded the flake into the briar bowl.

The silence continued as he struck a match and disappeared behind a cloud of fragrant smoke. After tamping the glowing surface with his forefinger, to ensure that none of the glowing fibres escaped he shook the match until the flame was out and dropped it into the ashtray.

He looked around the table as though he expected responses and seemed content when there were none. Finally, he addressed Charlie.

"Well now Charlie, that *was* balderdash. Congratulations."

Charlie acknowledged the gentle round of applause and began to remove the bandages. By then his two middle fingers were aching terribly.

Chapter Eight

The photograph of dad, or Charlie, if you'd prefer, still chilled me. He seemed so comfortable holding that weird-looking gun and then there was the dagger, strapped to his leg, just below the knee. I felt certain it was the one I'd found in the Chest. And why was he wearing a denim overall, instead of a uniform?

Then I wondered, was it even taken during his military service, or was he some sort of gangster? I chucked that thought out on two counts. Firstly, the idea was unpalatable, he was my father after all, but secondly, I thought that any heavily armed gangsters would have merited mention in the local archives; in fact enough of a mention to become an enduring lore. They've always been a bit thin on the ground in Hartshill and Mancetter.

Dad had been a member of the *Home Guard*, I was certain, yet that thought triggered a childhood memory I had never quite forgotten.

The *'Dad's Army'* episode.

Watching television in our house was as competitive as everything else that went on there.

We fought for the skin off the custard; it mattered how many prune stones you had balanced around the lip of your desert bowl and you did *anything* to ensure that someone else ended up with the crumbs and dusty dregs at the bottom of the cornflakes packet. All of the important stuff.

But television viewing never failed to bring out the worst in us.

The settee and two armchairs offered the most comfortable seating and in vantage terms, constituted the front row. Mum and

Dad had the armchairs, naturally, but the remaining three seats were always scenes of conflict.

Finally, in exasperation, Mum would declare the victors and the remaining three siblings were despatched to the loser's seats; a row of dining chairs lined up behind, where they would lean forward onto the back of the settee and rest their chins on folded arms in petulant defeat. Television viewing would begin at the same time most evenings and for the same feature.

The *'Tom and Jerry'* cartoon lasted for fifteen minutes every evening and was essential viewing for my father; I don't think he missed one. Hostilities ceased and silence reigned while it was on.

Tom was described as a 'mean stupid cat', bent on the destruction of Jerry, a charming, lovable mouse. Every dastardly attempt was thwarted by the mouse, using giant mallets, knives, frying pans, sticks of dynamite and a compliant bulldog named *'Spike'* who hated cats but had a soft spot for mice. The violence was so implausible and extreme it was funny. We all loved every minute.

On Saturday nights, during the nineteen seventies, it was followed by an episode of *'Dad's Army'*; a long-running series that featured a unit of the Home Guard, based on the southeast coast during the Second World War. For readers who have missed the repeats, and probably therefore, only just arrived on Earth, it was a wonderfully crafted comedy that chronicled the charming but often shambolic attempts of a home defence force, set up to help defend us from a German invasion, which in nineteen forty, after Dunkirk, looked set to happen.

On one particular evening the episode was particularly ridiculous; filled with calamities that might have stopped a Nazi invasion in its tracks, if comic disbelief had been a viable weapon. It certainly became one of ours.

Apart from Mum, whose silence granted us a tacit licence to continue, we all had great sport at Dad's expense; our very own member of *'Dad's Army'*. His lack of response only served to fuel an escalation of our taunting, until quite suddenly he snapped at us, "We were ready for 'em, in ways you'd never . . ."

He clammed up so suddenly that we were all stunned into silence. It was as though a gun had been pointed at him and even now I remember sensing that he was actually frightened by his outburst. After a few moments Alan, the eldest, sought more, "OK Dad, tell us then."

Dad ignored him and stared fixedly at the television, which prompted a chorus of demands from all of us. They continued to be ignored until finally, he leapt to his feet and headed out of the room with, "I'm going to prick-out some tomato plants."

At some level we must have all been aware of the *wrongness* of his reaction, it was so out of character, though as far as I'm aware, no-one pursued it, then or since.

The hoard in the Tack Chest wouldn't be denied, I knew that now. Any thought of leaving questions unanswered was out of the question. The most logical place to start was with Dad's service record and I soon discovered the web site for the *Army Personnel Centre*, which furnished me with an enquiry form to complete and submit with a thirty pound fee, along with a copy of his death certificate.

There was nothing else I could think to do and to be honest, the more I thought about it the more I realised how predictable Dad's reaction had been. Many young men in *reserved occupations* felt vulnerable to criticism for failing to sign up, notwithstanding the fact that he would have been sent home from the recruiting office anyway. It was all about public perception though, and his discomfort must have stayed with him for all those years.

Then there was the photograph. It suddenly struck me that the peculiar weapons and commando-like dagger might provide an explanation for the absence of a uniform. I fully expected his service record to show that he had spent a few days training with the main army, which would have explained why he wasn't wearing a uniform? They would have given him some overalls to wear.

It took ten days to receive a reply and two scans of the letter with my cheque stapled to it, to discover that they had no record of Charles Morcroft in the whole of the Home Guard, let alone the Mancetter Unit.

I have a very low tolerance of bureaucracy, particularly when they can't even find a name for heaven's sake, and on reflection, I might have been a little curt when I used the helpline number provided. A very nice lady suggested that we both spend a little time trying different spellings and numbers, which we did. Her patience was very calming and we tried every variation we could think of, but at the end of it she concluded, "I'm sorry Mr Morcroft, but there is no record of your father having served with any of the armed forces, let alone the Home Guard."

I wasn't prepared to accept it, "But I have a photograph of him, with five other men and they're all armed to the teeth."

She was being so patient, "Oh that's wonderful! Now, can you see any distinguishing badges or attachments that might help us recognise the regiment?"

"Err, no I can't I'm afraid." I certainly wasn't going to tell her he was wearing a pair of overalls.

"Do you know any of his comrades or is there anything in the background you can recognise?"

My answers became minimalist and we soon ended the conversation, leaving me to go through to the kitchen and report to Liz. By then, my spirits were sinking rapidly, not because of this failure *per se*, but because I realised that I couldn't drop it, the damned chest wouldn't let me. I might have had a knife and a photograph, but I didn't have a clue of what to do next.

It was the knife that marked the threshold of discovery, but it would be the gun that actually frightened me and revealed things about Dad I would never have imagined.

The weapon was scary in its own right though. Certainly not the fancy piece of metalwork you can buy from a French market stall; aimed at bolstering a computer warrior's chutzpah.

It was a dagger, or *poignard*, and looked as benign as a hooded cobra.

Years ago, I remember standing on the Portsmouth to Gosport ferry, which had stopped to allow a submarine enter the harbour. It was black and silent; in fact everything about it suggested stealth and menace, which I found unutterably sinister. There were no positives; it was a device used to hunt and kill, period.

Well that's how I still feel about that knife.

My finer feelings apart, there was research to be done, starting at my local library. I reckoned it must have been a Commando knife, but nothing there provided me with a perfect match. Either the pictures lacked enough detail or the author's focus was on the use rather than the aesthetics of the weapon.

Once again, Liz came to my rescue and as usual it was over toast and tea at the breakfast table, where she would ruminate on all manner of things, including stuff that was vexing me. If that conjures up an image of a cow chewing cud I apologise, particularly to Liz; perhaps I should have written, 'pondering whilst chewing scorched bread.' Take your pick, but if any belligerence is detected I need to add, that I am not a morning person. I'll go further, with less than an hour's consciousness and a few shots of caffeine, I am not a nice person.

"Try *Ebay.*"

Liz's suggestion came out of nowhere and gave my 'launch' button a glancing blow. I looked up at her as though she'd suggested giving me an enema sheathed in sandpaper, "What!?"

With casual disregard of the warning signs, she explained, "Try *Ebay*. You know, for World War Two knives, or commando knives. Someone's bound to be collecting them."

I ignored her of course. Any suggestions made at that time of day merit little or no attention.

But more caffeine and a pleasant lunch left me answering emails and trolling the internet. After a period of aimless searching I remembered Liz's suggestion and was delighted to have something specific to search for.

I found all sorts, from cutlery to speciality knives, for hunting, throwing, fishing and camping. One American supplier offered a huge range of 'spring-assisted' ones, which I took to mean flick-knives. None of them looked as deadly as mine, though some of the sales spiels promised the holder enough of a machismo quotient to dominate the World.

I should have done as I was told, of course, but I have my pride.

Even so, I eventually tried 'commando knife' on *Ebay* and there it was, time and time again. Some were genuine, some 'authentic copies' and many were accompanied with all sorts of accessories, including sheaths, camouflage uniforms and even knife sharpening kits, but I was amused to see first aid kits advertised below a copy of a wartime manual illustrating a variety of ways to despatch a German sentry; all with a dagger, of course.

One seller laboured the veracity of *his* knife and warned of the many copies being sold as the real thing. I opened the file and learned that it was a 'Fairbairn/Sykes' knife and the latest bid stood at a startling eighty pounds. I returned to the main page and found further evidence of it being a commando knife. Someone was trying to sell a picture of one, a commando that is, holding the knife between his teeth.

Now one thing I am certain about is that Dad was a farmer throughout the war which leads me to suppose that he wasn't a commando; I'm sure they didn't offer part-time positions. Yet the knife I had found in the chest was a specialist weapon issued to special forces and then there was that odd-looking gun. By now I had also concluded that *Home Guard* troops wouldn't have been offered weekends away with a Commando regiment.

It was time to *Google*.

I actually *googled* 'Fairbairn Sykes' and discovered a huge number of sites and most with illustrations. Like *Ebay*, some were selling the 'real thing' while others, 'faithful replicas'. One site featured interviews with old soldiers who had actually used the weapon and another gave tips on how to take care of it.

Another site, selling replicas, sought to illustrate the weapon's finer features by using terms like, *'martial elegance'*, *'pleasing to the eye'* and *'beautiful form and grace'*. Not the sort of phrases I would have thought of, particularly if I'd been on the receiving end. Those descriptions belong to a Rolls Royce, a bottle of champagne and a beautiful lady.

For the record, the men credited with the design were William E Fairbairn and Eric Sykes, so no cigar for guessing how it got its name.

I learned from one of the on-line dictionaries that these two designed the knife just prior to World War Two and it was immediately adopted by the British army, becoming the standard issue combat knife for the Royal Commandos, the SAS, and the US Marine Corps Raiders. A footnote added that it was also issued to the Churchill's Auxiliaries.

Who the hell were the Churchill's Auxiliaries? More *googling* was called for.

I was astonished to find there were hundreds of entries. One of the first read;

Churchill's Auxiliary Units or GHQ Auxiliaries were specially trained, highly secret units initiated by Winston Churchill in the summer of nineteen forty. Sometimes referred to as 'Stay Behinds', they were part of the British Resistance Movement, ready to act behind enemy lines if Germans invaded this country.

I spent the next hour learning about an underground army of saboteurs and assassins. They were highly trained, that much was clear, but very, very secret. So much so, that they remained under the radar until the late nineteen nineties; over fifty years after the war.

I discovered that an archive had been formed under the auspices of the *Coleshill Auxiliary Research Team, (CART)* and telephoned them. The chap I spoke to introduced himself as Steven and was extremely helpful. In the course of a twenty minute chat he gave me enough information to leave me in shock.

He was particularly interested to hear about my father and took his details, promising to get back to me with details of his service, if they had them, leaving me to work through the rest of their very large website, which included a list books on the subject; all published since the late nineties. I soon learned that my local library had one of them in stock and they had loaned it to me within the hour.

It was entitled, '*Churchill's Underground Army*' and written by John Warwicker. Whilst not a terribly easy read, because of the wealth of detail, it was as definitive a piece of work as I could have hoped for.

I lost myself on the web and in the book for three days and in the latter I found photographs of six-man units, albeit with an acknowledgement that such records were a direct breach of their strict rules of secrecy. Some of the men were in Home Guard uniforms, which I learned was a means of cover, even though they weren't serving members, though in fact most were recruited from the Home Guard. However, once the transfer had taken place all record of the men was destroyed.

I also found a photograph of a unit dressed in a mix of denim overalls and tatty jumpers. I had a photograph just like it!

They were so secret that even their wives and families remained oblivious. If the church bells had rung to warn of an invasion every *Auxiliary* would have disappeared underground immediately, without a word to anyone.

It *was* underground too, into a hideout called an *operational base* (OB). Just twenty one feet long and a little over eight wide, they were usually constructed by the Royal Engineers in isolated spots, well camouflaged and stuffed with weapons and explosives. But the conditions down there were pretty awful. Or at least they would have been if the OB's were occupied for a long period. That wouldn't have been a problem in practice, since their resident's life expectancy, once active, was around fifteen days.

The local Chief of Police was part of the initial vetting process and was therefore the only local to know their identities. I reckon he would have been pretty ticked off to learn that as soon as the balloon went up, each unit had a set of sealed orders that began with an instruction to assassinate him, using the .22 silenced sniper's rifle included in the OB armoury.

The only other sealed item, assigned to each unit was a gallon jar of rum, meant for the relief of pain following injury, or, and this one tickled me, to be taken when faced with imminent capture so that the inebriate might be better able to resist interrogation and torture. That one must have been thought up by a civil servant.

Probably the same one, who four years later, in nineteen forty four, demanded the return of those jars.

Whatever went back in those jars certainly wasn't rum, though it might have been, once.

When complete, the *Auxiliaries* numbered over three and a half thousand men and six hundred OB's. Each unit had an operational limit of fifteen miles radius, with targets that included railways, fuel and arms dumps, airfields, senior German officers and general supplies.

In essence, these men were required to go forth and commit illegal acts, (see the Hague convention on war), with such ruthlessness that many commentators would have described their acts as atrocities.

Many of the proposed tactics were aimed at damaging enemy morale. For example, despatching German sentries silently was a given, but it was deemed efficacious to disembowel him and leave his intestines in a pile on the ground, so as to enhance the visual impact of discovery by his comrades. Ah, bless.

The books also contained details and pictures of the boggling weaponry they were issued with, including the odd-looking gun my father was holding in the photograph.

It was, or rather *is* called the *Welrod*. I now know that it is a sound-suppressed handgun used for close-quarters assassination and my choice of tense is deliberate because it is believed to still be on the 'classified' list and was only recently withdrawn from service.

Rather than a pistol fitted with a silencer, it looks more like a very long silencer fitted with a handgrip and trigger. In fact, the handgrip is a six-round magazine and spent bullets were ejected and replaced by turning a gnarled knob on the rear of the gun.

They say that truth is stranger than fiction, but it was becoming a little uncomfortable too.

Just as I was beginning to think all this might have been possible, I received an email from Steven at *CART*, advising that he hadn't found any record of Dad in the *Auxiliaries* and for that matter, they had no record of a unit in the Mancetter area, though he did admit that many records had yet to be released into the public domain.

That left me with a mixed bag of emotions. Was I disappointed to find that Dad hadn't been an unsung hero or relieved to learn that he hadn't been a trained killer.

I telephoned Steven, nominally to thank him, but also to see if we'd missed anything. Perhaps there were other agencies I could contact.

Steven explained that, so far as current records showed, the *Auxiliaries* had primarily been set up along the south and eastern coasts, where the invasion was expected to arrive. There were also units in the borders region of Scotland and surprisingly in Worcestershire, where it is thought the Government and Royal family would have retreated, in readiness for their evacuation to America.

I was disappointed by the news but Steven had laboured the fact that a huge amount of information had still to be released.

So, I didn't have to let go, yet.

From the sound of it, inland units weren't deemed necessary, for the most part at any rate. So why would they want one in or around Mancetter? I scanned my notes for the *Auxiliaries* operational remit and soon found the answer. '..targets that included railways, communications, fuel and arms dumps, airfields, senior German officers and general supplies.'

We have always said how lucky we were, living in the heart of the UK's motorway and rail system. Getting anywhere is so simple. So OK, the motorways weren't here in nineteen forty, but the road, rail and canal systems were and even I can remember the days when the canals were primarily used for the carriage of goods.

Another visit to the library completed the picture for me. Nuneaton, which lies eight miles to the east of Mancetter, was a major market town, and still is for that matter. But by nineteen forty it had been a communications hub for over two hundred years and boasted three large marshalling yards that handled up to ninety thousand goods wagons per week. Throw in two Royal Air Force bases and a few dozen coalmines and there you have it; a cornucopia of targets.

So what did that leave me with? A smoking gun, that's what. No pun intended.

Even so, I had known my father for twenty five years; as a quiet self-effacing man with a keen sense of justice and now I had some cause to suspect he was a highly trained warrior and potentially, a very brave man. I had no official confirmation, yet, but I did own a photograph of him holding a weapon that was only issued to trained assassins and saboteurs.

Whatever the truth is, and I do now suspect that Dad was involved, the *Auxiliaries* weren't activated. For that I am grateful, given that I wasn't conceived until nineteen fifty one, well beyond the fifteen days he would have had left if the invasion had occurred.

Charlie
SCALLYWAGGING

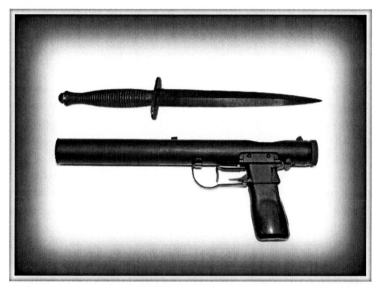

Two of the three men sitting in the bar were easily identified from their attire.

One, dressed in a check shirt, tweed jacket, moleskin waistcoat and heavy drill trousers that disappeared into leather gaiters couldn't be any other than a gamekeeper. In fact he was Edwin Beswick, the head keeper at Oldbury Hall, the stately place perched on the top of Purley Ridge at Hartshill. The lamb chop sideburns were an unnecessary overstatement, particularly when in the shade of the oversized deerstalker that lay on the bench beside him.

The second man was a bit of a giveaway too, given the khaki uniform, captain's pips and an army issue revolver. Captain Osborne's current role was labelled as an 'Intelligence officer', a conveniently misleading title.

The third man was much more difficult to identify. His complexion signified an outdoor life and his boots were scuffed and dirty, yet his clothes suggested a greater financial ease than most manual workers, few of whom would have worn a brown derby hat like the one beside him. Another discordant note in his attire was that it was the summer of nineteen forty, well into the dark days that followed Dunkirk. Could it be that the Captain was a recruiting officer and the civilian a rather tardy volunteer?

The landlord finally decided that was nonsense, after running those and other possibilities through his bored grey matter. They were more of a mystery than he normally came across, sitting in the far corner, chatting as though they were friends. No, that wasn't the word he was looking for. Minutes passed as he searched his vocabulary until finally, he had it. Committee! They looked as though they were having a committee meeting.

He wasn't too far off the mark, regarding the nature of the meeting, though he would never have guessed the occupation of the third man, Stan Broughton, and otherwise known as 'Master Blaster' at Man Abell Quarries over in Mancetter. He had followed in his father's footsteps and improved the inherited skills further as an explosives expert in granite quarrying.

The Captain had brought them out to the Horse and Jockey at Measham, well away from wagging tongues in their hometown.

"So you both seem to think he'll do."

Both men nodded at the Captain, though Edwin Beswick was the first to answer, "Charlie knows the land better than most, on both counts. He knows his way around the local countryside and he can live off it too."

Stan added, "He's my friend and I would trust him with my life and he has a flair with mechanical stuff too. He can mend anything. I've seen it and I reckon that if he can fix stuff he can unfix it too."

The Captain nodded, "Well, a pound or two of gelignite should help him along with that. In the meantime, I'll have the vetting done in the next few days." He addressed Stan, "Can you persuade him to join you for a pint in a week's time? I'll let you know where and I'll be there to meet you." He turned then to Edwin, "Just Stan, I think. No need to be mob-handed, though I'll be sure to let him know that you're the patrol leader."

Stan had a question, "How much longer do I need to turn up for Home Guard duty."

Osborne shrugged, "There's no real need for you to be there I suppose, but why do you ask?"

"There's an exercise this weekend, up on Grendon Common and if I'm not going to be there for much longer I don't see much point in spending two days camping in a field."

"Hmm, will Morcroft be there."

"Yes, I expect so."

"Then carry on as normal, for the moment. As soon as we get him on board I'll arrange for both of you to leave."

It wasn't what Stan had hoped for. Two days of being marched around the common by that pompous oaf, Hilliard was as welcome as having a tooth pulled. They all knew what to expect. It was the same venue, same agenda and same enemy; the Tamworth Home Guard, who they would attack on Saturday.

On Sunday, hung over from their Saturday night at several of the local hostelries, the Tamworth lot would be the attackers. That thought exaggerated Stan's chagrin further.

Major Hilliard, (Ret'd) must have taken the pledge,—on behalf of the whole unit it seemed, for no-one was given permission to leave the camp on Saturday night and their rucksacks were inspected for contraband. If that wasn't bad enough, *Silly Billy Hilliard* would no doubt get up in the small hours again and loose off a couple of rounds from his revolver, screaming "Stand to. We are under attack." Last time it caused pandemonium, with men running off in all directions, in the absence of any further intelligence. It could have been a submarine attack for all they knew.

* * *

Sure enough, at six-o-clock on Friday evening they were mustered at the church hall, after loading the ancient handcart they had on loan from the *Scouts*, who had also provided the great heavy bell tents, (2 off), groundsheets, (3 off), camp kitchen, clean, (1 off), *Tilley* lamps, (3 off), a large sack of pegs, (various) and large mallets, (2 off).

Stan made sure that he and Charlie took the shafts at the front for the hour-long march, so they could have a chat without being overheard by those pushing at the back, thanks largely to the clattering of the steel rimmed wheels. Hilliard, who was on horseback, took up the lead, looking better suited for the Crimean war than the one they were set to fight in. In any event he was in his own little world and wouldn't be listening to the likes of Broughton and Morcroft.

He led them south out of Atherstone, along the Coleshill Road, intent on taking them the long way round, past the Baddesley mine, but they had only covered a few hundred yards before the animal defecated spectacularly. Charlie and Stan side-stepped the mess but the men at the back didn't have the benefit of seeing what lay ahead and waded straight through it. Neither the horse, nor its rider showed any reaction to the howls of disgust and outrage.

Charlie nodded at the great rump ahead of them, "I wonder if a bit of black powder still upsets it?"

Stan gave him a sidelong glance, "Why?"

"Oh nothing, apart from the fact I'd like to see it take off up that hill like it did that day we blew the stumps up."

Stan chuckled, "Now that would be sight for sore eyes." They walked on a little further before Stan began his pitch. "Charlie."

"Yeah."

"Now I'm just saying, so don't go getting aerated, but if there was another outfit, Home Guard say, but much, much more serious, would you be interested in joining."

"What, you mean more of this?" He rolled his eyes from side to side and was about to say more when Stan interrupted, "Noooo, I'm talking about a unit that was a) secret and b) armed to the teeth."

They walked on in silence until Stan could wait no longer, "Well, what do you think?"

"What *I* think is that you aren't telling me something, that's what I think."

"No, I'm just being hyperthingy, you know, *in case* something like that came up."

Charlie decided to play along with his friend's attempt at discretion and sighed, "Stan, you know the answer to that; else you wouldn't be discussing it with me, so why don't you tell me the whole story."

"Bugger, I'm not very good at this secret stuff, am I?"

Charlie chuckled, "You just need some practice, that's all."

Stan told him all he knew, which at that point wasn't much, but it certainly served as a distraction and the marching was over before they realised it. By nine they had erected the tents and while it was still light, Major Hilliard ordered them to empty their belongings out onto the grass and stand behind, at attention, while he carried out an inspection.

It was a sorry collection of blankets underwear and shaving kits, for the most part, but Charlie's kit contained four tins of *Players Navy Cut* cigarettes. Hilliard tapped them with his riding crop, "Why so many cigarettes Morcroft. Expecting trouble? Bit nervous are we?"

Charlie spoke calmly, "No sir, I brought these extra ones in case any of the lads ran out and wanted to buy some, on account of us not being allowed out of camp while the exercise is on, Sir."

"So, planning a bit of profiteering are we?"

"No, sir. We all know the price of *Navy Cut* and it won't be a penny more than that."

Hilliard didn't like Morcroft but couldn't think of any other justification for censure, so he resorted to spite, "Well you won't be smoking many tonight my lad, not while you and Broughton are on sentry duty. Two 'til four for you two, understood?" Stan could barely contain his gasp at the petty injustice but Charlie continued to stare ahead as he responded, "Yes sir, certainly sir."

Somehow, Hilliard felt he'd lost some ground with that response and sought a closing advantage. He flicked the rope Charlie had used to close the throat of his rucksack, "Well I'm pleased to see you've put some new rope in that thing." With a curt nod he moved on to the next pile of kit and Charlie began to breathe properly once more.

Sandwiches and sweet tea were the first night's fare and at sunset, the men were dismissed to their tents for sleep. None were surprised when at one in the morning, two shots were fired and an alarm sounded, but they were all tucked up again by two-o-clock, except for Stan and Charlie.

As the moon crept out from behind a cloud Stan noticed that Charlie was wearing his rucksack, "What are you wearing that thing for?" He saw a flash of teeth before Charlie replied, "Give it another half an hour and then I'll show you, in fact I'm going to need your help."

Stan knew better than to pursue it, for Charlie loved his secrets, but thirty minutes later his friend appeared with the trenching spade they used to dig the latrine. He handed it to Stan with, "Here, lift a decent depth of turf on each side of the tents, two for each."

Stan wanted to know more, "What the 'ell are you up to?"

Charlie had removed the rucksack from his back and was on his knees, yanking the new rope from the eyelets, "Just making things a bit more realistic, is all."

Stan took a closer look and could have kicked himself. He of all people should have recognised fuse cord when he saw it, but then, folk didn't usually use the stuff to tie their rucksack up with, did they? This time he couldn't help the note of urgency in his voice, "Charlie, listen to me, what the bloody hell are you up to?"

By then, Charlie had folded the cord into four and was cutting it with his penknife. He lay the four lengths on the ground and pulled one of the cigarette tins from the sack. They both peered closely at it as Charlie picked at the paper on the lid until finally, he was able to peel it back, revealing a small hole that was just large enough to accept a piece of fuse. Once he finished inserting it, he held the device up for inspection and explained, "Not enough to hurt anyone, but some of 'em might shit themselves."

Stan tried to smother his burst of laughter, but in that moment he also knew that he had to try and talk Charlie out of it. "Listen mate, you can't do this." Any attempts at further dissuasion were ruined by involuntary giggling. It was *so* outrageous and so wonderfully wicked.

Charlie looked on in silence, as Stan's mix of fear, caution and hilarity played itself out. Finally, Stan squatted down in resignation,

"Alright, first, tell me how much black powder you've put in these and what time the fuses will give us. Then, *I* will place the charges. I know what I'm doing with this stuff. The full implication of that last statement wasn't lost on them and both tried to smother another bout of laughter.

Finally, Charlie agreed to lift the turf while Stan did the necessary with the bombs. The fuses were only a foot long, which at a burn rate of two seconds per inch would allow them twenty four seconds to find somewhere safe. With a small charge and in the absence of shrapnel they would be alright, provided both were responsible for two fuses.

A signal wasn't necessary, since the lighting of a match in that darkness, was signal enough.

As they ran for cover, they both started to yell at the top of their voices, "Take cover, take cover, artillery attack. Take cover!"

Shouts and groans were heard from inside the tents as the men struggled to understand what, if anything, was happening, until with timely eloquence, the first charge went off.

It sounded quite benign. A sort of buffered whumpf, but the whole side of the tent was blasted inward, snapping the guy ropes as though they were mere threads. The same thing happened, though in the opposite direction as the second charge went off and the whole process was repeated next door.

Inside the tents, beneath the weight of collapsed canvas, pandemonium had broken out, just as the bits of turf and debris began to rain down on them.

It was then that they heard the sound of a horse, galloping down the lane towards Grendon. Stan murmured, "Oh bugger me, we've done it again."

Major Hilliard, (Retd), was a reasonably intelligent man and by then, a magistrate, but he simply couldn't find words to adequately describe his feelings as he contemplated the wrecked site. Anger, humiliation and anxiety all featured to mind-numbing degrees.

His dislike of Charlie Morcroft was a given and deservedly so, it seemed, as his gaze fell on a ruptured cigarette tin; one that had returned to earth with the rest of the debris. He didn't even

Jeff Hawksworth

contemplate Broughton's role in the matter, for Morcroft was so obviously the felon and this time, the wretch had gone too far. Realising that the men would look to him for leadership, he sought some composure, until his fractured mental processes threw up the spectacle of having to report this incident to regional headquarters and then he lost control.

He pulled out his revolver and pointed it at Charlie, screaming, "You men, all of you, place that man under close arrest." His hand was shaking so badly no-one dared move, for fear of moving into the line of fire, notwithstanding the fact that most were still in their underwear and therefore lacked the military presence the arrest of a comrade called for.

In the end Charlie saved the situation, and possibly his life, by stepping over to the men and offering himself up for the arrest. Dawn was breaking by now and half the men struggled under the canvas to find their clothes and equipment while the others stood around Charlie, in a protective ring. A few men tried to erect one of the tents but soon realised that it was damaged beyond repair. Resignedly, they re-joined Charlie's encirclement and awaited orders.

Hilliard was making it up as he went along, with each strident edict adding to the many repertoires waiting to be delivered in the local pubs over the next few weeks.

When everyone was dressed Hilliard called out, "Right, form up around the prisoner and remove his jacket. He is no longer worthy of wearing the uniform of a British soldier!"

Charlie removed his jacket and passed it over as the squad was given the order to 'Quick march'. All the way into Atherstone, where the duty officer at the Police Station tried to point out that it was a military matter. Hilliard pointed out that as one of the local magistrates he didn't need to be lectured by a Police Constable. The prisoner was to be placed in the cells and charged with the *civilian* offence of 'attempted manslaughter' as soon as someone with enough authority could attend. He added that the appointed officer should attend him at Hartshill House, that very day, for a statement and if necessary, guidance in the matter. With that, he marched out of the building, leaving a troubled constable and Charlie to sort things out, starting with a cup of tea.

Two hours later, the Tamworth unit arrived at the field, intending to agree on the day's battle plan with the Mancetter bunch. They were mystified by the wreckage and one asked his CO, "Sir, I thought it was just the two lots. Mancetter and us."

The officer agreed, "So did I, but they would hardly do this to themselves would they? There *must* have been another unit involved."

Someone at the back piped up, "They did a bloody good job!"

The horse was still heading north and it was two days before someone found the animal, grazing with some new friends twelve miles away, in Measham.

* * *

Hilliard sent the men back to salvage whatever they could before returning it to the scoutmaster and then he secured a lift home, no doubt to begin work on his statement. Given half a chance he would have prepared a verdict and sentence too, but he knew that in declaring an interest in the case, he would be denied the pleasure of jailing the damned hooligan.

Meanwhile, Stan held back until everyone was out of sight before returning to the Police Station, but by then Charlie had been locked up. The constable apologised, but explained that until he could involve his sergeant, he would have to obey a local magistrate; at least he thought he should.

Stan knew that his friend shouldn't be in a Police Cell and pressed the young officer to telephone his sergeant.

"I can't do that. It's not even six-o-clock. Mr Morcroft will have to wait until seven thirty, like everyone else has to. In the meantime, I've given him a cup of tea." Stan could see that things were spiralling out of control. If Hilliard couldn't jail Charlie this way he would try for the military option and have him court-martialled.

It was time to make a call.

* * *

Captain Osborne waited until eight-o-clock before calling the duty sergeant, who in turn, was waiting for the arrival of his inspector before committing any due processes into action. Blowing up campsites was an area of the law he hadn't had any experience of and like his constable, he considered the matter to be a military rather than civilian one.

Osborne confirmed it, with enough authority to assuage *any* doubts, though he was made to observe certain protocols.

"Good morning sergeant, my name is Captain Osborne, I believe you are holding a chap called Morcroft."

Sergeant Partridge assumed it was more of a question, "That may or may not be sir. What is your interest in the matter?"

"I'm from GHQ and since this is a military matter I will be calling in this morning to relieve you of him."

This news should have signalled a very convenient end to the affair but with the perversity of one who feels compelled to exercise his authority, Partridge held his ground, "With respect sir, we are not in the habit of handing prisoners over to all and sundry, merely because we are asked to."

"Ah, well, you see there's been a bit of a mix up. Morcroft's commanding officer hadn't been told about our arrangements for a little authenticity and was a little put out by them."

"By 'arrangements' I take it you mean the unauthorised use of explosives and by 'put out', I take it you're referring to his arrest of the culprit."

"Just so. Terrible misunderstanding, but I shall sort it all out, have no fear."

"In due course, I'm sure you will sir, but in the meantime anyone we have in custody will stay there until there are grounds for his release."

"As I explained sergeant, you have no grounds for holding him there in the first place. This is a military matter."

"Then I'm sure the magistrate will agree with you, when the time comes. A very serious charge has been made and other parties have to be considered." Partridge knew that he'd given too much away, but did manage to withhold the fact that Morcroft's arrest had been made *by* a magistrate.

Osborne knew that anyway and realised he was getting nowhere. He moved into territory he'd rather not have, but Morcoft had to be kept out of the papers and a magistrate's court, at least until they'd had a chance to have a chat. "Fair enough sergeant, then would you be kind enough to tell your inspector about this before you take any action." Partridge made to say something but Osborne cut him off, "You will understand the sense of that request in due course, in fact, as soon as you pass this message on." He paused, to infer that it should be written down and there was a rustling of paper before the sergeant said, "And what would that message be sir?"

"Tell him that Morcroft is one of my men. That's Captain Osborne."

"Very good, sir, I'll pass your message on."

"Oh, there's one more thing. Tell him I'll be collecting Morcroft at around noon. Please hang on to him until then."

When the inspector finally arrived, it was Saturday after all; he read the message and sent someone out for a cheese roll which was to be delivered to the prisoner with a cup of tea and news that his transport would be arriving shortly.

Inspector Wheatley was the only person in the area, save for the actual participants, who knew what Captain Osborne was up to, just as he now knew that within the next few days he would be asked to help with vetting Mr Morcroft.

* * *

Charlie thought Hilliard was a buffoon; an unfortunate legacy from the last war, but until that morning he had generally been able to best the man. That day though, scores had been settled, in full. Not that his punishment hadn't been called for, he knew that and had anticipated a future filled with extra duties, but he hadn't bargained on jail. Moreover, he'd never been in a prison cell before and in spite of the constable's attempts to cheer him up, the prospect of what his father would say and do filled him with dread.

There were more surprises to follow though. The first of which occurred three hours into his incarceration, when a different constable entered the cell with a cheese roll and cup of tea. Somewhat diffidently, the officer apologised for having to lock the door again, explaining that they were merely acting under instructions, though he should be sure to bang the door if he required anything. Moments after locking the door, the same officer hurried back in and apologised for forgetting to mention that his transport would be there at noon.

A little after noon he was ushered out to the front of the station and passed over to an army officer who gave him a smile in greeting and asked, "Where's your jacket."

Charlie wasn't going to be coy about it. Whoever this chap was, the chances were that he'd know what had happened that morning. "It was confiscated sir."

Osborne's expression confirmed Charlie's suspicion, "Ah, yes. Well we'll get that back for you shortly. In the meantime my name is Captain Osborne." He startled Charlie by extending his hand and as they shook hands he continued, "I've got a car outside, so we can pop off somewhere and have a chat. Follow me."

Charlie did and was startled to see a staff car waiting for them outside the front door, on Ratcliffe Road. Osborne opened the front passenger door and gestured for him to use the rear, which he did, to discover Stan, sitting on the opposite side and wearing a huge grin.

"What are you doing here?"

Stan feigned indignation, "Charming, what happened to 'hello mate, how are you'?"

"I can *see* how you are. You should be asking me that question; after all I'm the one who's been locked up." He slammed his door and the car moved off as Stan replied, "And it was me who got you out, so say after me, 'Thank you Stan'."

Charlie obliged and added, "So what's going on then?"

"We're just going to have a pint and a chat."

"A chat? What about?"

Captain Osborne turned slightly in his seat and spoke over his shoulder, "I shall be doing the chatting, but it can wait until we're somewhere more comfortable."

Charlie gave Stan a troubled look but his friend sought to reassure, "It's just a chat; nowt to worry about."

"What about Hilliard?"

"All sorted out, don't worry."

Charlie sat back in his seat and stared out of his window as they drove towards Hinckley on Watling Street; he was still a very worried man.

* * *

Osborne savoured the first quarter of his pint in audible gulps, before setting his glass down and favouring Charlie with another smile. "Stan tells me you farm and that you're a dab hand with machines."

Charlie's uncertainty was mirrored in his reply, "Some say so."

"So, my experience with farmers tells me that a few snares and your shotgun make sure you don't starve."

Charlie rocked his head from side to side, as if concede the point, but his reticence served to force the pace. Osborne decided to come straight to the point, "Stan's told me quite a bit about you. For example, I understand that you're a bit of an independent thinker and with a bit of imagination to boot. *Apparently*, you're pretty handy with machinery too, which I take to mean that as well as mending the stuff you'll know how to wreck it too,—with a few bits and pieces to help you, of course." He paused for effect and continued, "The thing is, how would you fancy doing something extra for the war effort?"

Charlie had begun by nodding slowly at Osborne's reference to machinery but was now nodding furiously.

"Good man, Stan said you would." Osborne leant forward, with his elbows resting on his knees, "First of all, I need to explain a few basics, so you can change your mind if you wish, but mark you, that's a decision you will need to make now, not later."

Charlie was still nodding and realising he'd begun to look like an automaton, he asked, "Sir, they don't send folk like you out to make me grow more 'taters so I reckon it must be important." He nodded towards Stan, "And anyway, if he's in then so am I."

Osborne nodded this time, "Right well, as I said, the basics. You will be required to sign the Official Secrets Act and abide by it, which means that from now on, everything will be top secret. One word or deed that breaches that rule will be dealt with in the most profound manner. In fact I'll probably pull the trigger myself. Do I make myself clear?"

Charlie nodded once more but was lost for words.

The officer continued, "If Gerry invades, you will be required to carry out duties that will be dangerous, very dangerous." He didn't add that if and when that happened, their life expectancy would be two or three weeks, provided they were outstanding. And lucky.

* * *

Major Hilliard (Retd), spent the morning writing and refining his statement, ready for a visit from the constabulary. There was also the question of discreet lobbying, given that he wouldn't be the presiding magistrate and there would be a need to ensure that an appropriate sentence was handed down. Well, an adequate one at any rate. The morning's work had a therapeutic value that didn't begin to wane until lunchtime and which by four in the afternoon, was lost completely to a livid disbelief. There was no sign of a police officer or even the courtesy of a telephone call to explain why not. At lunchtime, he'd considered telephoning the station himself, but decided that it would have been undignified, even improper, but now, he was beyond caring.

Inspector Wheatley weathered the storm, until finally, he was able to get a few words in, however disingenuously, "I don't understand Major, I thought you'd have been aware."

Hilliard snarled, "Aware of what!"

"Well, that it is now a military matter. An army Captain came and collected the prisoner at lunchtime. I assumed you knew."

"He what! Who was it and on whose authority?"

"One moment Major, I'll check." The inspector rustled papers and dropped books onto his desk in an audible pretence at searching. He hadn't had so much fun for ages. Eventually, he said, "Ah, here we are; Captain Osborne, from GHQ."

Hilliard was beside himself, "Who the hell is he? Under whose orders was he acting. They were not mine, I can tell you that! Dammit, who dealt with him and where are the orders?"

"I'm sorry to say we don't have a copy of the orders Major, though they were authentic, I can assure you. I saw the man myself."

This was getting worse, "And you didn't think to check with me! My God man, I arrested the man."

"Indeed Major, though we've been told, quite unequivocally, that it was and always should have been a military matter."

"This is an outrage. Utter incompetence and damned bad manners. You haven't heard the last of this Wheatley." Hilliard slammed the telephone down and moments later dialled the Home Guard Western Command. Somehow and against the odds he managed to be coherent enough to be understood and was eventually put through to a Colonel Baxter who already knew about the case. He sounded very urbane, "Hilliard, you say? Mancetter, yes, well, what can we do for you."

"I wish to report a disgraceful incursion into my command by a Captain from GHQ, which has flouted protocol *and* my authority." Home Guard Command was indeed separate from GHQ but before Hilliard could rant further Baxter interrupted, "Yes, I'm quite aware of the case, but I don't know the specifics, though I can assure you that everything is in order."

"In order! Heavens, I'm the man's commanding officer and no-one saw fit to tell me about it. With respect sir, that is definitely out of order. I believe I'm entitled to an explanation."

The Colonel knew about Morcroft's release but he had no idea what was going on. What he *did* have though, was enough wit to realise that if information was being withheld, he wasn't entitled to know more. Clearly, this idiot didn't agree. He allowed the man to rant a little more before trying to explain, "Look Hilliard, I realise it's a little unusual but we all have to toe the line. You must carry on as though nothing had happened. Discipline, you see."

It was the last straw, "Discipline! Sir, that's a fine thing to say, but what about the discipline and morale of my men. What do you expect me to do about that now?"

Colonel Baxter's tone implied that he was bored now, "What I *expect* you to do is to say 'Yes sir' and then obey an order."

"That is unjust sir and a terrible breach . . . , hello, hello." He rapped the cradle but the line remained dead. He stood there, staring at the apparatus in disbelief.

By God, he thought, Morcroft is going to pay for this one day.

* * *

Charlie's next encounter with Captain Osborne was much more business-like, with Stan and Edwin Beswick in attendance. They met in a small room at the rear of the Black Swan, in Atherstone and with the exception of their beers, it began as a somewhat sombre occasion, with Charlie's signing of the Official Secrets Act; a procedure granted additional gravitas by the revolver and holster Osborne had casually placed on the table.

As soon the document was signed, Osborne gathered it up and pushed the revolver towards Charlie, "There you go. It's a start at any rate. The powers that be have decided you should all have a revolver, but there will be lots more I assure you. For the moment I will give you a preliminary briefing but from now on you three will be working together along with three more, once we've found them."

During the pause, Charlie pulled the weapon from the holster and inspected it while Osborne explained, "It's a point three two Colt revolver." When he saw Charlie turn the holster over and study the embossed lettering, 'NYPD', he explained, "Just one careful owner, the New York Police Department."

He allowed a few moments to pass before starting his briefing, "Right, let's get on with it." He gestured towards the others, "These chaps will fill in the details but I'm here to explain that from now on, you are a member of a GHQ Auxiliary Unit. Everything you do will be top secret, from anyone who isn't a member and I mean everyone. For the sake of appearances, you will continue to wear a Home Guard uniform though as of today all record of you has been removed. So far as Major Hilliard is concerned, you've been transferred to another platoon; you can be fairly vague about which one.

On the subject of records, there will be none. In fact, if called upon, the government will deny all knowledge of you.

If Gerry invades, your job will be to disappear underground, literally, and to attack them from behind. In fact one of the names given to you lot is the 'stay behinds'. We will provide you with enough training and weaponry to kill and destroy in ways you couldn't have imagined. In fact some of the ways will be departures from the usual rules of war; illegal if you will.

We call it 'Scallywagging'."

That meeting marked the beginning of an intensive period of training which included taking delivery of an astounding quantity of ordnance. Machine guns, 'Welrod' pistols, grenades, knives, garrottes and even knuckledusters established an weaponry arsenal whilst their destructive capabilities were catered for with a range of booby traps, along with ammunition, detonators, timers, incendiary devices and over a thousand pounds of high explosives. All this posed a short term problem, in that they had to find somewhere safe to store the stuff, until the underground base was built.

Charlie solved that problem by clearing out the back half of the workshop at the farm and boarding the area off with some old crate panels. He told the family it was a mix of this 'n that from his Home Guard unit; camping stuff and the like. It seemed reasonable enough and since the boarding lacked a door, the stuff was left alone, or should have been.

One day, some weeks later, Charlie came in from the fields to find his father sitting on a milk churn at the vice and welding a tine back onto a fork. One of the boards to the store had been moved to one side, which explained where the churn had come from. It also told Charlie that his father hadn't actually looked in the churn for if he had *known* it was full of detonators, he'd have hardly been likely to roll it across the shed and sit on it. Worse, he was smoking his pipe and as usual, throwing used matches to the floor to burn themselves out; all within a few feet of the arsenal.

Charlie was aghast, "Father, it's probably best you don't smoke in here, *or* weld for that matter."

Albert Morcroft continued with his work as he spoke, "Oh and why would that be?"

"Well, see, I'm sure there's some flammable stuff in there and the CO said he'd come and carry out an inspection some time, to make sure I'm looking after the stuff properly. If he sees matches on the floor I'll be for the high jump." It was a massive under-statement since there was over ton of explosives sitting an arm's length away.

Albert's innate regard for the ruling classes, particularly those who might have survived the Great War found favour in Charlie's plea, which was a good job really, since a careless spark would have put Purley View Farm, barns and all, into the next county.

Some of the physical training took place at weekends, at Coleshill House in Oxfordshire and more often than not, Stan and Charlie went together. The format was always the same. They would travel by rail to the village of Highworth, where they called at the local post office and were vetted by the postmistress, Mabel Stranks. Once satisfied, she would make a telephone call to Coleshill House and transport would be sent down for them.

At Coleshill House, they were taught a myriad of ways to kill a man and in particular, at close quarters, along with all manner of techniques for blowing things up. Explosives, timers and booby traps were all included but they were also encouraged to come up with ideas of their own; something Charlie and Stan took very seriously.

But above all, they were taught to avoid all-out confrontations with the enemy. It was a creed for guerrillas.

On one occasion, they were introduced to a lunatic weapon that might have been designed by Major Hilliard (Ret'd). It was called the ST Grenade or more popularly, the 'Sticky Bomb', which was covered with a fearsome adhesive. The hapless user was invited to actually stick it to a German tank or at least get to within fifty yards and go for a throw, hoping of course, that neither the tank's crew, nor the few hundred German infantry following it, would notice anything suspicious. The act of letting go of the stick activated the five second fuse which in theory was a good time for it to happen.

Charlie proved the boffins wrong on that one.

A very large fallen oak was designated the role of German tank and the trainees joined the training sergeant in a trench that was situated a little over fifty yards away. Far enough away to avoid death, they were told, but close enough to shit themselves. There were only eleven trainees and all were given an ST Grenade but told to wait their turn before exposing the adhesive and lobbing it at the tree. Stan was number four in line and Charlie number five, but when the first two fell short of the tree Stan whispered out of the side of his mouth, "Betcha can't hit the tree."

Charlie was expecting it, "Three pints of bitter says I do an' you don't." They ducked as the sergeant yelled "Throw" to trainee number three and as the sods of earth fell into the trench they all peered over to see that the tree remained unscathed, albeit a tad soiled.

It came to Stan's turn and Sergeant Manners yelled, "Right Broughton, do as you've been told. Prepare the grenade, now!"

Stan exposed the adhesive and waited until the sergeant stepped to one side and bellowed, "Throw." Everyone had followed the same procedure and whilst his might have been a little closer to the tree, it was only an addition to the growing number of holes before it.

Charlie could already taste the free beer and eagerly waited for the sergeant's signal.

"Right, Morcroft, your turn." The sergeant didn't have chance to say more and watched his nightmare unfold as Charlie tore the protective globe off, pulled the pin and threw his arm back for an Olympic throw. Everyone watched on horror as the grenade made contact with the front of the sergeant's trousers and the man was dragged forward, off his feet, as Charlie attempted to launch the device. Charlie realised there was something amiss when the device became two hundred pounds heavier and very much larger. Any further thought was interrupted when the sergeant's mass collided with his back and threw him off-balance.

As he and the sergeant fell into the bottom of the trench a strong hand clamped over his, though he was too winded by the fall to notice either that or the scrabbling of feet as the other trainees tried to make their exit. One man, thought to yell "Grenade" at the top of his voice but by then it was old news. Charlie became aware of the sergeant's head pressing down on his and then the instructions, spoken with a desperate urgency, "Don't move! Don't . . . fucking . . . move. D'you hear Morcroft?"

Charlie spat some of the soil away and spoke from the side of his mouth, "Yish Sharge."

The sergeant paused to collect his thoughts before his next order, "Now listen to me, very carefully. If you let go of that stick you will blow yourself up and my balls'll go with you. Therefore, no matter what, you will hang on to that stick. Do you understand?"

"Yish Sharge."

"Now wait, while I think about this, just keep holding on to that bloody stick."

Thankfully, the sergeant was a logical sort of chap who soon concluded that the problem was twofold. One; the grenade was now permanently fixed to his trousers and two; he was in them. Conclusion; the primary objective was to solve problem two. In fact, by now, the device was sandwiched between them and firmly attached to both men's trousers.

He spoke into Charlie's ear once more, "Mycroft, I am about to shout out. Do not jump or let go of anything, do you understand?"

"Yish Sharge."

In spite of the warning, Charlie jumped as his new Siamese twin bellowed, "Volunteers, two of, over here, at the double!"

In time, an inordinately long one, it seemed, two shadows were cast into the trench; Stan was one of them and it was he who spoke, "Yes Sarge?"

Manners could only turn his head slightly and had to ask, "Who is it?"

"It's me Sarge, Broughton and Taylor from Littlehampton."

"I don't care where the fuck he's from, I want him to go and find the duty officer and get help. At the double now, move it!" As Taylor scampered off Manners continued, "Broughton."

"Yes Sarge?"

"Go and find the medical orderly and ask him for a large pair of scissors, the sort they use to remove clothing from casualties. In fact, tell him to get his arse over here too."

Stan ran off in the direction of the medical office, guilty in the knowledge that Charlie had got himself into this mess because of their daft bet and guilty in his sense of relief at exiting the scene. One that looked set to go bang at any moment.

An uncomfortable silence followed, in every sense for Charlie, who was struggling to breathe under the sergeant's weight, but eventually, they heard the sound of running feet. As Sergeant Manners explained what was required he continually broke off to remind Charlie to hang on to the grenade, until the medical orderly struggled into the trench and set to work with his scissors.

Given the proximity of high explosive, the process took some time, leaving the sergeant's green underwear in plain view from waist to knee. To his credit, the sergeant stayed with them even when freed, still holding Charlie's hand in place, though he shifted to one side so that the orderly could trim the excess material from around the grenade. Very carefully, enough material was removed from Charlie's uniform to enable the grenade to be held away from anything else.

Manners yelled once more, addressing any who might be within earshot, "Clear the area, at the double!" The absence of any sound suggested that the advice was needless so he moved on. As they helped the hapless Charlie to his feet, the grenade looked like an odd-looking khaki mitt but once upright he listened carefully to his sergeant's instructions. "Right then Morcroft, in a moment I will release your hand. You will continue to hold the stick tightly. Do you understand?"

They heard the medical orderly scramble frantically out of the trench and he was allowed enough time to flee the area before

Manners continued. "Right, Morcroft I am going to let go. What are you going to do?"

"Hold tight Sarge."

"Right you are." With that the sergeant let go and stepped away before, "Right then, Morcroft, I want you to face in the direction of the target." Charlie did so, correctly, which prompted the next order, "Now, when I say throw, you will throw that grenade at the target." After a moment, "THROW!"

Hitting the target would have been some consolation, but the aerodynamics were seriously hampered by the two pieces of khaki serge and it fell well short. Not that it mattered, for both men knew only relief, briefly.

A crowd had gathered by the time they exited the trench and the tension gave way to amusement as the sergeant sought some dignity, with half of his underwear in view. Any relief he felt soon evaporated in favour of fury, "Morcroft!"

"Yes Sarge."

"You are to run around the perimeter. Beginning now; go!"

"Shall I change first Sa.."

"As you are. At the double!"

"How long for Sarge?"

"Until I think of what else to do to you, you cretin. Now go!"

An exhausted Charlie was allowed back into the barracks in time for the evening meal, by which time Sergeant Manners had discovered an entirely appropriate retribution.

The following morning the men assembled in the yard and waited for news of the day's programme, though the murmured conversations still centred on Charlie's escapade, who in turn, thought he'd gotten off fairly lightly.

All fell silent as Sergeant Manners strode into view, accompanied by two others. One they all knew was a PT instructor, but the other chap was new; an army captain who looked to be in his mid-fifties and too old for military service. In fact, he looked more like an army chaplain than a combatant. The absence of a dog collar signalled otherwise, but the lambs in front of him had no idea how much of a one-man army he was.

After calling them to attention, Manners began, "This morning you will be taught a good deal more about close-quarters fighting. You will benefit from the experience of our guest, Captain Fairbairn, who along with a Captain Sykes, designed the knife you've been issued with. I'll leave him to continue."

Captain Fairbairn stepped forward, almost diffidently, as the sergeant retreated and began to speak with a quiet calmness which gave an ironic weight to his words, "Gentlemen, you are, or will be, specialists. For you, there will be no artillery build-ups, no armoured support and no masses of troops and therefore, normal military training would be wasted on you. You must be able to kill and destroy without being caught and that means getting up close to your enemy. Therefore, you will have only one set of rules. Get tough, get down in the gutter and win at all costs. I teach what is called 'Gutter Fighting'. There's no fair play, no rules except one. Kill or be killed."

He smiled then and referred to a piece of paper in his hand, before, "So let's get started shall we? Sergeant Manners tells me that Private Morcroft has a particular need for training so we'll start with you. Please identify yourself."

Charlie stepped forward in the knowledge that his punishment had only just begun.

Captain William Fairbairn never drank or swore or boasted of his thirty two years with the Shanghai Police. There he had suffered so many injuries; being left for dead on at least one occasion, that he studied and mastered a number of martial arts. Well enough that is, to acquire almost mythical fighting abilities. None of the trainees knew that in the course of his career with the Shanghai Police, Fairbairn had survived over six hundred street fights with some of the World's worst criminal gangs, but by the end of that morning they knew *how* he'd done it.

A regular army officer once summed Fairbairn up with, "The man has an honest dislike of anything that smacks of decency in fighting."

On the train home that night, Charlie's take on the day was more personal as he nursed the cuts and bruising, "That bloke is just a killing machine."

Stan nodded, though his injuries were far less, "Too true. Mind, my instructor was nearly as bad. I spent the whole time trying to protect my privates."

* * *

By the end of nineteen forty there were three thousand five hundred auxiliaries, in six hundred operational bases, though each six or seven man unit continued to be autonomous and their identities remained secret, from other units as well as family and friends.

Charlie and Stan were 'transferred' to the Nuneaton Home Guard, as continuing cover and the means of separating them from Major Hilliard, which meant that they still had to turn up for duty; something neither enjoyed. When not on duty there, they would hone their particular skills in a variety of ways, particularly since their armoury continued to grow.

All manner of home-made booby traps were designed and they were familiarised with the marshalling yards at Nuneaton, the layout of the local Royal Air Force bases and even the plans of the local stately homes, having special regard for the principal bedrooms; the ones most likely to be occupied by senior German officers, who would be targeted for assassination.

The gamekeeper at Arbury Hall never knew that he'd been stalked to within twenty feet on a number of nights, or how many ways he could have been despatched had he been wearing a German uniform.

Above all, though he never spoke of it, Charlie knew that if the balloon went up, he *would* disappear without a word; he *would* kill as many Germans and destroy as much as he could and—he *would* almost certainly be dead within two weeks.

Ironically, whilst Mary stopped short of open criticism, there were times when he felt her resentment; one that would have undoubtedly been accompanied by guilt. But while her brother seemed to be enjoying the protection of his 'reserved occupation' and playing at being a soldier in the Home Guard, his friend, Arnie Blake was now established as her beau and serving with the Royal Artillery. For the time being he was stationed in Northern Ireland and she prayed that it would stay that way.

She was never sure whose idea it had been to sign up in October nineteen thirty nine, but they sent Charlie home to carry on being a farmer. When Arnold told her of his success in volunteering, she delivered a roundhouse punch that dislodged a tooth and screamed, "You stupid, stupid man!"

It was the second and last time she hit him.

Chapter Nine

My researches into the world of farming continued to throw up surprises. For example, did you know that soil has four main ingredients?

They are; rock particles, organic matter, air and water. Besides plants and burrowing animals, it also has a bunch of other things living in it too. One teaspoon of the stuff is likely to contain a few hundred nematode worms, a million single celled dudes called protists, a million fungi and we mustn't forget the billion bacterial cells of ten thousand species.

Just saying.

* * *

I'd flicked through the photographs from the chest a number of times and of course, most of them involved the farm. The picture of *Dolly Grey* was probably the most striking but others struck chords. The ubiquitous Border collie was featured in one, with the name 'Jack' printed neatly on the back.

That reminded me of dad's shock when mum suggested trying a different breed and we all shared his horror at the mere mention of a spaniel. When asked to justify his choice of border collies he would say, "They come with brains," and after owning a number of them I wouldn't argue with that.

I also remember dad mentioning a dog that was devoted to Aunty Mary. He said it was a little eccentric, but woe betided anyone who threatened or upset her and for all I know it may have been the dog in that photograph. The neat writing was more likely to be Aunty Mary's, since dad's was chaotic.

As I'm writing this, it occurs to me that there were relatively few pictures of animals, which is surprising, since they had so much livestock. Perhaps that's reason enough; they were too ordinary a part of life.

Funnily enough, I never heard him speak of *Dolly Grey*, yet her picture shows how impressive she was. Maybe it was because dad was always a machine man. Moreover, from what I've learned, he effectively managed the transition from horse to machines.

I would have liked to have known more about her though. In generic terms, I know they are the gentle giants of the equine world, weighing in at around a ton and standing at sixteen or seventeen hands.

They were incredibly strong too. In nineteen twenty four a pair of shires pulled an approximate weight of forty five tons; the reading on the machine they were using for the test didn't go high enough to provide a precise figure.

Dolly's head seems just a tad small for the great arch of neck, but her eyes and face spoke of intelligence and a benign temperament.

There were also a few photographs of the Morcrofts standing in front of the kitchen porch with different groups of people who I didn't recognise, though they were probably relatives paying a visit and being subjected to Mary's *box brownie* photography.

The wedding photos were expected, for what photo record could be without them and I already knew that Dad and Aunty shared a joint ceremony, down at the Methodist chapel, aptly sited at Chapel End. Mum and Aunty Mary wore light coloured suits that had obviously been made at home and both men wore suits that were no doubt reasonable for the time, when almost everything was still on ration, but the material looks poor and the wide trousers would look strange now. I remember Dad once saying that the turn ups used to collect great quantities of cigarette ash, no matter how careful he was.

There weren't many in the group but I assumed that there would have been other group pictures that he hadn't stashed away. There could have been two hundred there for all I knew because they never talked about their wedding day; not that I can recall at any rate.

Apart from Mum's appraisal of Dad's 'cockerel' legs that night of course.

Charlie

THIS n' THAT,
AND WEDDING HATS

It was in the year that Mary left school and assumed responsibility for the milk round that she saved Jack's life; in fact she brought him back from the dead.

Now that they'd gotten rid of the sheep, there was little call for a sheepdog and passengers weren't welcome on the farm. *Bill,* the Jack Russell, would serve as a guard dog and continue earning his keep ratting and *Meg* the border collie didn't have many years left in her. This last time in whelp had almost been the end of her, which would not have been unwelcome, in Albert's view.

As for the pups, well that was a matter he *could* deal with.

He hadn't intended to keep it from Mary, in fact he hadn't given that matter any thought, it was simply a case of having five minutes to spare; time enough to get the job done.

Meg whined and gazed at him anxiously as he bundled her young into a burlap sack. Then she followed him into the yard where he dropped them into the water barrel. He didn't even give it a second thought when he saw Mary walking along the drive, on her way back from school and simply gave a casual wave as he made his way down to join Charlie, who was repairing the fence in the lower pasture.

Neither spoke, for idle chatter was never encouraged, but as she reached the kitchen gate, Mary noticed Meg at the side of the barn, whining loudly and running to and fro in an arc around the water barrel that stood against the wall. At first she thought the dog had chased a rabbit, or rat, behind the barrel, but there something wrong. Whatever she was excited about lay *in* the barrel, not behind it.

She called Meg, who ran a couple of yards towards her before turning back and this time, Mary realised the dog wasn't excited, it was crying in distress.

She moved towards the animal, with a question rather than a call, "Meg?" This time the dog gave her a glance that said, 'hurry'.

Both of them cried at the sight of the sodden little bundles of fur, pitifully small and so dependent on those around them. Now they were cold, lifeless bodies being licked and nuzzled by their mother.

Mary hadn't thought to mention how much she wanted one of the pups because she never imagined that her father would have done what he had, not to the lot of them and not without mentioning to the family first. Meg had been a loyal friend and worker; it was only right that they should have kept one of her last litter. Besides, they were so young. She was used to life and death as part of farming life, but there was usually a special regard for newborns.

It was a sad little tableau, with Meg trying to revive her pups and Mary sitting back on her knees, trying to collect herself, until suddenly, Meg started. One of them had moved.

The dog began to lick the pup again, but Mary intervened and gathered the little bundle up. She'd seen enough calves born to know what was needed; a mix of blowing through the nose and massaging the body. After a few moments she gently poked a piece of straw into the snout and was rewarded with a sneeze, followed by an indignant squeak. Meg answered with a whine and gratefully gathered the pup in her mouth when Mary set it on the ground and hurried back into the barn. She returned moments later and inspected the other five but after licking them for a minute or two it was obvious, even to Meg, that they were dead. There was just one to care for now and she looked at Mary with an unnervingly eloquent gratitude, before walking back into the barn. Mary knew one thing for certain, that pup now belonged to her and would be protected.

His eyes were still closed when all that happened, but Mary always said that Meg had taught him who he had to thank for his life. That was a matter of conjecture but there could be no doubting his devotion to Mary, even though he sank his needle sharp puppy teeth into her hand as soon as they were long enough to do damage. That called for a name change, though still in keeping with Mary's policy of naming her animals after famous people. Her original choice had been 'Dick', after the highwayman Dick Turpin, who reputedly had a narrow escape at The Red Gate Inn, two miles away on the Watling Street. But the new name would prove to be far more appropriate. It was 'Jack' as in *Jack the Ripper*.

As for the biting, she remedied that by biting him back, on the tail and left him alternately yelping at the pain and chasing it to give comfort.

Meg wasn't with them for much longer, which left just the two dogs, Jack and Bill, the argumentative Jack Russell. They'd had a few scraps but Jack developed an air of disdain in the matter and ignored the pugnacious midget.

In time, Jack adopted the practice of accompanying Mary down the drive as she set off with the milk dray and would lie just inside the drive watching the world go by, until she returned. On the outbound leg he would trot alongside, companionably, but he was always allowed to leap aboard for the ride back.

At most other times he tolerated the rest of the family and almost always did as he was told, but Mary could do anything with him, which wasn't always good news. Somehow or other, she acquired a box brownie camera, when one of the aunts in Birmingham died and subsequent trials included dressing him up in bonnets and shawls. Charlie had watched on one occasion and later swore that the dog was smiling for the camera.

Other experiences were less benign; like the time he was caught trotting out of the barn with a dribble of egg white hanging from the mouth. Both the chickens and their eggs were for humans, not dogs. Mary strode indoors where she emptied an egg into a bowl and refilled it with English mustard, before tying it carefully back together. Jack wagged his tail cheerfully when she called him and even allowed her to open his mouth wide, but when the egg was stuffed in there he really did try to resist the strong hands that clamped his jaws shut on the smashed firebomb. She didn't let go until he had swallowed the lot and then he was allowed to run off to find a great deal of water. Needless to say, he never touched a chicken egg again.

The experience didn't lessen his devotion to Mary though. On one occasion they demonstrated a new trick to Charlie and Arnold while they were teasing her. She pointed at Charlie and said, "Bite him." Jack promptly did and from that day on they were a little less inclined to harass her when Jack was around.

He did have one profound weakness in that he was terrified of sheep. No-one knew why, but when they visited a neighbour, who owned a sizeable flock, a few sheep confronted Jack and stamped their feet. More joined them when he showed no inclination to join in the stand-off and minutes later, he was being chased across the field by over a hundred sheep. It must have been a fine day for them, but it was a pretty ignominious experience for Jack.

Curiously, though Albert knew what had happened that day at the water barrel, nothing was ever said about the rescue or Mary's claim to Jack. It just was.

Twelve years later she harnessed up the dray and gave him a ride on the outbound leg for the first and last time. She buried his body at the farm entrance, at the spot he used every day of his adult life, waiting for her to return and later she was heard to say that he was the first true love of her life.

* * *

Years slipped by with ever-present workloads, sprinkled with adventures and calamities, but Mary's worst ordeal began in nineteen thirty nine and lasted for six years. Though the first four and a half passed by with the comfort of knowing that Arnold was in Northern Ireland, comfortably clear of any Germans, but in January nineteen forty four he turned up at the door, on leave. They were posting him down to somewhere in Devon which prompted some merriment. Charlie said, "Arnie, you've dropped a tanner and picked up a shilling I reckon. Four years of drinking *Guinness* and now you're off to Devon for some cream teas."

Arnold already had an inkling of the truth but kept it to himself, "P'raps you're right and don't forget, they have cider down there too."

Mary scolded him, "Don't you go turning into a fat drunkard Arnold Blake, 'cos if you do I shall have little to do with you. It's bad enough that you've taken up smoking."

He didn't respond with the obvious, but like most soldiers, he thought cigarettes were a lot less harmful than German bullets.

Marriage was mentioned just fleetingly, during that leave, but Mary was terrified of tempting fate, and it was placed on hold.

* * *

In February, three weeks after Arnold had departed for his new billet, April arrived, half dragging her suitcase along the drive and looking hot and dishevelled from the exertion. As Agnes answered the door April announced, "Hello, I'm April Kiteley, I'm here to help out." She saw the puzzlement on Agnes's face and explained, "You know, Land Army!"

"Oh, I see, we weren't expecting anyone until next week."

"Humph, I wasn't expecting to *be* here until next week, only things happened." She added brightly, "So it means you get help sooner rather than later, ay?"

She was invited indoors and offered a cup of tea while Agnes explained, "I haven't got your room ready yet. It needs an airing and the bed will need making up."

"That's alright, point me at it and I'll see to it. There's nothing like making your own bed, then lying in it, as they say. Anyway, it'll help me settle in."

Agnes was a little nonplussed by the encounter, though she was sure to hide it. April whatever-her-name-was, had plenty of confidence with some to spare, but a little humility might have served her better, at least at the outset.

They went upstairs where April was given bed linen and shown to her room. Little had been changed from when Uncle Edwin had slept there. The same bed, chest of drawers and the shelved alcove, screened off by a curtain, though a new counterpane which a floral pattern had been laid on the bed which helped to brighten the room.

Agnes felt obliged to say, "It's a little musty in here. You might want to open the window for a while."

"Yes, perhaps I will; thanks." April cast her gaze around the room before announcing, "It's nice this is. I'll have it as cosy as anything, in no time."

Gesturing towards the bed, Agnes asked, "Are you sure you don't want any help making that?"

"No, I'm fine thank you. When do you want me down for lunch?"

"Oh, when you hear the others get back." She was about to say 'I'll have the meal ready by then', but stopped herself, for she was beginning to feel more like a servant than the matriarch.

Lunch proved to be equally startling.

Conversation had consisted of little more than polite enquiries from which they learned that her parents were two of the five hundred and sixty eight who were killed during the Coventry blitz in nineteen forty one. The Morcrofts and many other locals remembered going up to the top of Purley Ridge to watch the glow in the sky from thirteen miles away, as the firestorm took hold.

April seemed to take a pragmatic view of it as she explained, "Funny really, me dad spent all his time at work at the munitions factory, making things to blow people up, then it happens to him." She continued in the same vein, "With me parents gone and the house a pile of rubble, I had to find somewhere to live, preferably away from any future bombing targets, so somewhere in the country seemed the safest bet. The *Land Army* offered me that much, with accommodation thrown in, so that was that."

She'd lived on two farms and justified her departures with some candour. Apparently, the old man at Willow Tree Farm had sought relief in an extremely unpleasant form while the man at Hartley Farm kept stealing her dirty underwear.

Stunned into silence, the Morcrofts found focus in their teacups, until April decided to make her position clear. She didn't mince her words, "If any of the males here want me to do any favours of a personal nature, forget it. I'm not that sort of girl and never will be." She turned to Agnes, "See, Mrs Morcroft, I know I could have told them that in private, but I thought, if I said it now, with you present, it'd put your mind at rest as well." She smiled sweetly and stood, "I'll get started on the washing up then."

Albert and Agnes couldn't even exchange glances as they considered the spectres of illicit sex and adultery, respectively, but Charlie was tickled by his parent's discomfiture and rose from the table to help with the dishes.

Meanwhile, Mary saw everything she wanted to be in April. She was confident, wilful and determined; if they were friends, they could take the world on.

It would have made for a happier stay if all of the hurdles April had created on that day had been beaten down, but instead, her influence proved to be divisive, at least as far as Agnes was concerned.

During the day, April worked outdoors mostly and treated the hardships with the same pragmatism she'd used to deal with the loss of her family. Albert was only concerned with her ability to do the job and to that end, he was pleasantly surprised. He'd heard stories from other farms, of women who were signally unsuited for the work so when Agnes suggested getting rid of her, he urged otherwise.

As the weeks rolled by, the three younger people became firm friends. Mornings were more often spent with Charlie, but the afternoons were largely spent with Mary, once she had returned from the milk round. On a couple of occasions, Albert sent them both out on the round so that if Mary was ever unable to do it, they would have a standby that knew and was known by, the customers. Those were the times she first demonstrated a theatrical talent at mimicry, creating caricatures of the customers who warranted it.

When they returned from their second outing, Mary insisted she perform her mimicry of Major Hilliard. April, who had already been told of Charlie's encounter with the man, carried out her act with a cruel piquancy and vicious glee that attracted uproarious applause.

She was quick-witted too, as Albert noted when a man drew into the yard in a van and beckoned her over. He was clearly a trader of some sort and therefore a potential customer, so when he asked, "'Scuse me miss, is this Purley Ridge Farm or Purley View Farm?" she didn't miss a beat, "Both!"

But there came a time when Mary needed a shoulder to cry on. There had been talk of an invasion for a long time and evidence of a build up everywhere. Even as far inland as Astley; just three miles away, there were American tanks lined up on the side of Nuthurst Lane. Everyone assumed that the crossing would be from somewhere around Dover to somewhere around Calais, but in May, Mary heard someone mention an enormous amount of activity in Hampshire and reference to the family atlas established that Devon lay just two counties away. Her Arnold had been moved from one of the safest postings in the war to one of the most dangerous.

On the sixth of June she felt faint at the news. They said it was the greatest invasion in the history of warfare and her Arnold was part of it

It became the living nightmare faced by so many women at that time and Mary desperately needed to talk about things, though with a friend rather than a parent and certainly not with a brother. Should she have at least said yes to Arnold's tentative proposal or would that, as she feared, have sounded his death knell? What about 'the other'? Should she have conceded that much at least?

April provided the shoulder to cry on along with her own special take on things, such as, "Listen love, if you'd have given him a taste for that sort of thing there'd be no telling what he'd get up to with all those French women. What he's never had he won't miss. Besides, if anything did happen, not that it will of course, but *if* it did, then raising a bastard isn't going to go down well with your parents. The notion might sound romantic but I don't think the reality is.

The continual work on the farm helped to ease the passage of time, particularly things like haymaking. By then, April had firmly established herself at Purley View, with two friends, a satisfied boss and an implacable enemy in Agnes. The dynamics were set to change further.

The word 'haymaking' has a number of connotations, with good reason. It was hot and sweaty work that called for stripping down to bare minimums, albeit within the boundaries of decency, but unbuttoned blouses, already dampened by sweat and glimpses of female underwear have predictable effects on male companions.

Charlie was twenty nine years old had known love and sorrow on a scale he could not contemplate again, yet he also knew raw arousal when it leapt at him. In truth, therefore, he was only answering his body's demand for carnal knowledge when he asked April out to the cinema; alone, without Mary, but his aspirations were short-lived.

She allowed him to hold her hand, after the woman behind had moaned about him blocking the view, when he placed an arm over a shoulder. But when he allowed his hand to fall on to her knee, her hand dropped gently on to his. The gentle encouragement he'd hoped for became an agonising wrench to his little finger; easily capable of breaking it, and caused him to lurch forward from his seat and gasp in pain. She promptly released him and he shot back into the upright position as she leaned over and whispered, "If you ever do that again, without being invited, I'll break that finger."

After a moment she leaned over again to add, "And anything else I can get hold of."

'Anything else' had suddenly become distinctly unbreakable.

It was therefore something of a surprise when she put her arm through his as they left the cinema and tapped his shoulder with the side of her head, "Come on, you paid for the pictures so I'll buy the chips." She was grinning and nothing in her voice suggested that the incident in the cinema had earned offence. In that moment he realised how happy that made him and how much he wanted to be with her, in a very romantic sense.

The family had gone to bed by the time they got home and April heated some milk for night time drinks. They had already talked enough about the film and being together every day left little else to discuss, so April decided it was time for action. She stepped around the table and signalled for him to swing his legs out before planting herself down on his lap. "Now it's time for me to say thank you for a lovely evening." She draped her arms over his shoulders and his arms encircled her waist as she leaned forward to kiss him. Neither mentioned the burgeoning erection that made its presence known, but it did serve to call a halt to the proceedings. With a parting peck on his nose, she said, "Time for bed," then realised what she'd said and quickly added, "Each to their own, as they say."

Their relationship continued, with a curious sort of 'half life', for neither wanted to isolate Mary, who was alone and terribly anxious. Kisses and hugs were exchanged in the mornings when Mary was out and they were alone, but other signs of affection were largely reserved for when they were out. Not that Mary was unaware of the budding love match for their nights out alone were sufficient evidence of that, but it would have been much more difficult if she'd had to cope with a couple of lovebirds smooching around her.

Agnes had tired of her children's choice of admirers, though this time, she and Albert were in agreement. Charlie was old enough to know his own mind but this was clearly a distraction, while the World sorted itself out and an easy opportunity for female company lay to hand. Soon, Germany would be beaten; *she* would go back to Coventry and all would return to normal.

Though she never gave voice to the thought, Agnes did consider the possibility of Arnold failing to make it home and then all her anxieties would have been needless.

* * *

Arnold never was much of a letter writer and when any did arrive, they told Mary very little, not that she wanted to know overly much, but the eighteen months following D-Day passed in a frightened blur. Even after VE day there were reports of casualties, often caused by our own unexploded ordnance, but finally, almost unbelievably he was coming home.

His demob suit looked further out of fashion than the one he'd bought for the charabanc trip in nineteen thirty four but Mary didn't notice. The whole family had stepped out of the house to greet him as he strode up the drive and watched Mary run down and fling her arms around him.

Life had treated them both kindly, for whilst he'd seen some dreadful things, most of his time was spent in the quartermaster stores he'd been posted to. He hadn't shot a man and more importantly, he hadn't been shot. The Arnold that came home was close enough to the Arnold who went away.

The war had been over for five months and April was thanked for her service but politely asked to leave. It was a naive thing to do, for she had expected as much and spoken to Charlie about it. She had already arranged to rent rooms in Chapel End and within a week of leaving the farm she had secured employment at the hosiery factory on School Hill. Her independence, own home and the proximity of a barber shop that sold condoms, enabled the sexual aspect of their relationship, which would have added further to Agnes's woes, if she'd learned of it.

Now things were different in every way, in that they wore their affections on their sleeves and often went out with Arnold and Mary, as a foursome.

In February, they called at the *White Horse* for drinks and in time, the men had to visit the toilet. They were standing at the urinal when Charlie said ruminatively, "I suppose we'll be expected to propose soon."

Arnold nodded, "Reckon."

"How do you plan on doing it?"

"Well I'd planned on seeing how you got on. Then, with her brother getting wed, I'm sure Mary would want to follow."

Charlie pursed his lips, "Why don't we suggest it now, together."

"What safety in numbers you mean?"

The reply was accompanied with a grin, "Sort of."

They returned to the table with another round of drinks and soon, Arnold gave Charlie a nod of encouragement. Something was up, the girls could tell and April gave her man a gentle kick, "What are you two up to?"

"Well Arnold and me thought it might be time to think about getting wed." He held up a placatory hand, "Only if you two were in agreement mind."

April feigned offence, "Oh, that's very thoughtful of you." She turned to address Mary. "We don't need to be afraid of being kidnapped and carried off to Gretna Green then."

Mary rolled her eyes, "Heaven forbid. This is so much more romantic." She stared at Arnold, "So is this why you two were in the toilets for so long? Planning how you could get it over and done with?"

Arnold looked crestfallen, "We've waited long enough love."

It might have been heart-melting if April hadn't interrupted with a more practical take on the matter. "Well the sooner the better, I say, those blooming condoms are costing too much."

Mary's jaw dropped in shock. She had no idea that they had been doing that sort of thing and she certainly hadn't let Arnold near her.

April continued as a comical thought occurred to her, "So, you agreed all this in the gents then. Don't tell me you shook on it."

This time the men looked shocked and Mary covered her mouth with a hand to smother a bout of giggles.

April stood her ground, "Don't you be high and mighty Charlie Morcoft, or you Arnold Blake. Neither of you will be thinking of saying vespers on the wedding night, I'm sure."

It took a few moments for the men to realise that however clumsy or unromantic, their marriage proposals had been accepted and both grinned broadly.

Mary spoke to Arnold, "We worked out what was taking you so long in there, but I didn't expect you to do it like that."

It was Charlie's turn to ask Mary something, "What about Mother and Father?"

A blanket of concern fell over the four of them, while they considered their options. Mary spoke first, "They're not going to give us their blessing Charlie, so don't expect it. But I for one have waited long enough for this. We've made our choices; there's no going back from that."

* * *

Agnes and Albert were unequivocal in their opposition to both matches, but both children were of *full age* and there was nothing they could do. The relationships had been allowed to continue for so long their objections held little sway anyway, and there were practicalities to deal with too.

It became clear that Arnold would be allowed to live at the farm, whilst Charlie already had his accommodation organised, thanks to April. Beyond that, no money would be provided to assist with any aspect of the relationships, including the marriage ceremony, which they had no intention of attending.

Two weeks before the wedding Mary asked April to go for a walk with her. She knew the principles, but knew that more was expected of human females, beyond an encouraging kiss and cuddle. April told all, in graphic detail, though at the end of it she cautioned, "Don't go in for all that in the beginning, you'll terrify him. Just be prepared to follow him there when he suggests it."

Mary had another issue she wanted to raise, "Doesn't it bother you that you've both *known* each other before getting married."

April seemed genuinely shocked, "Heavens no! Now he knows what's expected of him."

Mary looked at her friend aghast, until she saw the grin, "Now you're making fun of me!"

"I know, I'm sorry, but the honest answer to that one is that now, we *both* know what to expect."

Two days later, the status quo had been remedied. Both brides would walk up the aisle on an equal footing.

In the meantime, Charlie had moved most of his possessions out of the farm and into April's flat. The bed would remain at the farm until after the wedding, for the sake of appearances but he did surprise Agnes when he gave her *Dolly Grey's* old tack chest. He'd laid claim to it years earlier but now seemed happy for it to stay where it was; on one condition, "Please promise me Mother, that you will not sell or give this away. If you no longer have a use for it I shall have it back. It holds memories of the old days for me."

Agnes thought of the horses and of the early years of farming and knew what he meant, or thought she did, "Of course, son, I shall use it, you can be sure."

* * *

The weddings were a modest affair for all manner of reasons. Many items that might have been bought for such an occasion were still rationed and the guests reflected the division that had occurred at Purley View farm. The older relatives felt unable to demonstrate support for the younger generation, in the face of such opposition from Albert and Agnes and there were only a limited number of personal friends. Arnold's mother was there but his father had been persuaded not to attend. He'd already indicated a degree of discomfiture at Mary's pedigree, perceiving it to be part of the ruling class, no matter how modest, and by that token, they all knew he would become belligerent with a few beers inside him.

Stan Broughton acted as best man for both grooms and knew the tensions and dilemmas as well as any of them, so it was a given that his speech would have to deal with things delicately.

He stood when the time came and looked around the small gathering before turning toward both couples and asking, "Are you sure you put stamps on the invitations?"

Chapter ten

Not all the photographs I've looked at recently came out of the chest, but the ones showing Dad on tractors prompted me to dig out some of the more recent ones we'd found in his wardrobe after he died.

Some of those were similar, showing the same tractors and with a simple note on the reverse; *Purley View,* but whilst he looked happy in them, he never made any secret of the fact that he'd left farming by choice and never regretted it.

Most of the photographs had notes on the back, but this one didn't need one. It was a group photograph, of men who were dressed in ill-fitting suits, though after a more thoughtful appraisal I decided that it was the men that didn't fit the suits very well, rather than the other way round. Most of them had pint beer glasses in their hands and there were a few glassy smiles too, but my dad was standing at front centre, holding a small placard and a medal in one hand and his boss's hand in the other. In a handshake, I mean.

I recognised his boss, Alfred Wright, from when I used to call at the council yard and I knew it was dad's long service do, commemorating twenty years, because that's the number shown on the plaque.

I also knew a number of the men, who were unfailingly kind to me when I called down to the council yard.

Dad started work at Nuneaton Borough Council in nineteen fifty, shortly after the farm sale. I've seen a copy of the sale catalogue and was astonished by the amount of equipment they had, all built up over many years, I don't doubt; generations even.

I don't know much about the early part of his career there, since I was only minus one and a half then, though I know he started as a general labourer.

By the time I started calling at the yard, fifteen years or so later, often to cadge a lift home, he was foreman fitter in their vehicle workshop so I just remember the smell of diesel oil and his over-alls. The council arranged to have them laundered every week, but within a day they would be shiny with black grease. We knew this because he used to come home in them and stuff them under the sink. For years he used to come and go on a moped and thinking back, I'll bet he never needed waterproofs, but when he did even-tually get a car, he used to cover his seat with a sheet of polythene rather than change at work.

There was always lots of banging and crashing in the workshop which is probably why I heard some men address him as 'Ammer; it certainly couldn't have inferred that he was violent because I only ever knew him as a reticent chap, but a great dad.

Whilst we didn't have a car when I was young, lots of family friends did and they all seemed to visit at the weekend, with a list of faults. Dad would clamber into his overalls and disappear for a couple of hours during which time mum would be raising hell, for he would never charge them anything, saying that he would rather be in credit with everyone, in case he needed a favour sometime. Of course, he never did.

I remember him saying, in the later years, how his job had altered, with developments like ministry testing and health and safety; which were growing more onerous with each year and on reflection, I realised what he meant and how much of a strain it was becoming. I know he lacked any formal qualifications in vehicle maintenance but he was still a superb mechanic.

Like the time they rebuilt the twelve cylinder engine out of the bulldozer they used on the refuse tip. It was a monster and the components covered two thirds of the workshop floor, yet he put it all back together, perfectly.

That said, I also know that he was an incredible bodger and I don't mean that unkindly. No matter what he was confronted with, it would be fixed; sometimes with the most bizarre bits and pieces. Or in other words, there was nothing that couldn't be fixed with a bit of chewing gum and string, metaphorically speaking.

I remember the time someone reversed over my bicycle, when I was out on the paper round. I used to do it at the trot and was in the habit of just dropping my bike on the pavement outside each delivery. I was distraught.

I was eleven years old and it was my first new bike, given as a reward for getting into the grammar school. The frame had been twisted so badly, that when I pushed it home the wheels left two tracks in the rain, about nine inches apart, instead of one. Dad had a calm manner when he considered these sorts of problems and was best left to work them out in his own way, without suggestions, advice, or hysterics. Within minutes he'd set the frame on its side, on to several piles of bricks of varying heights and once satisfied, stood on one end and flexed his weight, up and down; just shy of actually jumping. A few more adjustments, followed by tribal-like dances and hey presto, I was back in business.

As I wrote this it occurred to me that these days the car driver's insurance company would end up paying for a new bike and compensating me for my distress, with additional punitive damages for making me walk home that night. As it was, the driver told me off for scratching his paintwork and I felt compelled to apologise, for not looking where he was reversing, I suppose.

In fact, my *first* bike, the predecessor to the new one, was a conglomeration of bits that the dustbin men had fished out of their loads over a period of months and not all of them fitted together effectively; as I found out the first time I tried it. It was incredibly heavy, with great big wheels and just front brakes; which were operated by rods rather than cables. I discovered that the rods were fractionally too long for the frame when I tried to stop at the bottom of School Hill and careered across Coleshill Road before crashing into the front of Croydon's grocery store. They were capable of stopping me on level ground but one in ten inclines called for a better fit.

Another time, dad intercepted and 'fixed' a full size recreation slide that was deemed beyond repair and removed from the municipal playground. It was around fifteen feet high; with cast iron framing that needed concreting into the ground and a stainless steel slide that could be lethal in wet weather. It almost filled our yard, which the local kids did as well, whenever they were given the chance.

Good memories; good times.

I won't call them failures, but there were, shall we say, flawed successes as well.

I remember when they introduced a new scale of water rates and dad decided to organise his own supply, by divining for one. I actually watched him do it.

He bent two brazing rods over at right angles and rested one on each hand, before slowly pacing the garden. As he neared the wall at the side of the greenhouse they shot across each other and ten minutes later; just three feet down, he was in water. The next day he went around to the stores where they found a great pile of antique, cast iron water pumps tucked away in the back of beyond and still wrapped in the original waxed paper. He paid ten bob for it and never needed tap water again for his plants. Unfortunately, his excavation changed the water course and within weeks we had rising damp in the house, on an almost biblical scale.

He got into a lot of hot water about that.

Charlie

CHARLIE THE 'AMMER

Albert was beside himself, barely able to vocalise his anger. They were selling a couple of calves and he'd taken Charlie to Atherstone cattle market as a treat, not expecting the stupid boy to actually *bid* for something. Worse, it was something utterly useless.

He'd actually bought two crates full of scrap metal, or at least it might just as well have been, with a *maiden* bid and he was only fourteen years old! The auctioneer had promised that it was complete, which meant that all the parts were there, but they weren't connected.

Once they had paid for it, father and son presented the receipt to one of the attendants who authorised them to take the two crates away, as well as the two fly wheels that lay close by. They were heavy too, needing both of them to lift each one and as they heaved them onto the trap Albert said, "When I get you home Charlie my boy, you'll feel the full measure of my disappointment in you."

He was right, Charlie felt every stroke.

The crates were left in the corner of the tool shed and would probably have remained there until the farm sale, over twenty years later, if Sidney Lockyer, the agricultural engineer hadn't needed to apply heat to a stubborn bearing off the seed drill. Such repairs were too technical for Albert to take on, but the expense of employing anyone from outside was always unwelcome and boded ill for the future. These people were generally keen to keep their secrets too. Sidney seemed to be an exception, but the previous summer, when the tying mechanism on the binder played up, that contractor refused to work with anyone looking over his shoulder.

Albert regarded it as a 'black art'. He was a horse person through and through and could school those animals as well as any man. There was a comfort in working with them too, one that was founded on a *relationship* as well as trust, where only occasionally would a vet be needed, but for the most part care and feed were enough. Now it was all about speed and efficiency, with equipment that was fickle and needed outside contractors to maintain.

Dolly Grey and *Nelson* were part of his life *and* a living farm, but tractors were taking over and he knew that if they were to survive, he would have to commit to the concept, one day. Fordson were boasting that they had sold over six hundred thousand tractors, worldwide and had introduced a new model two years earlier, at a price of one hundred and seventy five pounds.

In the meantime, there was a seed drill to repair. They had taken the part into the tool shed, where the welding equipment was tucked in behind Charlie's crates and when Albert and Charlie moved them out of the way Sidney said, "My word, that's a *Petter*. Damned fine engines they are. Run all day on a cup of fuel and don't cause any bother."

Albert was dismissive, "Well that one won't run anytime soon."

"Nonsense, I could soon have that running for you." He peered behind the boxes, "And you've got the flywheels with it too."

"No, no, thank you. It's cost me quite enough as it is."

"Well, let me know if you change your mind."

Albert promised Sidney that he would and promised himself that he wouldn't, but Charlie lingered until his father left to attend to another task and then asked, "Excuse me Mr Lockyer."

"Yes Charlie, what can I do for you?"

Charlie began by explaining how they came by the machine and how much it had cost him personally.

Sidney chuckled, "So how much *money* did you pay for them?"

"*Dad* paid two guineas."

"Then I would say you have an eye for a bargain Charlie. That engine would have cost sixty eight pounds when it was new. Seems to me that someone started a job and lost interest, or lost their way more like."

Charlie asked, "Do you think *I* could get it to work."

Sidney turned his mouth down, "Depends how good you are at reading manuals. Was there one with it?"

The lad looked into the crates but was already certain of the answer, "No, nothing like that."

The mischief in the notion appealed to Sidney, "Well, tell you what, I'll drop one off for you tomorrow; only on loan mind. Keep it for a month, then if you haven't made any progress with it by then I'll have it back off you and if you want, I'll take that lot off your hands for a guinea."

Charlie was delighted, "Thank you Mr Lockyer, I'll have a go at any rate. As for buying it, you'd have to speak to Father about that. He paid for it."

Sidney chuckled again, "Sounds like you both paid for it one way or another, but anyhow, I should like to see you get it working and to see your dad's face when you do!"

As a traveller loves studying maps, Charlie lost himself in that manual.

Sidney had dropped it off as promised, together with a sheet of gasket paper and a tube of sealant, but he cautioned against a premature start, "Get to know the parts first lad. Dig them out of the boxes and make sure they're all there and then look at the book to see where they go. *Then*, see if they will!"

Charlie soon discovered that he had a natural ability to look at the exploded views and *see* the poetry of design. The process of assembly rested in his mind's eye as easily as a course would appear to a navigational officer in the navy, which was not to say that it was easy. Nevertheless, Charlie heeded Sidney's advice with a logical determination, and step by step, over a number of weeks, he managed to re-assemble the beast.

Albert watched on in growing amazement as a shiny machine began to materialise on the workbench, until the day they heard Charlie cranking it over. It was on a Sunday afternoon, so the family were to hand and soon they assembled at the door to watch.

Nothing happened though. Wheels, cranks and levers all seemed to move as they should, but try as he might, Charlie couldn't get it to start. Eventually, soaked in sweat and severely disappointed, not to say embarrassed, he conceded defeat, albeit a temporary one.

Albert walked down to the canal repair yard first thing the next morning and made a call, which was answered later that morning in the person of Sidney Lockyer, who stood before it with his hands akimbo, "Charlie, Charlie, I am impressed, yet somehow, I knew you'd get it put together." He did a complete external check; often muttering, "Well, well, well," and finally turned the crank slowly, while listening for any unfortunate noises, but there were none.

Satisfied that it was safe to do so, he began to crank the engine over in earnest; explaining, "Make sure you turn it over eight times before you flick the compression lever over." Which he did, but the engine flopped through a couple of compressions before coming to rest. He checked the fuel tank and tap before trying once more, with the same result. Finally, he asked, "Did you bleed it?"

Charlie replied uncertainly, "No."

Sidney nodded sympathetically, "No, well, the manual doesn't mention that, 'cos it's a general thing that applies to all diesel engines, so they take it as read, that folk will do it. So, how about I show you how to bleed a fuel system?"

Ten minutes later, Sidney began to crank the engine over once more but stopped suddenly, "Whatever am I doing? Charlie, you should be doing this, come on lad." As Charlie took hold of the cranking handle, his new mentor reminded him, "Eight revolutions, before you push the lever over."

Albert didn't realise that he was holding his breath, until he saw the lever go over and the machine cough two gouts of black smoke from the exhaust, causing him to gasp also. Charlie turned to Sidney, with his mouth open, as if to say, 'did that really happen', but the man grinned and nodded at the machine, "Again."

The same thing happened, twice more and Charlie began to fear the worst, but he would never forget his fourth attempt. It coughed twice and then uncertainly, a third time, before finding a beat that became a regular and beautiful, donk, donk, donk.

Incredibly, Albert was put in mind of a new born calf, struggling to breathe as it struggled clear of the sac.

Sidney, on the other hand thought it was absolutely wonderful, and funny. He knew that Albert was a proud man and wouldn't have appreciated someone having sport with him over the matter, but he also knew that at some point, Albert would need to make it good with his son.

Two weeks later, they took the machine back to the Atherstone market. In spite of the success, they didn't know how it could be used on the farm, though in coming years, they would regret getting rid of it so hastily. Somehow though, it seemed the appropriate thing to do.

Sam Bostock, the auctioneer, was known for his haste and anyone interested in a lot had to be on their toes or the hammer would have fallen before they realised it. It was a sound strategy too, for more often than not, it excited feverish bidding. But when Charlie's engine came up he paused to check his schedule and called out, "Gentleman, the next lot is a *Petter* stationery engine, recently re-built and in perfect working order. Is Charlie Morcroft present?"

At that moment, two attendants wheeled the engine in on a heavy duty trolley; just as Charlie and Albert held their hands up.

The auctioneer called down, "Charlie, if you please, we would appreciate a demonstration."

The place was almost silent as Charlie stepped forward, save for the few who were out of 'the know' and being advised. He grasped the starting handle, as he had done so many times in the previous fortnight when it had never failed him, but this was different and if anything *could* go wrong, it would now, he knew.

Everyone watched the fourteen year old youth crank the engine over eight times before flicking the compression lever over, at just the right moment. With an enthusiastic *chuff* of black smoke it gathered its skirts up and ran beautifully.

Everyone, including the auctioneer applauded, except one, who looked on in awe. Albert felt extremely proud. He felt humbled too and a little ashamed.

It sold for twenty six guineas.

They said little on the way home, until they reached Mancetter Green, where Albert pulled off the road and halted in front of the manor. He could not go any further without speaking his mind, "Charlie, I wronged you in this matter, though I hope you will understand how my doubts were justified at that time. But I believe that the leathering I administered has given you some rights in this matter. After the auctioneer's fees and the two guineas I paid for it, there is a profit of a little over twenty three guineas. I believe you should have half of it."

It hadn't even occurred to Charlie, "No Father, I don't want it."

"I must tell you lad, I would not be comfortable keeping it as my own, so what would you suggest we do with it"

Charlie was stuck for a moment, until an idea came to mind that was magnificently appropriate.

"Well Father, why don't we put it towards a tractor?"

Albert would have continued to waver, but now he'd been influenced by Charlie's success. If a fourteen year old could master machinery there was little excuse for a grown man to avoid it.

* * *

It was still two years before they could afford one. Sidney Lockyer was called in again, for they could think of no-one better to help them select a tractor, though in agreeing to help them he added a wry caveat, "I shall have to charge you for my time Albert, because I suspect that your Charlie will ensure that my future rewards stay at a minimum. I mean no harm in that, for I feel that I've had a hand in his development and am proud of it." He didn't add that the local farming community knew it too, which had already proven good for business.

The tractor was four years old and cost the staggering sum of eighty eight pounds, or as Albert pointed out, a man's wage for a year and that would be from seven until five for six days a week, which was a sight more than they could expect from the machine.

Sidney assured them that it had seen little use; partly because the previous owner had been ploughing with it when the share caught on a large rock, causing the tractor to rear up and throw him off. If he hadn't been quick on his feet, he'd have been ploughed under himself and whilst he went on to use it for more modest work, he'd never trusted it since.

It was a Fordson 'N', a much more reliable beast than its predecessor; the Model 'F' *and* it even had mudguards. Pneumatic tyres were an optional extra that few first timers could afford, so it had the more usual steel wheels, though they purchased a set of wooden 'road bands' from Sidney, which came with a large box of nuts and bolts.

They were soon to discover that the problem with those lay in the fact that no matter how tightly they did the nuts up, the bands would shake themselves loose within half a mile and the driver would have to get off and tighten them all up again. Predictably, Charlie was always given the jobs that entailed roadwork.

They learned to manage its idiosyncrasies as well. It had two fuel tanks; one for petrol, which was used to start the engine and warm it up, before switching over to the other tank, which contained 'TVO', or tractor vaporising oil; a sort of paraffin. Since petrol was an added complication and expense, Charlie discovered that if everything else was set up perfectly, not least of all the timing, he could get it started without using petrol, though the yard would be filled with a great cloud of oily blue smoke until things had warmed up. They also learned to use the starting handle with their thumbs tucked in. Many farmers who didn't, would discover that if the timing wasn't set exactly right, the engine would deliver a kick that broke or dislocated unprotected thumbs.

And there were more, but to Charlie, they were mere foibles waiting to be dealt with and managed.

Albert's misgivings were well-founded though, even if he couldn't have identified the specifics at the time and notwithstanding the fact that they had no choice in the matter.

With the tractor, came the need for all the machinery and implements needed to accompany it and as such, marked the beginnings of a new era, which in time would engender concepts such as 'capitalisation', 'amortisation' and above all, 'viable acreages'. Quite simply, the ever-increasing demand to mechanise brought with it a need for larger farms, to justify the investment.

The Second World War exaggerated the cycle further, with a heightened need for domestic productivity. In that time, Charlie's flair with machinery became established, confirming Sidney Lockyer's forecast that he would see little custom from the Morcroft farm.

* * *

Finally, in nineteen forty nine, Albert decided he'd had enough and announced his retirement. Little had been said since Sarah Jane's death and now that Charlie had a wife and children there was an unspoken belief that he might continue with the tenancy, but it was a forlorn hope and arrangements began for a farm sale.

Charlie had waited for fifteen years to exercise his oath and wasn't to be swayed. Now that his father was getting out of farming, he would too.

Arnold and Mary also showed little inclination to continue farming though she and Charlie stayed on to ensure the farm was as it should be for the day of the sale.

It was a traumatic experience for them all and when finally, it was over and everyone had gone home, the place had an air of desolation. Even the kitchen lay empty. Any furniture they were keeping had already been moved to the new houses and the rest had been sold. Without fire the *Aga* was simply a lump of cold metal, it was as though the heart of the kitchen had finally stopped.

Then, when the opportunity arose, Charlie went for a walk, down to the field that ran alongside the canal and allowed his own special memories back for one last time.

But life had to go on. He and April had two children with another on the way so he had to find a job.

He had no qualifications. His skills with machinery were part of the local lore but they with without formal accreditation and he had no intention of signing on as a farm labourer, though in effect, that was all he was; an able labourer.

Which is why Nuneaton Borough Council set him on as one.

* * *

The fitters from the workshop looked a little disconsolate when they entered the canteen at lunchtime. All manner of trades were represented there on most days, since councils didn't outsource much. They had their own plumbers, carpenters, bricklayers, electricians, drivers and labourers. Officially, after just over a year, Charlie was still at the bottom of the pile, but lately, Alf Wright had been giving him driving work, when he could and had inferred that an upgrade would be on the cards, next time a vacancy came up.

One of the carpenters called out to the fitters, "You lot look like you've lost a shilling and found a farthing."

One of the fitters shook his head and pointed a thumb over his shoulder, towards the workshop. That bloody tractor, I don't know why they bought the thing. We've been on it for over an hour and *can't* get it to start. I'd put a bloody match to it if *I* was given the chance; give me a *Fergusson*, any day.

They continued to discuss it amongst themselves while they unwrapped their sandwiches, but no-one had anything new to offer. Calling the agricultural engineers in from Hinckley was unthinkable, but the foreman announced his intention to call them as soon as they'd had lunch, to see if they would offer some guidance on the telephone.

Charlie quietly left the canteen and crossed the yard, around to the back of the workshops, where the wilful tractor stood, as though it had been waiting for him. It was a *Fordson E27N*, a later and upgraded version of the *Fordson N* they had owned at the farm, but he was delighted to see that the magneto remained unchanged, with the *Impulse Assembly* on the front of it.

The unit contained weights which were thrown out centrifugally to engage with a coupling that produced a denser spark for starting, when the engine was being cranked over. Starting the engine was still a manual process, using a starting handle, for starter motors were a luxury that had yet to appear on tractors, but those weights, or toggles, were prone to getting gummed up with oil and dirt and short of dismantling the thing the only solution was to belt it with a two pound hammer.

Charlie wandered into the nearest workshop and borrowed one.

The mechanics were still eating their lunch when a blue cloud of smoke appeared from behind the workshops and the foreman leapt to his feet, "What the. . . ."

He got no further, for just at that moment Charlie appeared at the wheel of the remarkably healthy-sounding *Fordson* and wearing a huge grin.

He was promptly set on as a mechanic and remained there for the rest of his life, though he would always be known as 'Charlie the 'Ammer' or 'Ammer for short.

Chapter Eleven

I never knew the farm and have no recollection of Albert, my grandfather, because he keeled over with a fatal heart attack when I was two years old.

They'd already sold up then and were living in Hartshill, in a detached house with a large kitchen and a *very* large garden. I think they must have chosen the house for its kitchen since it had an *Aga* stove and a big table, just as I imagined they'd have had at Purley View.

I never thought of Gran as cuddly sort of person; at least she never cuddled me, but she was still a kindly sort. Always polite, but never outgoing with strangers around and if she found something funny it would merit a gentle chuckle rather than outright laughter. In fact, thinking about it now, the thought of Gran guffawing seems improper.

Folk they knew from the farming community would often call in and bring with them some game, or vegetables, fresh from the fields, so the kitchen was always filled with wonderful aromas.

I remember calling in on her with a school friend one day, when we were out on a bike ride. The weather was terrifically hot and I knew she would let us have a glass of water.

Phil, my companion, was more of a 'townie' than a country boy so now when I look back on that day; I can barely imagine the shock that awaited him.

I tapped on the door and opened it, as usual, poking my head inside and calling, "Hello Grandma, it's only me." 'Me' could have been any one of a score of folk but it didn't matter. She would usually be halfway out of her chair by then and would say, "Come in, come in and shut the door."

On that occasion, Phil followed me in and I explained, "Hello Grandma, we've been on a bike ride and I wondered if we could have a glass of water please."

She gestured to the wall cupboard at the side of the sink, "Help yourself, while I see what's in the cake tin."

I hadn't told Phil about the cakes, though I knew there would be some. Shortly after, we were seated at the table with our glasses of water, having declined the offer of a cup of tea and watched her slice into a wonderfully moist and fragrant fruit cake. As usual, the tin was left open and to hand.

She showed polite interest as I told her about our ride, including a description of the dead pheasant we'd seen on the road. When I mentioned the prospect of bringing such finds back for her she gave one of her wry chuckles, "You'd do better leaving it where it is. If a car hit it the bones'll be smashed into fragments. Best leave it for the fox." She struggled to her feet and walked into the larder, re-appearing moments later with a brace of pheasants in one hand, "Now these are as they should be. A bit of shot in them, but ready for the pot; or they will be when you two have finished." She dumped them on the table and explained, "The arthritis in my fingers makes it difficult for me to pluck birds these days, but they came as a gift so I couldn't ask to have them plucked and drawn as well."

Phil's face was a picture. In the first place, I was sure that he wasn't accustomed to such close contact with dead animals; he would do no more than poke the road kill with a stick, and then he voiced his second concern as he looked at me in horror, "I've never done this before."

Grandma's wry chuckle preceded her confident forecast, "Then today shall be your first time."

Shortly after, we were positioned on chairs with a large bucket between our legs and a pheasant on our laps. She was a patient teacher and before long I had the knack of it but poor Phil treated the carcase as though it could return to life and fight back. These days he'd probably need counselling, but all he received that day was a handful of tail feathers to take home to his mum.

On reflection, I'm sure there was a smidgeon of mischief at play, though Gran would never have admitted it and she did at least spare us from drawing the guts. Phil would have fainted, I'm certain.

I think most of us would have liked a cuddle at some point but that simply wasn't her nature, though I never doubted that she did love us, in her *own* way.

* * *

Now this is where things become tricky for me and hopefully, it'll be a cathartic exercise. This tale began a few months before Grandma passed away.

As I've already mentioned, the family's farming connections were maintained, to the extent that we were offered half a carcase of beef, though not for free, obviously, but the price was keen and the source impeccable. It was before legislation decreed that stock had to be taken to massive abattoirs for slaughter, pumped full of *valium* and put through a trauma that rendered the meat as tough as beef jerky.

This one was to be slaughtered locally, in an entirely relaxed way. (I'm talking about the animal, not the slaughter man.)

Nevertheless, that represented an awful lot of meat and a considerable sum of money; so two things were necessary for the project to be feasible. Firstly, there had to be enough people to cover the cost and secondly we would need a large kitchen to butcher it.

First thing on the morning of delivery, the extended Morcroft and Blake families, of all ages, assembled in Grandma's kitchen.

To begin with, there was a carnival-like atmosphere, but once the carcase arrived and work started the kitchen became like a charnel house, filled with piles of meat joints as one group butchered and the others wrapped and sorted the cuts into even piles, ready for each family to take home.

It was messy and smelly, but still a bonding sort of experience, which included two visits to the hospital in Nuneaton for stitches and tetanus jabs.

But the beef was superb.

* * *

Grandma's passing was unexpected, though we all agreed that the carcase incident had nothing to do with it.

The funeral was on Thursday, but it was customary in those days, for a remembrance service to be held on the following Sunday; ironically, in the same Methodist chapel that Dad and Mary were married in.

After the service, family and close friends retired to Grandma's house for a cup of tea and biscuits. Once again, the venue was chosen because of the large kitchen.

It was a gentle family affair, without the formalities of the funeral, with people sharing their memories of Grandma and of course, oft repeated snippets of family lore.

Inevitably, someone bemoaned the fact that we only seemed to get together for baptisms, weddings or funerals and that we should have gatherings for other things as well.

I agreed and voiced a thought that sprang to mind, "Well, all we need is another dead cow."

Nobody said a word, or made eye contact with me. In fact, I think everybody avoided eye contact with *anybody*, but the silence was deafening.

Even now, years later, the cringing horror of that moment ambushes me as a waking thought in the middle of the night.

It wasn't one of my finer moments.

These days, I have a name for such aberrations; it is *'freewheeling'*, or 'mouth in motion before brain in gear'.

Charlie
AGNES

She was born in eighteen ninety two, as number eight in the Ashcroft family.

Though small, she was a robust infant with a decent measure of luck by either surviving or escaping measles, consumption, scarlet fever and diphtheria, though a bout of whooping cough caused concern, along with the inconvenience of the ringworm she caught from the cattle when she was seven years old.

They had a small farm in the Peak District, just outside Leek, where they were grateful for summers but life was too harsh for appreciation of the beauty around them. Instead, that season was simply the time to prepare for winter, when the tops would turn white in October and within a couple of months, bitter winds would leave snowdrifts that cut them off for weeks at a time.

Everyone, from the age of five on, had work to do and still they barely survived. But the children kept coming.

Agnes knew nothing of procreation then, and she knew little about her father, for he was a distant figure, yet with enough presence to subdue the family into silence around the table.

An outsider might have thought him mean in spirit, but few would ever know how mean he was in other ways.

Once, Agnes's mother said that she wanted to go down to the market for some bits and pieces; things he felt she could do without, but when he forbade her to go she demonstrated enough sullen resentment to cause him anxiety. He had work to do outside and could not stay to watch over her, but in any event, his word should have been law.

The kitchen had a central oak post that supported part of the first floor and gave him the means to solve his vexation when he grabbed his wife and wrenched her skirt open. Women wore long, ankle-length, wrap around skirts at that time; made of warm, thick, but coarse material.

He was a strong man and she might have expected an enforced sexual encounter had it not been for the three of the children watching what was going on. Instead, her back struck the post with enough force to wind her and before she could react, he had retied the skirt around both her and the post, knotting it with enough force to ensure she couldn't undo it. Not that she would dare to, after such a show of displeasure.

When he returned to untie her, four hours later, she could barely stand unaided, but the market was over and his authority affirmed.

Expenditure of any sort was frowned upon and clothes were always handed down from child to child, becoming a little greyer each time. One day, an Aunt called on them and saw the state of the shoes being worn by two of the children. One pair were obviously too small and the uppers of the other pair were tied to the soles with strips of hide. It was too much, and a few days later she returned with new shoes. Agnes's mother was terrified and tried to refuse them but the Aunt would have none of it, though she believed it when she was told he would cast them out on principle.

Finally, they took the shoes out into the yard and scuffed them against the wall before rubbing them into the mud. By the time they had finished, the shoes looked like wrecks and it worked too.

Though Agnes remembered incidents such as those she didn't think them strange or unduly severe. They were simply part of their lives, which were as bleak and grey as the stone walls that surrounded them in winter.

She met Albert at church and in spite of his natural reserve, she thought him generous in spirit and nature, as well as handsome of course. He was a farmer too, which found favour with her father, particularly when it was discovered that he was the only son and therefore in line to inherit the tenancy. Moreover, his father was in his seventies and a widower.

Their wedding day was as bare as her childhood, which in itself had ensured that she had few friends to invite anyway, but at least the day contained the promise of a new life, with some degree of affection in it.

They lived with his father for three years, until he died, leaving them the farm and a significant sum in savings. By that time Mary had been born and Albert had declared his intention to seek better farming in the south. Soon after, they learned about a hundred and ten acre farm to let, near a village called Mancetter, in Warwickshire.

Albert attended an interview and was successful, but the move and equipment necessary to meet the demands of a different type of farming, took almost all of his inheritance. Some of the stock came with them, including sheep, but a large part of the farm was arable, which called for seeds and labour as well. The next time they would have savings to spare would be in nineteen forty nine, when they sold up.

So her life was still one of hard work, but at least she had a man who was considerate and two children who would never know hunger or a cold that could kill.

She was thankful for that.

Chapter Twelve

So there you have it, there wasn't a slick beginning, developing middle or even exciting end. There wasn't even a strict chronological order, though my trail of discovery did start and end with Grandma, or Agnes if you'd prefer.

For those who hoped for a dramatic climax I am terribly sorry, but family histories rarely finish that way, in fact they rarely finish at all. They just go on. My family is still making history and I hope it will continue to do so for many more generations.

Of course, some do include epic highs, lows, heroes and villains, but for most of us, it is a journey which is littered with small stuff, that might seem important at the time but looks trivial in hindsight, when age is accompanied by wisdom.

As Sue, a friend of ours said, "Sixty two; I don't give a shit."

That said, I also believe that most families know love, kinship, friendship and fulfilment. My wife and kids are a case in point. Once Liz had accepted my proposal of marriage, the rest wasn't that much of a surprise, though on reflection, her forbearance has been. That she came into my life in the first place was just dumb luck on my part.

Life *does* have surprises and secrets too though. The chest certainly had enough of them for me and it still had one more in store, which is why you are reading this.

I thought I'd finished this story, or at least as much as I could have done, over three weeks ago and celebrated by taking the dog for a walk the next morning. When we got home I took the chest downstairs, from beside my desk, where it had lain for almost a year.

Both the dog and chest needed hosing down, but only the chest was going to be treated with paint stripper first. The dark brown paint, or varnish, looked faded and scratched but it took two applications of the strongest paint stripper I could buy before getting down to the original material. I love working with wood, but this had an extra dimension. I could *feel* a connection with Dad; see him jointing the corners with dovetails, hear him sanding it down and smell the varnish he was brushing on.

That 'connectivity' felt quite timely, as though he was encouraging me to keep going and not just with the chest itself. I'd learned a great deal from the secret hoard, but it had provided as many secrets as well and I knew that I couldn't stop looking for answers now. There were still clues to follow and archives to search.

The next day, I set about removing the wallpaper lining that was definitely a nineteen forties vintage and browned with age. It had almost certainly been put on with flour and water as well, which is why it took repeated soakings with hot water and a stiff scraper to get it off. Bits of paint stripper had leeched through the seams from the previous day, to dry as dark brown blobs, which took a wire brush to shift. It was inside and on the base, so I wasn't too concerned about the finish though I was keen to get the whole thing dried off and sanded.

It was definitely pine, that much was obvious from the knotting, which I thought would look quite striking when treated with Danish oil.

But first I had to give it a final rinse off. The boards on the bottom had shrunk, leaving gaps at the seams but they were too small to drain the water quickly enough, so I upended the chest to speed things up. As I rolled it back I caught a glimpse of shiny metal and guessed it was a wayward nail, so I wandered into the garage for a hammer and screwdriver. It would either come out or go in a little deeper; didn't matter to me.

Yet on closer inspection, it didn't look like a nail. For one thing, it lay parallel to the frame instead of at right angles, which a nail hammered through the side would have done and I realised that it lay in line with the direction I'd taken with the wire brush

It also lay beneath the surface of the surrounding wood, but inside a large knot, which I assumed had been fractured by the passage of the metal. It was enough to justify having a poke around with the screwdriver, at any rate.

Knots in such old timber invariably shrink and often fall out so I was startled when it held firm and only a small part crumbled. I picked the bit up and rubbed it between my fingers to discover that it wasn't wood at all. In fact, it felt like a compound.

I used a much smaller screwdriver to ferret out the rest, but once, when it slipped, a fresh shiny scar appeared. It was then that I realised what I was looking at. The object was soft; almost certainly silver, because I hadn't been using any force with the screwdriver, but more importantly, it had been hidden deliberately.

He had done a wonderful job of it too, for a niche had been carved into the frame to house half of the treasure and the other half disguised as a perfectly formed knot, but made with stained filler rather than wood. This much became clear as I cleared the area and lifted the silver locket from its resting place.

It was heart shaped and a plain thing really, but it opened easily to reveal a lock of dark hair. I closed it before checking the other side, to see an embossed pattern of leaves and flowers, with a heart-shaped panel in the centre, where someone had used simple punches to stamp the letters *S J* on it.

I still have no idea who 'SJ' was, but she must have meant a great deal to my father.

Books by the Same Author

Graham's Chronicles
A Heart Warming Trilogy

A Child's Eye View
Graham's Chronicles I

Graham Parsons is a *man ordinaire* whose well-ordered life is changed beyond measure when he witnesses the manslaughter of a 7 year old boy, Christopher. Whilst holding the dying child he experiences a profound out of body experience and minutes later suffers a life threatening attack, leaving him with permanent disabilities.

His recovery brings with it a telepathic connection with children who need help. An affinity which threatens his sanity, marriage and eventually his life.

This tale of discovery begins with a fearful and confused denial which takes him to the edge of reason until eventually, he accepts and employs his remarkable gift with a charming pragmatism that disarms doubters and helps to salvage blighted young lives. His simple, candid honesty wins the support of four friends from very different backgrounds; Christopher's mother, a GP, a Child Protection Officer and a Detective Sergeant.

This story chronicles the shocking, moving and yet sometimes heart-warming episodes in his new life.

Graham's Gang

Graham's Chronicles II

Graham has come to terms with his special gift. A telepathic connection with children who need help, but his efforts to help them are often accompanied by calamity.

The tiny group who know his secret decide he needs their protection, but just how effective can Nancy, his partner, a GP, a social worker and an overweight detective sergeant be?

They are joined by Harvey Calder, a wealthy business man. He and his wife Audrey are indebted to Graham for saving their granddaughter's life, which prompts them to give Graham, Nancy and their foster child, Jimmy, a holiday of a lifetime. But *'life'* takes on a whole new meaning when Graham confronts an American, set to become a Senator, who will do anything to discredit and remove a threat.

Graham's false imprisonment does just that and the situation seems back under control, but no-one has told the Senator about the Hell's Angel, 'Big Bob'.

Help Out House

Graham's Chronicles III

Graham Parsons is back in England, a fugitive from US law, but his freedom is still threatened by a vengeful US Senator and extradition.

His life goes on hold, in a stasis of anxiety while in America, Chrissy Haddon and her mother confront their own demons of abuse and alcoholism. Is it time for Senator Haddon to answer for his deeds and make amends?

The 'Gang' rally to Graham's side once more, with support and practical help on both sides of the Atlantic that become quite extraordinary. But like Graham, with his telepathic connection with children needing help, they all know others would think their experiences were no more than fiction.

As things begin to fall apart help comes from an unexpected source and the US State Department are persuaded to join in.

Meanwhile, in Leicester, Lori is a frightened fifteen-year old, trapped in a world of drugs and prostitution. Yet in the darkness shines a tiny glimmer of defiance. Only she knows her real name is Marya, until she sees Graham's advertisements and 'puts her message in a bottle', triggering a dreadful reaction which causes Graham to suffer one of his worst nightmares.

Graham's Chronicles

Reader Reviews

Review #1

'A really good read. The subject matter could have been daunting but it is handled with sensitivity and grace. You soon get caught up in the story and its many facets. Humour, tragedy, pathos, fear and whimsy are all to be found in these pages. I found myself feeling great empathy with the characters, particularly with Graham and his plight. You will care about these people and want to know what happens to them.'

Review #2

'A thoroughly enjoyable Trilogy. The characters are true to life, Graham and Nancy in particular. The books are well researched and written and contained all the elements that keep you turning the pages from wit, humor, violence and death. I laughed and cried throughout and I actually miss my morning read now I have finished all three books. Highly recommended and I look forward to any new material in the future from this talented Author.'

Review #3

'What a great series of books! The characters in the books are so well developed you feel as though you know them personally. The books are filled with comical incidents as well as the deep sadness that dealing the subject of child abuse automatically brings. It would be great to bring these characters to life as the story-line would make a superb TV series. I look forward to reading any future works by this author.'

Review #4

'I have read all three of these books and was hooked after reading the first 10 pages - absolutely enthralling. Although the subject matter can be harrowing it is such an up lifting and positive story which leaves you with a good feeling thanks to the wonderful main character Graham!Well done to the author I will look out for more of his books in the future.'

Review #5

'Read this on the kindle because of the write ups and loved the story line. Went on to books 2 & 3 and also bought copies for a friend's birthday and she enjoyed them just as much well done and something a bit different.'

Review #6

'This is an incredibly well written story. I was hooked before I finished the first chapter and read the whole thing in days. Such a clever take on a story like this. Recommend to anyone who fancies something a bit different.'

Review #7

'Top draw, huge intensity with clear visual feel, love the twists and turns, should make a best seller in my view. I produce films and this would make an excellent project.'

Review #8

'As an avid reader of novels I do tend to stay with certain authors and read all their works before moving on to the next. I have read all three in this trilogy, I don't know where the inspiration came from for this story but ten pages into it and I couldn't put it down. This first book, Through A Child's Eye View' left me wanting more and when 'Graham's Gang' came out I wasn't disappointed. When book three 'Help out House' was released I wondered where the Author was going with it, it soon became apparent. The storyline is not without an element of truth so praise to the Author for the lengthy research he must have carried out to write such a feasible story, sometimes amusing, sometimes harrowing and sometimes sad, you've got to be good to bring me close to tears! Sorry I haven't explained what the story is about, that's for you to find out but well done the Author on an outstanding first novel, I can't wait to read your next work.'

Review #9

'This book is pacey and punchy. The author is an accomplished story teller who juggles the story lines in America and England to keep them all on track to their conclusion. I think I enjoyed this book the most out of the three, perhaps because I had become so involved with the characters and was desperate to find out what happened in the end. The author slightly changes his style again to match this stage in the story and you can see how his confidence has grown as a writer. In this trilogy, he has steered us through the events in the life of these people, tweaking his writing style to give three very different types of books which seamlessly follow on from each other through the characters and their growing relationships and the very strong central story line. Very clever! Highly recommended!'

Jeff Hawksworth

After thirty years in the insurance industry, latterly as a pensions consultant, Jeff decided to take a gap decade.

His life has been filled with formative influences, such as those imparted by his woodwork teacher, 50 years ago, who gave him a lifelong love of wood and taught him how to work it. You might say Mr Dunkerley was Jeff's *Mr Chips*. (No pun intended).

Not forgetting Pam, his wife of 40 years, his son James and daughter Kim.

More recently, a master carver named Mike Painter taught Jeff how to carve and so wood carving has filled a significant part of the 'Gap', along with coach driving, here and on the continent, (boys toys). Speaking of continent, there is the new found love of France; it's culture, food and of course, wine.

Felling trees, cooking and a short but very enjoyable spell as an examinations officer at a local college also helped to fill time but the real surprise was fiction. Writing it that is.

What started as a vivid dream that stayed with him, became a four year journey of discovery that resulted in the publication of Graham's chronicles, *A Child's Eye View*, *Graham's Gang* and *Help Out House*.

Oh, nearly forgot, Jeff is 63 and 9 years into his gap decade. Watch this space.